the man in
THE BLIZZARD

NOVELS BY BART SCHNEIDER

Beautiful Inez
Blue Bossa
Secret Love

bart schneider

the man in
THE BLIZZARD

a novel

 Three Rivers Press · New York

Copyright © 2008 by Bart Schneider

Published in the United States by Three Rivers Press, an imprint of the
Crown Publishing Group, a division of Random House, Inc., New York.
www.crownpublishing.com

Three Rivers Press and the Tugboat design are registered trademarks of
Random House, Inc.

Permissions acknowledgments can be found on page 292.

Library of Congress Cataloging-in-Publication Data
Schneider, Bart.
  The man in the blizzard : a novel / Bart Schneider.—1st ed.
  1. Private investigators—Fiction.   2. Pro-life movement—Fiction.
3. Attempted assassination—Fiction.   I. Title.
  PS3569.C522374M36 2008
  813'.54—dc22   2008006865

ISBN 978-0-307-23813-9

Printed in the United States of America

DESIGN BY ELINA D. NUDELMAN

10 9 8 7 6 5 4 3 2 1

First Edition

To the poets and all their mysteries

Even his tracks are gone!
And, of course, his shadow . . .

—**Thomas McGrath**

the man in
THE BLIZZARD

BEFORE SLEEP

I don't know when I first discovered that Detective Bobby Sabbatini, of the Saint Paul Police Department, had a photographic memory for poetry. He always tucked a couple of slim volumes of verse into the flapped pockets of his silk jacket, or curled them into the pouches of his bomber.

I heard that the stuff came spewing out of him all day. He'd recite Ginsberg or Gary Snyder to some kid making espressos at Dunn Bros. A bit of a blue-collar poem, by Philip Levine, to an ancient gal scanning groceries at Kowalski's. Everybody loved it, because Sabbatini did it with a light touch.

A tall, slender man, with silvered temples, Sabbatini dressed better than any cop I've known. Dude was his own man. Played viola in the university orchestra at Michigan State, just as I played cello at Berkeley. He was also a long-distance runner during college. Claimed he kept himself going by humming bars from Bartók's third and fourth string quartets.

I got to know Sabbatini before his poetry conversion, in the late 1990s. We met at the murder scene of one of my clients. A week later we played quartets together. I was still grieving for my client and craved some musical solace. I gathered a couple of fiddle players I knew, both pharmacists, and the four of us made a few righteous runs through Haydn's String Quartet in D, "The Lark." I fell in love with the Adagio Cantabile. The first violinist, the pharmacist with the longer nose, had a lovely tone. The second fiddle, Sabbatini, and I strung out some sweet chords. Of course, Bobby and I had smoked down a nice nugget of hash before we started playing, and the pharmacists clearly had their own secrets.

I'd never really thought of Sabbatini as a priestly man, but shortly after 9/11, when he had his prostate problem, the poetry hit him like a calling. Another cop might have gone and drowned himself, but Sabbatini embraced the poetry like a man with a mission.

Despite the fact that this story begins with a troubled violinist and ends with gunfire and protest songs, I'll remember its sound track in verse. Sabbatini was quite persuasive with the stuff and infected more than a few of us.

It so happens that I smoked a goodly amount of weed during this time. I feared it would erase hunks of my memory if I let it. So when I went to bed at night, I forced myself to remember the day and find the right title for its key episodes. Finally, after I'd come up with a few decent headers, I could fall asleep.

MIRACLE WRAP

All I can say is that I was amused when, in early August, I saw the first buses in the Twin Cities wrapped in a lush lake landscape. They looked like a Hamm's Beer commercial from the 1950s, heading up the street.

Except that a message in a dripping font overlaid the lake image: THE MIRACLE IS COMING.

Pretty soon a small fleet of miracle buses made its way across Minneapolis and Saint Paul. THE MIRACLE IS COMING. I smiled at the evangelical boast. At the notion that anything can be bought for the right price—our public space, our curiosity, even our souls.

In less than a month the Republican National Convention was coming to town and all hell was going to break loose.

The buses kept rolling. Finally, a date was attached to the claim: THE MIRACLE IS COMING ON LABOR DAY.

Good, I thought, *I'm gonna be out of town.* But, of course, I wasn't.

THE VIOLINIST

On a sultry morning in mid-August, the door to my Loring Park office opened and a bright-faced blonde, who couldn't have been much more than thirty, stepped inside. She carried a violin in a canvas-covered case. I took a good look at her. Green eyes and a sweet mole just north of the bridge of her nose.

"Mr. Boyer?"

"How do you do?" I stepped from behind my desk and extended my hand. "August Boyer. They call me Augie."

The violinist held out a soft hand with nails trimmed to the nubs. "I'm Elizabeth Odegard."

The woman had sprayed on too much Ysatis, a cloying, citrus fragrance from Givenchy that my wife began wearing just before she left me. But what really grabbed my attention were my visitor's shoes, a wondrous pair of turquoise missiles that narrowed into long, impossible snouts. I thought of a pair of ferrets.

"So, did you come to play me 'Happy Birthday'?" I asked, nodding toward her fiddle.

"Is it your birthday, Mr. Boyer?"

"No, but people are always sending me strange gifts out of the blue. Have a seat, Ms. Odegard." I pointed toward the teak sofa, a garage-sale Danish modern relic that I spent a fortune having re-covered. I did a few daft things after Nina left, but the remake of the sofa was the costliest. What kind of crazy fuck spends nineteen hundred bucks to cover an uncomfortable salvage piece in leather the color of summer squash?

I leaned back against the edge of my desk and watched the violinist bend her long frame into the teak rack. She parked her violin at her feet and clicked the sides of her ferrets against the case.

"I'm on my way to rehearsal," she said. "I play in the Minnesota Orchestra and live a few blocks away—on Willow and West Grant. I thought I'd walk today."

"Isn't Orchestra Hall in the opposite direction?"

"Yes, but I came to see you. Do you mind if I stand?"

" 'Course not. That's a pretty uncomfortable perch."

The violinist strolled past my Bob Dylan calendar, on the south wall, and stood face-to-face with a framed photo of Rose, belting out a song with her band.

"My daughter," I volunteered.

My visitor squinted at the photo. "She looks like she might be a handful."

"She's out of my hands," I said, suddenly lonesome for Rose. "Actually, she's become quite the star."

"Really."

"Yes. So what can I do for you, ma'am?"

The violinist spun around and looked at me. "It's my husband. I need to get away from him."

"Is he dangerous?"

The violinist didn't answer. I watched her for a moment and then studied the long snouts of her shoes. I wondered how she walked around in those things. They didn't seem the right shoes for a woman who was trying to get away.

The violinist came back and sat on the edge of the leathered teak. "My husband has a habit of straying."

You'd have thought she was describing a lost tabby.

The violinist leaned forward and I got another whiff of her perfume. Definitely Ysatis.

"But I'm not really interested in his extracurricular escapades. I haven't let him touch me for a couple of years. I don't care who he sees or what he does with them, but it might be wise to document the whole dirty business for the sake of the divorce."

"You're planning a divorce, Ms. Odegard? Is that what you're after?"

"In part. Please, call me Liz."

I had no interest in calling her Liz. I wasn't usually bored in the company of nice-looking women, but this one made me drowsy. I strolled around my desk and rummaged through the top drawer, finally pulling out a tin of Altoids. "Look, Ms. Odegard, maybe what you need is a divorce attorney. I can recommend a few."

"My husband's business has been very shady lately."

"What kind of business is he in?"

"He trades in violins."

"He's a dealer?"

"Not in the traditional sense. He doesn't have a shop. He has a collection of fine violins that he's procured over the last decade. He shows them only by appointment. He lent me one to use in my first season with the orchestra."

"Kind of him."

"It's not uncommon. I got into the orchestra straight out of Oberlin, and I'd been using a violin on loan from the conservatory. That's what led me to Perry."

I opened the lid to the Altoids, plucked out a couple of pellets, and dropped them on my tongue. Nasty as ever. "I'd offer you one, Ms. Odegard, but they're stale. I've had these rolling around in my desk for an age." I nodded toward the violin case. "So is this the violin?"

"Yes."

"What's its value?

"It's a pretty decent instrument. Giovanni Rogeri, 1712. From the Amati school."

"And its value?"

Elizabeth Odegard lifted the violin case onto her lap. "Would you like to see it?"

"No, I don't want to see it."

The violinist, poised to unzip the brown canvas cover, seemed surprised by my disinterest.

"What did you say your fiddle's worth?"

She bit her lower lip. "I didn't say. It's a very rare instrument. Perry only deals in rare instruments. I can't say what it's worth exactly."

"Give me a ballpark."

"It's insured for $350,000."

"I see. So it's not a student model."

"No." She laughed. "Not a student model. By the way, Mr. Boyer, I hear you play cello."

"I'm a rank amateur. How did you hear about me, Ms. Odegard?"

"An article in the *Star Tribune*."

A few years earlier, with help from the violin dealer Lionel Ross, I'd located a symphony member's "lost" violin, a Matteo Goffriller valued at more than $275,000. The fiddle, owned by the dapper Pieter Haus, disappeared from the musicians' lounge at Orchestra Hall and turned up in Dallas, where a twelve-year-old girl, who had trouble keeping it tuned, played it in her junior high orchestra. A human-interest story about me, and my good fortune in tracking the violin, appeared in the *Strib*.

"I rarely do that kind of work, Ms. Odegard. That was an aberration. My stock and trade—infidelity and insurance—isn't so glamorous. And even infidelity, or at least the desire for proof of it, has tanked. I spend most of my time on workers' comp cases."

Elizabeth Odegard sat up straight, the way a person is meant to on a piece of Danish modern furniture. "I think my husband is involved with something illegal and very dangerous."

"Maybe you should contact the police, ma'am."

"I don't want the police. I want you to follow him. I've noticed an urgency about Perry's activities in the last couple of weeks. He's usually pretty laid-back. He likes to think of himself as a businessman of leisure."

"Like a pimp?"

"Violins are far more profitable than whores."

I was surprised by how easily the word rolled off the violinist's tongue.

"But Perry hardly seems like a man of leisure these days. His phones are ringing all the time. When he's not out on the terrace playing with his iPhone, he's poking at his BlackBerry. Sometimes he's got them both going." She reached into her bag and pulled out a photo. "Here's a picture of Perry, just so you know what he looks like."

I was a little surprised to see a nicely tanned man, not yet forty, standing beside a tropical swimming pool. He was wearing nothing but a pair of snug swimming trunks. A Speedo. "Are you sending me on a Club Med trip to track your husband?"

"It was the only photo lying around. I overheard him telling somebody that he'd meet them tonight after dinner, but I don't know where."

"You want me to follow him tonight?"

"Yes. He likes an early dinner because he often does business at night. What else can I tell you? He drives a white Jaguar, an SJ8 sedan. We live just around the corner at 115 Willow. Le Palais."

"I know the building."

"Good. I'll give you a call before he finishes his dinner."

I handed back the photo of her husband. "I require a three-thousand-dollar retainer," I said, hoping to put her off with some inflated numerics, "and I charge two hundred dollars an hour. Expenses are extra."

The violinist pulled out a pen and a checkbook. "Will you accept a personal check, Mr. Boyer?"

"Of course."

"One other thing," she said. "I picked up a violin case he left by the front door this morning. It felt funny. Instead of a violin, there was a gun inside."

RATIONING THE WINGS

Late that afternoon, on my way back from checking on a comp claim in Richfield, I stopped at Shorty & Wags on Nicollet to pick up dinner for a couple of nights: two pints of collard greens with turkey, a side of okra, a half pound of chicken gizzards, and a twenty-four-pack of wings. Enough fried food to kill a man my size, and I happen to be rather large. I told myself I'd have to ration the wings; no more than eight at a sitting.

I brought the grub back to the office, cleared my desk, and spread the front and back pages of the *Star Tribune*'s Metro section across the desk. The five-day forecast called for hot.

I grabbed a roll of paper towels, plucked out exactly eight wings from the Shorty & Wags bucket, and opened a pint of collard greens. With any luck, I'd finish my supper before the violinist called. I decided to leave the other pint of collard greens, the okra, and the gizzards in my pint-sized fridge, where I found a chilled bottle of Negra Modelo.

I dipped the first wing into a cup of hot vinegar, tore into it, stabbed my plastic fork at the sharp greens, had a sip of beer, then went for another wing. I nodded across the desk to Dylan, who was decked out in a white hat and shirt—the back photo from his *Love and Theft* album—for the August calendar page. Dylan, with his silly mustache, didn't nod back. The sight of him reminded me of the road trip Rose and I took to Memphis to see the man, a couple of summers earlier.

I dripped a little hot vinegar from my second wing onto Dexter Dunn's column, "All but Dunn," across from the weather page. I used to read Dexter as soon as I got to work in the morning, but I'd recently weaned myself off anything related to politics. I did it for my health. I'd get so wound up about the damage George and the Bushies had done, I thought I'd blow a coronary. And when the election season kicked in, a year and a half ahead of the election, I got strung out watching debates, reading reams of analysis, and firing off pithy posts to the blogs.

During the early debates and preprimary babble of smear and bullshit promises, I'd stand in front of the TV and scream at most of the candidates. When the plague of political ads started up in earnest, I threw spitballs at the screen. For a while, I wiped them off before I went to bed at night, but by Super Tuesday, the TV screen, lumpy with layers of spitballs, had evolved into a trophy of pop art.

Come March, I was in full moratorium mode. No more radio. Only the sports and weather in the newspaper. I'd wiped the *Times,* the *Post,* the *Guardian,* Reuters, *Slate, Salon,* and the *Huffington Post* off my Google landing page. No more political teasers.

I plucked another chicken wing and dripped a trail of vinegar across an article next to Dexter's column that caught my attention. Apparently, a fleet of antiabortion trucks had started driving around the Twin Cities. I'd yet to see one. According to the piece, these trucks were being sponsored by the same organization, Born Free, that was behind the large antiabortion rally slated for Labor Day on the state capitol grounds.

It wasn't until I'd stuffed the sixth wing in my mouth that I realized the great "Labor Day Miracle" advertised on city buses was linked to the Born Free rally and to the Republican convention, which commenced the same day.

Through the grease, I made out the title of Dexter's column. "Holsom—Born Free, Home Free," a reference to Minnesota governor Jim Holsom. You had to love Dex. After all the mergers and buyouts he was the last old-school lefty at the *Star Tribune.*

Everybody knows about the ambitions of our puckish governor. Yes, we know that he's angling for the vice presidential nomination.

As a comely Republican governor in a traditionally Democratic state, Holsom's demonstrated that he can do any damn thing he wants. Just as he vetoed bills that would have raised taxes for education and highways right before the I-35 bridge collapsed. Just as he hosted a Christian revival on the state capitol grounds during his first term. Just as he showed off his dimples during his recent policy speech against illegal immigrants. "I've got nothing against wetbacks," he said sweetly, "but it's time to hand them each a towel and send them back home."

And now, in his most audacious play, right during prime time, Holsom is betting that the Labor Day save-our-babies spectacle on the capitol grounds will mollify the Rush Limbaughs and firm up the Republican ticket's conservative bona fides.

By the way, word's out that Born Free, the organization behind the rally, will be bringing in pregnant woman willing to be induced. They'll be giving birth in medical tents on the capitol grounds. It's being sold as the patriotic thing to do. The pro-life thing to do. The idea is to imbue "Labor Day" with a new meaning. Our pretty-boy guv thinks it's a Holsom idea. He'll be there to kiss the babies.

I tossed aside Dexter's horror show of a column and roared through some more wings. Might as well make it a dirty dozen, I reasoned, before wrapping the leavings in the sullied newspaper.

Meanwhile, I debated whether I wanted to click onto Rose's blog. I sometimes had trouble reading it. It wasn't that I minded the kid's voicing her feelings, but did she have to post them for the rest of the world? Throughout her adolescence, she railed about "boundaries." They were the centerpiece of her personal theology.

You can't go into my room. Period. I'm talking about boundaries here. Talking about mutual respect. Good fences make good neighbors. That's Robert Frost. The Great Wall of China, ever heard of it? And don't look so smug, Dad. You know what you're doing if you let the mother cross the threshold—you're enabling her.

Rose was bigger on the language of recovery than anybody I'd kept company with during the years I went to meetings. But now that she had a little fame, she'd forgotten all about boundaries. When Rose launched her blog, Nina referred to our daughter as "the slut of free speech." Rose's song "Mothers, Daughters" sent Nina up a wall.

Mothers and daughters, they aren't meant to mix.
Especially when the old one's in such a bad fix.

The woman's gone off on an evil bender
Must be because she's afraid of her gender.

I did my damnedest to calm my wife. "It's a fictive mother and daughter; she's not talking about you."

"Of course she's talking about me," Nina exploded.

I remember how odd it was to hear some of the lines the first time on the radio and realize that it was my young daughter who had written them and sang them.

It's so hard to groove on a mentality
That's spooked by your basic sensuality.

Hey there, good women, don't fall under that hex
There's nothing wrong with a little good sex.

More recently, since so many of Rose's songs had become overtly political, she didn't get much radio play on the mainstream stations. They wouldn't touch songs like "Ballad of Abu Ghraib" or "Tricky Dick Deuce on the Loose." Fortunately, Rose didn't need the radio, not in the age of MySpace and YouTube, not when music sites like Pitchfork championed her. The band's own site was hugely popular, with free downloads and a culture of bulletin boards swirling around each of Rose's lyrics.

I peeked at Rose's blog, skimming over her account of taking a one-hour bus trip, during some flight of fancy, from downtown LA to the beach in Santa Monica. In the last paragraph, I found myself characterized in a way that embarrassed me.

The beach was pretty raggedy-ass, with litter blowing all over, but I was glad to be there. There were some poor Latino families, the kids running through the white water, getting their shoes and pants all nasty, but having the time of their life. I realized that those poor families were far happier than my family, which has gone on sad times, the old folks separated now. What can I say? The mama bear went out on her own. I'm all about liberation, though I'm sorry for the damage done to the sad-sack dad, and to the yours truly of the tale.

CUL-DE-SAC

The violinist was breathless when she finally called. "He's just about out the door, and he's taking the violin case with the gun in it." *Great,* I thought, *I'm really in the mood for tailing boy-beautiful and his violin gun.*

Perry Odegard's creamy white Jaguar was a virtual beacon leading me west out 394, south on 10, and west again on County 5, until he vanished for good somewhere among the cul-de-sacs near Deephaven. I inched through the maze, searching for the sleek, white Jag for a while before I lost heart.

I lit up a half-smoked joint, flattened by a roll of parking meter quarters in the ashtray. After a half-dozen tokes, I noticed that I was being followed by a private security guard who fixed a spotlight on me as I limped along in my rusted Mazda, my beloved forest green 626 with the yellow passenger-side door that I'd never bothered to have painted since getting broadsided a few years ago, in the suburb of Savage, by a teenager masturbating while driving his mother's Cutlass.

The bulbous-nosed guard buzzed down the window of his Skylark. "What are you doing out here, chief? Teaching yourself how to drive?" I didn't have the heart to tell the old guard that I was just a little dick who'd lost his way, so I simply asked for directions back to County 5. Rose's sad-sack dad. The detective who'd lost his way. I winced at the thought of the song my daughter could write about this episode.

TESTOSTERONE

I had a little trouble getting myself going the next morning. Twenty-four deep-fried chicken wings and a tub of gizzards will do that to a guy. After the debacle in the suburbs, I ended up with a compelling case of the munchies. There was nothing to do but return to the office and polish off the remaining wings.

I showered until the hot water ran out, brushed my teeth, then broke open a couple of packets of AndroGel for my testosterone deficiency. I rubbed the clear, cold jam across my hairy paunch. The humiliations involved with this daily ritual were legion, not least of which was making my belly shine with gel each morning as I faced the bathroom mirror. All this, because blood tests associated with a routine physical in early July showed my testosterone numbers slumping.

Dr. Jacks, the sixty-something endocrinologist, a feel-good "our-hormones-are-our-buddies" kind of guy, wanted me to keep a journal from the day I began applying the goop. Fat chance.

"The changes can be very subtle at first," the doctor said, "and I'd like you to participate in every part of the treatment. One of the best ways for us to do that is to become dedicated observers." I made a point of watching Dr. Jacks's prominent

Adam's apple as he spoke, convinced that the guy had gone into his specialty because of issues he'd had with his own "buddies."

"So this stuff's not going to turn me into a bar brawler or some kind of a cretin flaming with road rage?"

"Not unless that's what you were to start with."

"You'd have to ask my ex-wife."

Dr. Jacks laughed. "You should feel a difference; you should feel a little bit more like this," he said, throwing three or four hard right jabs into the air. "You should feel a little more pop, a little more bombs away, a little more bring 'em on."

"If this is the hormone they've been feeding George Bush, I don't want any."

"No, no, no, no, no," Dr. Jacks said, his Adam's apple going off on such a spirited bounce that it looked as if it might somersault out of his throat, "I'm only trying to describe the kind of pick-me-up you might feel. On the other hand, you may not feel anything."

"Then why would I do it?"

"We can't know until we try." The doctor threw his fists in a right-left-right combination. "The upside is that you may feel . . . you may feel more . . . verve for life."

"Isn't that an existential concern, Doctor?"

"The body and the spirit are not unrelated, Mr. Boyer."

"And the downside?"

"I don't see a downside. But let me be clear: you don't need to do anything. This is simply a quality-of-life consideration. You can stay the way you are and it won't be the end of the world. Of course, it's a bit odd for an otherwise healthy man of fifty to be running low on testosterone. But not to worry," the doctor said, nodding his head meaningfully. "We're all missing something."

Somehow, that comment didn't comfort me and I found myself wondering what I'd trade to have back a full measure of my manliness—a bit of my hearing, my sight, maybe my sense of smell? But the notion of swapping one ill for another brought me back to myself, and I thought of the sick convoy of medical curiosities on its way to pick off all of us. Half the people I knew had cancer.

When I asked Dr. Jacks what had caused my drop in testosterone, he threw up his hands. "We don't know. It could be stress. It could be grief. Have you had any unexpected losses recently?"

Although I was tempted to say that my entire life had been an unexpected loss, I shook my head. I didn't care to discuss, with the good doctor, the fact that my wife had left me for another man. Or that my career had already peaked, and it had never been very distinguished at that. As to the testosterone, my most recent theory was that smoking too much marijuana is what had nudged my numbers lower.

Standing in Dr. Jacks's office, I tried to conjure up an image of my father at age fifty, ten years before he dropped dead on the sales floor at the Emporium in San Francisco while helping a customer into a suit jacket. I could see my father, walking home from the bus stop in his overcoat and wool cap. "Another day done," he'd say once he got in the door. "Another day further in debt." Surely, by fifty, my father's testosterone level had dropped as well.

After more than a month of laying this jelly across my tummy, I could testify to experiencing no added pop or pick-me-up or verve. The only thing that had increased was my self-consciousness. I doubted myself now more than ever. Would Nina have left me if I had maintained the hard-jab certainty of my manliness? And worse yet, I'd begun to have trouble staying hard with my girlfriend, Erica. It was the first time in my life I'd had that difficulty. I felt certain that the problem was more in my head than in my body. Dr. Jacks had planted a worm in my brain and I rubbed on the jelly.

IMAGINARY FRIEND

I glanced a little sadly at myself in the mirror and recited my daily portion from the epic poem I was memorizing, "Letter to an Imaginary Friend," by Thomas McGrath. Bobby Sabbatini had got me hooked on memorizing verse, but I did it on the sly. I didn't want to give him the satisfaction of thinking he had another convert. I figured I'd spring the poem on him once I had it down. But since it had more than ten thousand lines and I was memorizing at the rate of nine or ten lines a day, it was going to be a while.

I'd seen McGrath in the flesh more than twenty years ago. I hadn't heard of him, but happened to wander into Hungry Mind Bookstore one night when he was reading from his epic. Dude wore a black glove on his right hand and looked as if he was aching for a cigarette and a blast of bourbon. Fifteen or twenty people were sitting on folding chairs and a funky sofa, listening to this sour-looking old sucker read a long, heavenly passage about a small boy being pulled on a sled through open country in North Dakota on Christmas Eve.

Years later, after finally having fallen under Sabbatini's sway, I decided to look for McGrath's poetry. Somehow, I'd managed to remember his name. By then the poet was dead and the bookstore defunct, so I went by Micawber's, in Saint Anthony Park. When I mentioned McGrath, one of the guys brought me a fat volume and said. "The greatest poet that nobody's read."

"Have you read him?" I asked.

"Not me."

McGrath seemed like the perfect imaginary friend for me—the kind of dead man who'd talk back to you. I nailed my daily portion, nine lines from the fourth section, where he talks about the "immortal girls" of his North Dakota youth.

> *And under the coupling of the wheeling night*
> *Muffled in flesh and clamped to the sweaty pelt*
> *Of Blanche or Betty, threshing the green baroque*
> *Stacks of the long hay—the burrs stuck in our crotch,*
> *The dust thick in our throats so we sneezed in spasm—*
> *Or flat on the floor, or the back seat of a car,*
> *Or a groaning trestle table in the Methodist Church basement,*
> *And far in the fields, and high in the hills, and hot*
> *And quick in the roaring cars, by the bridge, by the river. . . .*

No testosterone problem for young Thomas.

I dressed quickly in a pair of clean khakis and a rayon shirt that sported a pattern of dominoes. Popped a multivitamin, a fish-oil capsule, Lipitor for high cholesterol. and Lisinopril for high blood pressure. How high could it all go? Twenty-four deep-fried wings should have taken it to the roof. I drank a tall glass of water, gobbled down a low-carb energy bar, and spilled exactly ten roasted almonds into my left hand. I munched them slowly. It was time to go on the diet for real.

Next, I checked the plants. Since I'd lived alone in the house, the same house in which Nina and Rose and I had lived together, I'd been filling it with plants, taking a crazed pride in the fact that everything seemed to thrive. My African violets were still going since last spring, and the large topiary rosemary, which the florist had doubted would make it past the New Year, was continually sending out fresh shoots. The crotons and the Norfolk pines loved the south windows of my dining room. My gorgeous, bent-trunk cypress took my breath away some mornings. It occurred to me that I should get a few grow lamps and raise a crop of cannabis, despite the fact that I enjoyed the monthly ritual of buying my stash from Conrad, my hipster supplier.

Almost out the door, I paused by the hall table, slid open the wooden lid of my scarab stash box—a vintage tobacco container from Indonesia. Getting low. Time to call Conrad. I rolled a fatty and slipped it into my shirt pocket.

WORKING MAN

Despite all my morning rituals, I still made it to Minneapolis by seven. Not bad for a Saturday morning. Who said I didn't have a work ethic? The Odegards' condo was in a small pretentious building, Le Palais, located beside the seven-floor nameless complex that dominated the street. I had bad associations with Le Palais.

Instead of open parking around the rear of the building, the joint had a gated garage. The night before, when I waited for Perry Odegard's Jaguar to emerge from the garage, I sat a ways up the street in my Mazda, aiming a homemade code grabber at the garage's electronic eye.

Now I parked in front of my office on Harmon Place and walked around to the Odegard condo, carrying an old canvas book bag, featuring a moo-eyed cow, from Hungry Mind Bookstore. The bag held the code grabber and a few other tools of the trade. I aimed the device at the double doors of the Odegards' garage and pressed the soft black button. The doors whined for a couple of seconds before sliding open. I pulled on a pair of white silk gloves and took a look around before entering the garage. There were only eight units in the building, and the association hadn't sprung for a security camera.

The Jaguar was protected by a red Club locked across the steering wheel. An antitheft sticker, Twitchell Covers Your A, featuring a black-gloved demon, was posted on the driver's-side window. I held my white gloves up to the devil. Good meets evil. I wanted to get into the car without tripping the alarm. I thought about it for a minute, but I no longer had the nerves for this kind of work.

At 7:30, I called my sometime assistant Blossom Reese in Saint Paul and asked if she could meet me in a half hour.

"You're going to get me out of bed on a Saturday morning, Augie?"

"I need your help, Blossom."

"You're lost without me, aren't you?"

"I'm wandering in the desert."

"Buy me breakfast at that Cajun joint, Boudreau's, up on Hennepin."

"You need breakfast first?"

"Hey, I only operate as a well-oiled machine, Augie. I'll be there by eight."

THE ARMAJANI

To kill time, I climbed the stairs to the iron pedestrian bridge that crosses a dozen lanes of traffic to the Walker Art Center. The quirky bridge was among my favorite places in town. I'd become a fan of the architect, Siah Armajani. I once stood behind him at the cash register in Hungry Mind, though I didn't know who he was. He had a pile of books worth a couple of hundred bucks and I remember craning my neck to make out the odd philosophy and archaeology titles and gazing with wonder at his heaping stack of poetry volumes. The guy looked like a middle-aged Persian pothead who might bounce a check. But he and the owner, Unowsky, grinned at each other and exchanged pleasantries. I knew Unowsky pretty well—we'd chattered about baseball, and civil liberties, and books that neither one of us had read. So, when his eccentric customer left, I said, "Hey, Uno, who is that dude?"

Unowsky grinned at me and shook his head with admiration. "That's Armajani," he said, "the Persian prince of public art."

Next thing I knew, the Walker bridge was erected and, though it was named for some donor, I've always thought of it as the Armajani. Now the Persian prince has pedestrian bridges in Nashville and Strasbourg, and he's acclaimed for his poetry parks and gazebos.

I spent a lot of time on the Armajani right after the I-35 bridge fell. I figured that the best way to contemplate the collapse of one bridge is to stand in the middle of another.

Now I stood atop the bridge, admiring the long poem that

inches its way in a relief of white letters across a sky blue steel girder spanning the bridge. The poem, by a tripper named John Ashbery, says something about arriving at your destination, or not. It's a little deep for me. I always read it as if I'm seeing it for the first time, despite having memorized it years ago. My hope is that someday I'll actually get it and discover that I'm a deeper person than I knew.

Standing at the absolute middle of the bridge, suspended above so many lanes of traffic, was electrifying, even at 7:45 on a Saturday morning. I pulled the fat joint from my shirt pocket. After struggling to get it lit, I took several deep tokes and looked down to the sculpture garden, watching a few lone souls walk by. The views of traffic through the girders made the bridge the most magnificent sculpture of all. Cars fired off in a dozen directions, each bearing a primal urgency. They might as well be a Milky Way of shooting stars, I thought, or countless spermatozoa, hauling their spineless tails.

I turned to face the leafy neighborhood west of the Walker and thought of Nina for a moment. We hadn't yet bothered with a divorce. Not divorced, but estranged? I liked to think of Nina as estranged. She had an apartment not far from the Walker. It pleased me that I didn't have the slightest inclination to boost myself over the side of the bridge and leap into traffic.

Bells in the distance tolled the hour. I faced Loring Park and the massive basilica beyond it. Such sober stateliness. Although I'd never been a believer, I had a genuine fondness for the grand church.

NINASHAME

Before I could do a damn thing to avoid it, I saw her—long-legged Nina in running gear. She was heading in my direction but was in the zone and hadn't yet noticed me. What's to notice? A familiar shape on the bridge. An oversized gargoyle. A man she once loved. She gasped when she recognized me, but didn't break stride, running right past me. I imagined that she'd run for the rest of the morning, up and down blocks of Kenwood mansions, around Lake of the Isles, then Calhoun, finally collapsing in a heap after rounding Lake Harriet.

I turned to watch her and then she was gone. Another man might have bit down on his lip and decided to run after a woman he once loved, a woman he might still love. I relit the joint between my lips. Another man might have called her name and gone panting after her. I drew as much smoke into my lungs as I could swallow.

It made sense that she ran past me. She'd pretty much done that during our life together. It was me who was supposed to have the shining career, although that impression was based on little more than my own bullshit, back in the day. I talked about making a genuine contribution in the field of criminal justice. I just happened to be too lazy to stay in law school.

I always knew that Nina was the one who'd shine. She didn't believe in downtime, couldn't enjoy herself unless she was getting something done. She'd stand in the checkout line reading pop psych books. I used to try and get her high, but she didn't care for it. Nina stayed home the first few years after Rose was born. Then she went to grad school. Before you knew it, she had a successful therapy practice going. She read heavily, took one workshop after another, and carved out a rich territory for herself. She really tapped the zeitgeist with Anger. You've got to hand it to her for spotting a growth area when she saw one. Pretty soon she was giving workshops, then the first couple of books came. Her last one, *I'm Going to Kick Your Ass: Anger and the American Dream,* did so well, along with the lectures and workshops she gave, that she could afford to quit her practice. But as far as I knew, she kept it going. The damn woman probably had another book in the works.

I looked out past the sculpture garden. Nina was long gone. She'd left me for another man. I carried the knowledge like a stripe of shame that ran vertically through my body. I'd even given it a name: Ninashame, which sounded to me like something from the Indian subcontinent, a curried dish, perhaps, that eats you from the inside out.

HELLO, BLOSSOM

By the time I arrived, Blossom was already forking her way through an enormous stack of flapjacks, dripping syrup and blueberries. On one side of the pancakes was a stainless-steel platter, greasy with a half-pound andouille patty. On the other side, a huge caramel roll, a swirling Russian church of caramel that still seemed to be rising from its perch on the lunch plate, a couple of dozen pecans shining atop the shellacked double dome.

"Looks like you've gone off the Atkins," I said, sliding in across from Blossom.

She offered a faint smile, then pushed in another mouthful. The joke was on me—Blossom, tall and lean, couldn't have weighed much more than a hundred and twenty. I liked to watch her eat. Her lips had a way of enveloping food; she seemed to enjoy it more than us mere mortals. She took another big round bite, her blue eyes staring through me. If she really wanted to unnerve you, she'd aim them at you sideways. All this took place under her hood of spiked red hair. Whenever I tired of watching Blossom eat, I'd study the homemade tattoos on her hands and think how glad I was not to have known her in the days when she hurt herself.

I'd met Blossom eight or nine years ago, not long after she got out of prison. Bobby Sabbatini introduced me to her one evening at the Poodle Club over on Lake. It was karaoke night at the Poodle and the crowd was randy, hollering in support of whoever was at the mike.

Blossom had been a good girl from South Minneapolis. Working-class clever. She'd gotten decent grades and she'd run cross-country at South High. But the summer after her graduation, before she was to head to college at the University of Wisconsin-Stout, she met a freckly-faced monster named Kevin who charmed her into a few seasons of bondage and a hearty drug habit. She spent the next decade either as a living ruin or in prison.

I remember my first sight of Blossom, perched on a bar stool at the Poodle. Her fright of straight rusty hair nodded to the beat of some nasty grunge. But no matter what she did to herself, she couldn't erase her sexiness. She had the kind that kept surprising you. It started with her lips. They were juicy whether or not she wanted them to be, but she knew how to work them.

Bobby Sabbatini sat beside her. He'd dressed down for the occasion in a knit shirt, linen slacks, and a pair of Bally loafers. I could see by the way he smiled at Blossom that he had a terrible crush on her.

At some point, he put his arm around her and said: "This woman is a picture of rehabilitation. Next thing I'm going to do is get her to memorize some poetry. She's got no problem with song lyrics. I think I'll start her out with some Robert Creeley."

Blossom shook her head.

"I got one," I said, and smiled at Sabbatini before shifting on my stool to face Blossom. "Couple of years ago, Bobby told me that if I wanted to keep his friendship I had to memorize a Creeley poem." Then I commenced to recite the only lines of Creeley I've ever known.

"As I sd to my
friend, because I am
always talking,—John, I

sd, which was not his
name, the darkness sur-
rounds us, what

can we do against
it, or else, shall we &
why not, buy a goddamn big car,

drive, he sd, for
christ's sake, look
out where yr going."

Sabbatini was ecstatic with my recitation. "Is that not the great hipster poem of 1956?"

Even Blossom gave me a smile and pushed out her lips a little. I figured I was helping Sabbatini court her. I probably should have been courting her for myself, but I was still a very married man back then.

"That's Creeley's 'I Know a Man,'" I said, tipping my Twins cap to the poem.

"Can you hear that coming out of Blossom's mouth, Augie? I can't wait to see it coming through those beauteous lips."

Blossom again shook her head. "Forget about it, Bobby."

"I'm threatening to take her to a Robert Bly reading," Sabbatini said.

"I'm not going, Bobby."

Sabbatini slipped into a righteous Robert Bly impression, snooty with nasal inhaling. "Oh, you'll love Bly. He's quite the trickster. You're going to groove on his ghazals."

Blossom wore black, fingerless gloves in those days to cover her tattoos. She swatted a gloved hand at Sabbatini as if he were a fly, then lifted her tumbler and sipped, a twist of lemon tipped on the far rim of the glass. "Yeah," she said to me, "I'm totally rehabilitated—I drink my tequila neat."

"Well, I'll join you in that," I said, signaling the bartender, "if you don't mind me having a couple of cubes of ice."

It was about then that the DJ called Blossom and she walked up to the mike, a little shy, and sang a surprisingly plaintive version of the Ramones' "I Wanna Be Sedated." Although she didn't have much of a voice, she pushed out her lips like Mick Jagger and projected an eerie intimacy that quieted the place.

A couple of weeks later, I had the two of them over to the house for dinner, after which Sabbatini and I headed into the living room to play some scrappy cello and viola duets, with Nina as our only audience. Blossom went with Rose to her room. The two redheads became fast friends, listening, no doubt, to one nasty CD after another.

Now Blossom looked up from her stack of pancakes and offered me a ripe-lipped sneer. "I get out of bed to meet you and you're not here."

"Sorry; I took a walk over to the Armajani. Must have lost track of the time."

"You got high."

"A toke off a roach, that's all."

"Really, Augie, at seven thirty in the morning."

"Time's a moving target," I said.

"For you. Okay, so this guy wild-goosed you out in the suburbs."

"Yeah, cruel and unusual."

"Were you high?"

"Nah, you know me and da burbs—no love lost. I had him coming out of his garage, followed him all the way out to Deephaven. Lost him. I've got a device to track him now. Just need to get inside and release the hood. He's got a bit of an alarm. That's where you come in."

Blossom nodded and pushed the plate with the caramel church toward me. "Here, have this while you wait for the server."

I shoved the plate back. "No, thanks." My appetite rose to attention, but I vowed it wouldn't get the better of me at Boudreau's. Worse came to worst, I'd stare at Blossom's tattoos.

Blossom spun the plate, admiring the caramel roll from all sides.

"So you free to work this little job with me, Blossom?"

"How little?" Her eyes shot at me sideways.

"I think there's something here. Clearly more than the client's letting on. Woman's odd. She's got the aura of a prodigy gone sour."

"That's what I am, dude—a prodigy gone sour."

"You're not sour, Blossom."

She did her damnedest not to smile, and pushed the caramel roll toward me again. When I again declined, she said, "What's the matter with you, Augie, are you on a fucking diet?"

"Nah, I'm just a bit hungover. Last night I scarfed down twenty-four juicy wings from Shorty & Wags."

"Way to go, Augie. Enough estrogen in those birds to start growing breasts. Who knows, maybe you'll grow some hair back."

My hand flew up to my head and measured my diminishing hairline. I pictured it as a tide on a curving shoreline, a tide that only goes out. In a few years there might be nothing left but a little sea wrack. I was so undone by thinking of myself as a man turning bald that I put back on the baseball cap I'd taken off when I walked into the restaurant.

"Hey, Augie," Blossom said, "you're a Twins fan, aren't you?"

"Yeah."

"Then why the hell are you wearing that Cincinnati Reds cap?" Before I could answer, a waitress with a face full of piercings stepped up to the booth and handed me a menu. The young woman had rows of ball bearings pocking each brow, clusters of tiny rings at the corners of her mouth, and a shiny silver post running through the cartilage beneath her nostrils. *Quite the presentation,* I thought, recalling one of Nina's damning phrases.

I flipped dutifully through the menu. I used to worry that Rose would become a nightmare of piercings, but she seemed to be past that. In photos of the band on the website, Rose appeared alert, her eyes fixed on the audience, her hair either hanging in ringlets or tightly braided.

"So, you eating today, sir?" the heavily pierced waitress, name-tagged Rory, asked, "or you just getting off vicariously?"

"He's already had his vicarious meal," Blossom offered.

"Vicarious man," Rory said in a breathy whisper, some sort of rip, I guessed, on how sexy I wasn't. I asked for two poached eggs, à la carte.

"À la carte?" she said, incredulous. "No home fries?"

"No."

"No hash browns?"

"Nope."

"No toast or caramel roll?"

"No."

"No hickory smoked bacon, no ham, no andouille?"

"Nothing."

"Just the eggs for you today," she said, regarding me as if I were missing a gene.

"Hey," I said, fixing my eyes on the silver post running through Rory's schnoz, "toss a sprig of parsley on those poachers, if it makes you happy."

NUTS WITH THE POETRY

Blossom, in a second pair of gloves from my Hungry Mind bag, got in and out of the car quickly without a peep from the Twitchell alarm. I planted the chip under the hood of the SJ8 and dropped the hood gently. There was only the slightest gurgle of an echo in the garage. Satisfied, I dragged a gloved hand over the polished right flank of the Jag. I'd now be able to track Odegard, no matter how deep into the suburbs the fucker went.

Blossom backed away from the car like a seasoned crook, as if she'd never seen it before.

I shot her a smile. "You made that look easy."

She slipped off her gloves. "The dude must have already snipped the Twitchell, probably sick of tripping it himself."

Blossom and I stood there a moment, looking at the bugged Jaguar. We should have gotten out of the garage, but neither of us was in a hurry to move. I was still goofed up from seeing Nina, and Blossom was sucking whatever was left of my high off me. I figured she had such a rich deposit of narcotic radioactivity left inside her that a little mooch here and there could light her up again.

"Hey," I said, "I meant to ask you to pop the trunk."

Blossom flipped me off. Then took a lipstick tube from her purse, pulled off its cover, and drew a couple of broad stripes over her lips. It was a reddish-orange that matched her hair and gave a sheer shine, even under the dim garage light. Blossom pulled the gloves back on. "You're going to owe me big-time, Augie, and I plan to extract."

"We talking pound of flesh?"

"You're putting me in harm's way, dude."

"I've got you covered, Blossom."

"I've never liked breaking into a car a second time."

"Look, it's Saturday morning; everybody that lives here is still in bed."

"Where I should be." Blossom stuck out her tongue at me. "I've got a record, man."

"Hey, you're working for me."

"Like that means dick."

"You've been hired by someone with a license."

"Who himself is engaged in an illegal activity."

Blossom glided back toward the car with her fists clenched. She was fun to watch. Lean and tall, at thirty-four, part urban model, part tomboy, and part prison girl.

"You've got nothing to worry about," I said. "Your boyfriend's a police detective."

"He's not my boyfriend."

"All right, your sweetheart. Your man."

"He's too weird, Augie. A cop's not supposed to play viola and recite poetry. Dude drives me nuts with the poetry. He's a fucking evangelist. All he wants to do is recite poems to me."

"And you're complaining about that, Blossom?"

"My big fear is that he's gonna start writing the shit."

"Hey, so Bobby's reborn to the poem."

"Try ten thousand of them," she said, wrinkling her nose.

I thought about Blossom nursing Sabbatini after his prostate business. He'd never told me if it had taken anything from him. But Blossom seemed to me a satisfied woman, despite her prison-yard scowl.

I flashed Blossom a big smile; I was happy for her. "You know he's going to get you."

"Is not."

"Oh yeah, he'll have you reciting poems in the end."

That shut her up and I saw that after years of resisting, Blossom Reese had finally started working up a couple of poems.

Blossom sneered at me. "Yeah, so how's it going with your attorney, lover boy?"

"She's too good for me."

"They're all too good for you, Augie," she said, slipping inside the car to pull the trunk release.

A FUCKING GUADAGNINI!

The trunk, rather than popping open, lifted slowly like the creaky lid of a coffin in the cartoons. After taking a quick look behind me, I pushed open the lid. The Jaguar's gaping white trunk was illuminated by a number of recessed lights that gave it the quaint feel of an underground living room. Three violin cases with zippered cloth covers were wedged together in a row.

I reached into the trunk and touched one of the cases. "Does the guy actually keep violins in the trunk?" I asked, as Blossom stepped around the rear of the car.

"Maybe he's just got empty cases."

"Could be."

"Pick 'em up, Augie."

I bent over the trunk and lifted one case at a time. "Feel like fiddles in there. Sure the insurer would love to know where he keeps them."

"Why don't you take one, Augie? He might not miss it. Could buy you a lot of poached eggs and killer weed."

"Nah, not my style."

I pulled one of the cases out of line and laid it flat in the belly of the trunk. Then I unzipped the cloth cover, flipped open the two latches, and lifted the lid of the case. An elaborate green paisley cloth, backed with black velvet, covered the instrument. I pushed off the cover and the Jaguar's soft trunk lamp shone on the reddish-brown varnish of the violin. I lifted the instrument, admiring the elaborately carved scroll and the beauty of the pur- fling, so close to the edge. The back looked like a one-piece maple with a lovely curl to the grain.

"Is it the real thing, Augie?"

"Either that or a wonderful fake."

I tilted the violin under the lamp so that I could peek at the label through the F hole. With a braided border, the label read pretty clearly, though a few letters were obscured by a speckling of black marks and yellowing.

JOAN ES B PTI TA GUAD GN NI
CREMONENIS FEC T TAURINI 1777

A fucking Guadagnini. During the time I worked to recover Pieter Haus's violin, old fiddles became a bit of a hobby for me. I picked up a few pricey books on Italian violins and sat for hours flipping through page after page of glossy photos of rare instru- ments as if I were gazing at pinups.

"What the hell's that worth, Augie?"

I sighed, and considered the Guadagnini. "Let's put it this way; if the other two are in the same ballpark, this joker's got a million dollars' worth of fiddles in his trunk."

THE ITCH

Erica greeted me at the door with a kiss that evening, and I handed her a couple of bottles of California Syrah that I'd spent too much money on.

"Look at you," she said. "You've dressed as if you meant it."

"What's that supposed to mean?"

"You look like you've come a callin'," she said with a laugh.

I winked at her. "Hey, I know a good thing when I see it."

Erica threw her arms around me. "Oh, Augie, you're such a charmer."

"That's me."

She grabbed hold of my shoulders and held me at arm's length for a moment. "You look good," she said, and clicked her tongue.

I wasn't sure what had gotten into me. I'd shaved and showered in the late afternoon, then dressed in a freshly laundered oxford-cloth shirt, a pair of pressed Dockers, and a raw silk sport coat. I guess I'd finally begun to realize that Erica was the best thing to happen to me in ages.

I also had to do something to compensate for the itch. For the last week, I'd woken every night scratching my arms and legs. At first, I did my best not to pay attention, but a dry rash had developed on my inner thighs and there were red blotches now on the undersides of my arms. I described my condition to the phone nurse at HealthPartners and she ruled out shingles because it's exclusive to one side of the body or the other. Fortunately, my malady affected me everywhere. When I named my meds, the nurse guessed that the testosterone was the culprit and suggested that I stop rubbing it on. Did this mean that my manly days were over? Just as I hadn't told Erica about my deficiency, I tried not to let on about the itching.

Neither had I mentioned the device in my coat pocket. How it could buzz at any time, as soon as Perry Odegard got into his car. I'd apologize profusely and claim that I was like a doctor on call. A spy-doctor, I'd say, and at least Ritchie, Erica's nine-year-old, would understand.

Erica led me into the kitchen and I followed obediently behind. She was a lean beauty, who wore a snug tee that was short enough to show a couple of inches of flesh above her waist, including the very top of the floral tattoo that adorned her spine. Who'd have guessed that I'd find myself with a woman who wore skimpy T-shirts? I used to holler at Rose to cover herself whenever she wore a shirt too short.

"So, how do you like your steak, Augie?"

I forced a burst of excitement. "We're having steak tonight?!"

Ritchie bopped into the room, sporting the earbuds to his baby blue Nano.

"Hey, Ritchie," I said. "You having steak?"

"Are you kidding me?" Ritchie said with a bit of swagger. "I'm having Ball Park franks and I'm grilling them myself."

"You don't say?" I put out my palm for Ritchie to slap five and the kid slid the heel of his hand along mine and then did an elaborate twirl. I did my best to match it. "Soul five," Ritchie said.

I wondered which of Erica's former boyfriends had shown Ritchie that trick. "So what are you listening to there, sport?"

"Green Day."

"Aren't they a little passé, Rich?"

"No, you're passé."

"Touché, boyo."

Erica laughed. "He doesn't know what he's saying."

"He knows exactly what he's saying."

I watched Ritchie dial up the volume on his Nano. Oblivious to his mother and me, he grabbed a spoon from the silverware drawer and headed to the freezer, pulled out a pint of Ben & Jerry's, and spooned in a few mouthfuls of AmeriCone Dream.

"Rich, put the ice cream away," his mother said.

"Are you kidding me?" the boy said, continuing to spoon the Ben & Jerry's into his mouth.

Erica spoiled the kid. What sensible parent gives a nine-year-old an iPod and lets him eat directly out of an ice cream container right before dinner?

Erica slipped on a fetching yellow apron. "Augie, how do you like your steak?"

"Somewhere between rare and tartare, not to put too fine a point on it. I like it bloody," I said, clowning for Ritchie's benefit.

"Gross!" Ritchie screamed.

"Do you want me to grill it at all, Augie?"

"I can do it if you like."

"No, I want to do it for you."

As I fought the instinct to scratch my right thigh, Erica slipped her long fingers under the starched collar of my shirt. Ritchie pulled out his earpods and parked his Nano in the dock on the far end of the kitchen counter. Pretty soon Ritchie took hold of my hand and smiled up at me. "Mom says we can play cards on the deck, if it's all right with you."

"After we eat."

"Yeah, after we eat."

"Sure." I tried to understand the meaning of all this affection directed my way and realized I might as well give into it. I threw open the refrigerator. "Hey, what the heck can I do around here? How's about I toss a salad?"

"That'd be great, Augie."

"I'll even make my famous vinaigrette."

Ritchie tugged on my hand. "What makes it famous?"

I bent over and whispered in the boy's ear. "It's the Dijon mustard."

"Are you kidding me?" he screeched.

I watched Erica, with her yellow apron flapping, hoist the platter of meat and head out the back door to the grill. What would happen now, I wondered, if Odegard climbed into his car and lit up the little device in my coat pocket?

CAPTIVE

A few hours later, after we'd eaten our steaks and wieners, coleslaw and salad, and gone through a bottle and a half of Syrah and two bottles of Stewart's root beer, after we'd cleaned up the mess we made and played hearts on the deck until the mosquitoes began to eat us alive, after we tucked Ritchie into his bed, and made love in Erica's bed, I lay awake, scratching my thighs. I was troubled again by my performance. Erica, with her lips formed in a pout, slept on her back. Downy-skinned, and with her intense green eyes shut, Erica seemed as if she'd slipped back into her girlhood. I had trouble seeing her as the woman who'd just been so rapturous, or as the high-powered attorney who represented insurance companies in personal injury cases. As Erica tensed up in a flash of dream, I dropped my hand lightly on her forehead. She responded with a sweet, gurgling sound in her throat.

I turned to my side and thought some more about my failure in the sack. I'd been taking her from behind, fucking merrily away, and then went soft, just as Erica got fully aroused. A hormone deficiency or the brain? It hardly mattered. I'd saved the day, as had become common, by going down on her. In a matter of months, I'd become a specialist. What once had been a rare pleasure for me had turned sour. I began to feel like a captive of cunnilingus. Tonight, Erica couldn't get enough of it and it took a good half hour of concerted effort to push her over the mountain.

The last time I saw Dr. Jacks, he offered to prescribe Viagra or Cialis—"Whatever's your pleasure"—but I wanted no part of such drugs. I was convinced my fortunes would soon change.

Erica woke from her fifteen-minute snooze and smiled up at me. "You're the one who's supposed to fall asleep."

"Why me?"

"The man, silly." She flashed me a coy smile. "You're supposed to fall asleep immediately after shooting your wad."

"I didn't exactly shoot my wad."

"Well, it was terrific for me."

"Yeah, I got that." I propped myself up on a pillow.

"You were great, Augie."

I ruminated for a moment about my greatness. How come I didn't feel great?

Erica snuggled close. "Augie, would you ever consider marrying me?"

"Nope."

"Why?"

"I'm still married, for Christ's sake."

"You don't have to be."

"Yeah, I bet you know a good lawyer or two."

"Don't be mean, Augie."

"Anyway, I'm too old for you."

"Who says?"

"You'd be tired of me in a week."

Erica stuck her tongue out at me and then reached under the covers and grabbed hold of my penis. "See, this guy is interested."

"I thought you were satisfied."

"I was satisfied. But that was then."

"I don't think I'd last three days with you. You'd throw me out."

"No way."

"I couldn't begin to satisfy you."

"You do satisfy me," she said, seriously now. She let go of my penis and kissed me tenderly above each brow. "You make me very happy. The problem is, I want to change the rest of my life."

"What are you talking about? Ritchie?"

"Not Ritchie. Ritchie and I are cool. But my job, I'm sick of my job. I'm tired of being an attorney."

"What would you do?"

"I don't know." She threw off the sheet. "I have to pee."

I watched her walk from the bed—her small, lovely breasts, the pink floral tattoo at the base of her spine. The first time we slept together, I asked her what the flowers were supposed to be and she pretended to get angry with me. *They're lilacs, dummy,* she said. *It's right out of Whitman: "When lilacs last in the dooryard bloom'd.*" I made a note that if things ever went south between Blossom and Sabbatini, I'd introduce him to Erica.

But the next time I saw her I brought her a gift: an oversized edition of *Leaves of Grass,* which I found at Magers and Quinn. The volume had rather cheesy illustrations by Rockwell Kent, but I liked the binding, a green, textured affair meant to simulate grass. By this simple gift, I entered into the realm of sensitive man, in Erica's imagining.

Now, scratching the rash on my right arm, I watched Erica walk loose-limbed back toward the bed, the blond plush of her dooryard glowing in the lamplight. My penis twitched and rose up with sufficient majesty. As Erica climbed into bed, I put my arm around her and asked, "So what's this about you're tired of being an attorney?"

"I don't want to talk about it," she said, turning her face away from me. "It's an awful job. I spend my time trying to screw guys out of what they deserve."

"But some of them are deadbeats."

She turned back to face me, her green eyes flashing. "Yeah, and a lot of them aren't. But it's my job to screw 'em all."

I knew what she was talking about. How odd; we both made our living off insurance companies. It was the doomsday scenario—the world had gone to hell and all that was left were the insurance companies.

"So, what do you want to do, Erica?"

"I don't know," she said, snuggling back into my arms. "It'd be great to do a job that meant something in the world."

"Yeah, I used to think like that."

"What happened?"

I grinned at Erica. "What happened? I got wise. I realized that

I'm a lazy ass by nature, and that it was the vanity of my youth that made me think I could make any difference."

Erica kissed me on the brow. "So you let the lazy ass win out?"

"Yep."

"I could learn how to be lazy."

I gave her a squeeze. "It's something to aspire to."

"How about I become a courtesan?"

"You want to become a working girl?"

Erica flashed her shiny white teeth at me, "No, I don't want to work. I just want to be kept."

"Right, and who would you find to do that?"

"You."

"I don't think so, honey. I can barely keep myself." You had to hand it to the woman for laying it all out there. *If I were truly clever,* I thought, tearing into my left thigh with my nails, *I'd find a way to be kept by her.*

I CELEBRATE MYSELF

Bobby Sabbatini came by the office early on Monday morning, dressed in a blue seersucker suit with a green silk tie that featured Whitman's fabled line "I celebrate myself, and sing myself" repeated a dozen times in subtle yellow script.

"What you doing over in Minneapolis?" I asked.

He sat on the edge of the teak sofa. "I've got some business here," he said vaguely.

"Business? Something top secret?" I said with a laugh.

"Hey, I'm going to level with you, Augie. Blossom wanted me to come by. She put me up to this, man."

"Put you up to what, Bobby?"

"She thinks you're smoking too much weed. She wanted me to talk about it with you. She says you have an addictive personality."

"She should know."

"Hey, I'm just leveling with you, man."

"What do you think, Bobby? You think I'm smoking too much?"

"I don't get into subjectives on this kind of shit, Augie."

"I try not to, either."

"What's to gain?"

I pulled out a juicy cigarillo of a joint. "Care for a smoke, Bobby?"

"Sure."

I lit up and we passed the fatty back and forth for a while.

"So, you been reading any poetry, Augie?"

I wasn't about to let on about all the McGrath I'd been ingesting. "You know," I said, "a little Ashbery."

"Anything more than that poem on the bridge?"

"No, not really, but I've been reading it a lot. Almost every day. I usually read it in both directions."

"You've been spending a lot of time on that bridge, man."

"Bobby, sometime you should don your Armani and stroll the Armajani."

"It's a nice bridge, Augie, but I prefer 'em when they take you over water."

"Yeah," I said, and took a honking hit, letting the smoke out in sputters as I spoke. "So the other day I'm up on the Armajani, over a dozen glistening lanes of traffic. Pacing back and forth, puzzling over the poem, and Nina runs by. My fucking wife. I had half a mind to run after her."

"But you didn't use that half."

"Nope. I just watched her go."

Sabbatini took a long toke and expelled it in the air above his head. "Hey, don't get yourself down, Augie."

"I don't intend to," I said, and had another blast of the fatty.

"Maybe you should be reading some grief poetry, Augie. Emily's the best." Sabbatini closed his eyes and recited.

"Grief is a Mouse—
And chooses Wainscot in the Breast
For His Shy House—
And baffles quest. . . ."

I nodded, unsure whether "Grief is a Mouse" was going to do the job for me.

Sabbatini caught my vibe and said, "Another way people deal with grief is through intensive physical activity. I've got the perfect exercise poem for you, Augie. It's got just enough rigor for you."

Sabbatini grinned at me. "I love this one. It's from one of the Russian River poets, Pat Nolan, master of Monte Rio." Sabbatini intoned the poem's bare title—"Exercise"—with pizzazz, and then recited the poem carefully, as if it were a Zen koan.

"Just as I stood up
I sat back down
again forgetting
what I stood for."

I didn't mind Sabbatini's having a laugh at my expense. I grinned back at him as he slipped off his seersucker coat. Pretty soon I found myself staring at the gun bulging from his shoulder holster. I pulled a roach clip from my desk drawer, attached it to the hunk of missile that was left, and passed it to Sabbatini.

"You know what this town needs, Augie?"

I wasn't sure I wanted to know. I glanced over at Sabbatini. He went suck, suck, suck on the roach and settled back. He was the first person I'd ever seen who'd gotten comfortable on the teak sofa.

"What this town needs is a poetry bar. I'm not talking that spoken word shit. Nah, that's joined at the hip to hip-hop. What I'm talking about is a bar that has a karaoke machine with nothing but good poems on it."

"You could just use an overhead projector, Bobby."

Sabbatini shook his head. "No, I want something flashier than that. I want beautifully letter-pressed broadsides projected onto the screen. I want atmospheric music playing in the background of each poem. I want a place where a guy would feel safe and cozy reading Theodore Roethke poems through the speakers."

I liked listening to Sabbatini rap and saw it as a public service. After all, I was one of the few people he could let his hair down with. Strutting around as a poetry proselytizing police detective is a delicate proposition.

Sabbatini stood up and started pacing. "Can't you see some large-lunged dude coming in to rap a sheaf of Whitman or one of Pound's Pisan Cantos? And the women, channeling Sylvia Plath, Jane Kenyon, Mary Oliver? Think of the night when a table full of beautiful incest survivors do Sharon Olds. That's what poetry can lead to—transformation."

"That's right," I said, "they come in sipping sauvignon blanc and they go out quaffing dirty martinis."

"No, Augie, don't you see? The potential is unlimited." Sabbatini threw his arms into the air in glee. "Guys would come down for bachelor parties to perform W. S. Merwin's 'The Vixen.'"

Sabbatini's eyes misted up as he told me about a sergeant down at Rice Street whom he had memorizing Auden. But his joy was short lived. He leaned against the wall, closed his eyes, and looked troubled.

"What's the matter, Bobby?"

"I don't know, Augie. Sometimes I wonder why Americans are as afraid of poetry as they are of al-Qaeda. Screw the ones who've decided that poetry's an effete enterprise. Let 'em party with the homophobes. It's the others who concern me, the folks who claim they don't get it, who think they're too dumb to read poetry. Thing is, they're not willing to be dumb enough. That's their problem. If you want to get inside a poem, you need to dumb down to your senses. That's where the receptors are. You need to accept that you don't know. Why should you know? What's the matter with a little mystery? They think the poem's a theorem. If they can't solve it, if they can't control it, then they're afraid of it. It's so American to want it all or nothing. If you can't conquer it, what good is it? Americans have become so frozen with fear, they've lost their sense of play. It's time to lighten up and lower our expectations. It's time to rediscover our basic fluency. If a man's not fluent, if he ain't got the flow, what chance does he have to converse with his soul? Consider Jim Moore, the king of fluency, the master of Saint Paul, and his poem 'Invisible Strings.'

> *"I vow to write seven poems today,*
> *look down and see a crow*
> *rising into thick rain on 5th Avenue*
> *as if pulled up by invisible strings,*
> *and already*
> *there are only six to go.*

"That, my friend, is fluency."

"A question, Bobby," I said. "Having truly cultivated the dumb part of my brain and become a master at lowering my expectations, shouldn't I have a special aptitude for poetry?"

"Absolutely, Augie. Although it might be a while until you're dumb enough for Auden. Ah, but Sergeant Brunansky, he slayed me the other day with 'Elegy for Yeats.' He's working on the Freud elegy now. After that, who knows; maybe the Bucolics. The question is, where do I send him after he's nailed a bit more Auden?"

It seemed to be a troubling consideration for Sabbatini, but suddenly his eyes shot bright. He grinned at me, and whispered, "Milosz."

Sabbatini loved Milosz. He loved pronouncing the man's name. It was really a treat to hear him say the full name. Bobby immersed himself in the project, just like a method actor, and by the time he'd finished saying *Czeslaw Milosz,* he all but hailed from Kraków.

"With Milosz," Sabbatini said, "you tease them along at first with one of the two-line gems. I'm particularly partial to his poem 'Learning.'

*"To believe you are magnificent. And gradually to discover that
you are not magnificent. Enough labor for one human life."*

"So, Bobby, tell me the truth here, are you still in the magnificent stage?"

Sabbatini nodded. "Yeah, but I'm beginning to sense the shift.
Meanwhile, let me tell you about my new convert. I've been
working with an FBI agent named Francis Synge."

"You've got the FBI memorizing poems?"

"Oh, Augie, this guy is a quick study. I mean, in a matter
of weeks he shot through the Black Mountain poets. Olson.
Creeley. Levertov. Ed Dorn. Before I know it, he's asking questions about Olson's essay 'Projective Verse' that I can't begin to
answer.

"Sounds like he's ready for some Lorca," I said, talking out of
my hat.

But I got away with it. "Yeah, the Gypsy Ballads are a
thought."

I decided to pick Sabbatini's brain about the poet whose epic I
was memorizing. "So in the end, Bobby, what do you think of
Tom McGrath?"

Sabbatini thought I was suggesting McGrath as the next poet
for his FBI agent. "No," he said, "not McGrath. The poor man
had enough dealings with the FBI. After he stood up to the
Committee in 1953, they were all over his ass. Even though he's
gone now, I couldn't feed him back to the FBI."

"But what about him as a poet?"

Sabbatini's eyes brightened. He took a deep breath that made
him swell. " 'Letter to an Imaginary Friend,' " he proclaimed, "is
the greatest American poem of the twentieth century."

I licked my chops at the thought of springing all ten thousand lines of the poem on Sabbatini.

"We can't all be poets, Augie, I grant you that. But we can pick up other people's poems and wear them like skins. It's an improved way to go through the world. You're in communion with another spirit. You'll never be alone again."

"You're scaring me, Bobby. What's happened to you? You used to be this driven detective, who couldn't ever chill, opening dead cases whenever things went quiet. You hit middle age and turn into Walt Whitman."

"A lovely compliment, Augie. You see, a man also needs to become a detective to his own soul."

"I don't know if I'm dumb enough to try that, Bobby."

I stood up and threw an arm around Sabbatini. I needed to get rid of him. Stoned as I was, I had work to do. I suggested we go down to Joe's Garage for an espresso. It was a trick I'd learned from Hemingway. That's the way Jake got rid of visitors in *The Sun Also Rises*. I figured if it worked in Paris, it could work in Minneapolis.

GALACTIC PIZZA

After I bid adieu to Sabbatini, I spotted the violinist sitting in the driver's seat of a red Saab, parked directly across from my office. I ducked into an empty storefront, figuring I could see what the violinist was up to from there. I didn't think she'd seen me. There had been no word from her all weekend, and, if the planted device was working, her husband's car had never left the garage.

At 10:40, my client started up her Saab. I wasn't sure who I was trying to get the goods on, her husband or the prodigy, but I decided to follow her. Before dashing to the Mazda, I waited until she'd backed out of her parking spot and followed the one-way around the corner. Half a minute later, I spotted the red Saab stopped for a light near the basilica. I gave her six or seven car lengths and followed her up Lyndale. Just before Lake Street, she pulled into a parking spot. I parked a quarter of a block north of her and sat pat in the car. The violinist, dressed in a blue suit, plugged a number of quarters in the meter and then rummaged through her purse, finding a few more. Wherever she was going, she planned to stay awhile.

It made me wince to watch Elizabeth Odegard dash across Lyndale in the same ferret-snouted shoes she wore to my office. She was almost clipped by a little electric car from Galactic Pizza, the driver dressed in a green and silver superhero suit. Who knew that Galactic was out delivering pizzas before eleven in the morning? The violinist seemed impervious, like a sleep-walking character in a cartoon. I watched her pause to look at photos in front of the Jungle Theater, which, according to its billboard, was presenting Sam Shepard's *The Tooth of Crime*. The violinist had some time to kill. She moved on to J.P.'s, next door, and studied a menu in the window. If she'd asked, I'd have recommended the calamari with Thai dipping sauce. Best in town. And as for the duck confit, it was nothing to sneeze at.

The violinist was directly across from me now, so I slipped down in my seat and watched her stroll past Galactic Pizza and enter the two-story building next door. I whipped the Mazda around and double-parked north of the building. I hurried inside just in time to see a first-floor office door close behind the violinist and her shoes. Jules McCracken, PhD. The woman's shrink. Now I'd have to find out why she'd led me to Dr. McCracken.

Meanwhile, it took some serious willpower to walk past Galactic Pizza. My appetite was coming on strong and I had a major jones for Galactic's "Paul Bunyan," made with toppings, they claimed, native to the Minnesota ecosystem: mozzarella cheese, morel mushrooms, wild rice, and bison sausage. I loved what the wild rice did to the texture.

BECOME A KILLER

I thought about the pizza all the way back to my office, but then ran into something that took away my appetite. A converted bread truck was parked directly in front of the Beamish Building, where I had my office. Magnified and enhanced photos of bloody fetuses were spread across the body of the truck. Even though I felt like retching, I walked around the truck and studied the images. Large block letters drove home the point:

IF YOU LIKE HOW THESE HUMAN BABIES LOOK AFTER THEY'VE MET THE ABORTIONIST—BECOME A KILLER

The truck made me angry. I wanted to find somebody associated with it. The windows were tinted. I knocked on the driver's-side door, pulled at the locked door latch. Nobody answered.

The driver was either lying low or had scrammed. The damn thing struck me as a form of terrorism. Unlike the truck bombs that blew up in Iraq, the damage this truck brought escalated the longer it drove around. By remaining visible, by staying intact, it kept on exploding.

BELIEVER IN EVIL

A couple of hours later, the violinist called to say that her husband had left town unexpectedly on Saturday for Prague.

"What's he doing in Prague?"

"That's not the kind of thing he tells me."

"Do you ask?"

"I know when to ask and when not."

"When's he getting back?"

"Tomorrow night."

"That's a lot of jet lag for a few days."

"Augie," the violinist said, "I thought it might be smart if you came over to see what Perry might be hiding."

* * *

A former client of mine had been murdered at the violinist's building, Le Palais, shortly after it opened in 1995. Gregory Sands, a clean-cut young investment banker with a taste for bad boys, got himself caught in an affair that he no longer wanted any part of. Sands sensed that he was being set up by his chum Jimmy Garibaldi, a Best Buy sales associate, who dressed in tight leather pants and bright velour tops. The murder was particularly grisly, with Sands manacled to a chair while Garibaldi and his paramour, a masseur named Patrick Harter, played a video of Sands and Garibaldi having sex. They claimed they'd distribute copies of the video to Sands's bosses at First Bank if he didn't pay off.

During Garibaldi's testimony at the trial, he described the deceased as an arrogant queer who laughed at his blackmailers and shut his eyes, refusing to watch the video. Infuriated by this affront, Harter, who was pretty coked up, shot Sands through each eye, at point-blank range.

The whole business had unfolded quickly. Sands started seeing Garibaldi just before Christmas and, by late January, Garibaldi began bringing Patrick Harter to the Sands condo. Sands hired me in mid-February, and the murder was committed on March 1.

Sands walked into my office for the first time on Valentine's Day, a detail I remember because I happened to be sitting at my desk cutting hearts out of a sheet of red construction paper. The curly-haired young man introduced himself in a whisper, as if he were disturbing a man at his work. I motioned for him to sit. In those days, I had little in my office—a straight-backed chair, not unlike the kitchen chair Sands would die in, and a wall of red file cabinets. Once seated, Sands smiled at me, a big, white-toothed smile, one of his professional assets. "I've never seen a cop on TV making valentines."

"I'm not a cop," I said, putting down my scissors, "and I'm not on TV."

"You must have a few girlfriends."

"A couple—my wife and daughter."

Sands asked about my daughter, her name and age, her grade in school.

"You're a good father," Sands said, his eyes tearing up, "making a valentine for your Rose."

Then Sands said he'd seen my ad in *Lavender* and liked the line I'd used: "Boyer's Very Private Investigations—Twenty Years of Experience." Sands explained being set up for a financial shakedown. Then he asked me if I had any trouble working for a gay client.

"Not at all."

Sands smiled at me. "I know you put the ad in *Lavender*. But I like to ask. I like to be up front. I don't want someone working for me who doesn't take me seriously."

Sands said that his current problem had less to do with gay culture than with class. He told me about Garibaldi and his friend Harter. How Harter always had his massage table with him when he came by the condo, and that he got angry because Sands always declined the offer of a massage. He thought Harter, a big muscle guy, might be violent and asked me to find out what I could about Harter's past.

Sands's hunch about Harter was right. He'd been busted three times for aggravated assault and served eight months in a provincial prison in Saskatoon, where he'd blown out a knee playing minor-league hockey. The hank-haired slob ended up working for a number of trucking firms in a half-dozen states and provinces. In 1993, he was jailed again briefly after a bar fight in Minot.

Garibaldi, who'd been fired by Best Buy just after the New Year, had grown up in Northeast Minneapolis, getting by for years as a small-time hustler. He had a couple of burglaries on his sheet and had been busted three times in the early 1990s for prostitution. Despite Garibaldi's checkered past, he had no record of violence.

Sands was concerned about Harter and wanted a restraining order. I told him he didn't have grounds. Would the restraining order have saved Sands? Probably not. What pained me was that I hadn't taken the threat as seriously as I should have. The murder haunted me. Had Sands been a straight man or a woman, I might have responded differently. I had been duly warned, but in the end I'd regarded the poor man's concerns as at least one part homosexual histrionics.

The only good thing to come out of that grim incident was that I met Bobby Sabbatini at the scene. As an admired Saint Paul police detective, he was brought over by the Minneapolis crew to consult.

Dressed in a leather evening coat and a gorgeous pair of gray chalk-stripe pants, Sabbatini nodded toward the bloody corpse and said, "It makes you a believer."

"A believer in what?" I asked.

"A believer in evil."

MIRROR, MIRROR

The lobby of Le Palais was as I remembered it—filled with mirrors and shiny faux-marble floors that looked as if they were meant for an upscale LEGO set. But the lobby was only an overture to Elizabeth Odegard's condo. Mirrors lined both walls of the unit's narrow foyer, providing, in effect, a visual echo of an echo. A beautifully etched floor-to-ceiling mirror occupied much of the living room's west wall. The lovely objet d'art, hung in an ornate plaster frame above the fireplace, was not a painting but a Victorian mirror whose glass had clouded over at the corners. I kept myself from thinking about the reflections more than likely available in the master bedroom.

The violinist had changed her clothes since the morning. She greeted me in a matronly moss green linen dress that was too large for her. I thought Eileen Fisher, something Nina might wear for a long day of clients and consultations. As I watched her pad across the floor toward me in a pair of pink ballet flats, it occurred to me for the first time that my new client might possess a rich assortment of personalities.

She took my right hand in both of hers. "I'm so glad you came, Augie."

I caught a glimpse of myself in the floor-to-ceiling mirror. If I didn't know better, I'd have thought I was looking at a serious man. The guy was unshaven. His jaw set stiffly, with full lips, bunched halfway to a pucker. His brown eyes were large and steady—I'd have been tempted to say unforgiving, which is not how I think of myself.

The violinist motioned for me to sit on the large sofa, a cream-colored Italian leather that reminded me of automobile upholstery. Elizabeth sat across from me in a matching leather chair that swiveled.

"I looked your daughter up on the Web," she said with an impish smile. "I Googled Rose Boyer and ended up with her band. She really is a star. Minnesota Rose. And what a website she has. I listened to some of her old songs. One stuck with me. 'Imbedded.' It's quite catchy. I started singing it in the shower."

I took a close look at the violinist, trying to catch a wink in her expression, but she appeared to be playing it straight. I figured she was probably a Republican. Maybe she came from a long line of Daughters of the American Revolution. That would be enough in itself to explain a personality disorder.

"That's a pretty old song by now," I said.

"One of her greatest hits," Elizabeth said, again with no sign of irony. Then in a light, tremulous voice, that sounded nothing like Rose, the violinist sang:

"That's the thing about being imbedded,
you have far less chance of getting beheaded.

Once you make the choice to abdicate,
there's nothing left to do but fabricate."

Her face didn't reflect the words she'd just sung. It was like watching an Italian film poorly dubbed in English. There was something disembodied about the violinist. I wondered how she was medicated. I wanted to ask her about her shrink, Dr. McCracken, but decided to wait.

"Do songs that political get much airtime?" my client asked.

"No, I doubt that song was ever played. Too unpatriotic. The music-boosting sites on the Web really made that song."

"You must be very proud of Rose."

I nodded. I was ready to change the subject. "So, where should I begin looking, Elizabeth?" Maybe if I called her by her first name, I could keep her on task.

"Oh, yes. I think Perry keeps a lot of things hidden in his wardrobe closet."

I noticed a framed photograph of a young girl with a violin, presumably the prodigy as a child, on the wall behind her.

The grown-up violinist swiveled from side to side in her chair.

"It's very strange," she said, "to live with a man who's always locking and unlocking his closet door. He does it right in front of me. It makes me crazy. It's worse than his cheating."

I tried to gauge the sincerity of the violinist's voice as a bit of emotion crept into it. I noticed the bracelet on her left wrist—a charm bracelet with dangling silver instruments, linked eighth notes, key signatures, and treble clefs. The trinkets seemed the perfect link between the girl pictured on the wall and the woman swiveling in the chair in front of me.

"Let's go have a look," I said.

"I'm afraid I don't have a key."

"We might be able to get around that."

The violinist led me from the living room, past a good-sized study—her music room. I glimpsed a pair of rosewood music stands and a gallery of violinists in framed photos. Beyond the study, I nodded to myself in another floor-to-ceiling mirror.

"Like what you see?" my client asked.

"I don't know; the guy could use a shave."

"I like the look," she said with a teasing, take-me-I'm-yours expression.

I turned to face the violinist. If I had complimented her on her looks, the afternoon might have taken an odd twist. But I knew better, and she didn't exactly call my name.

"You have a lovely studio," I said.

"Thank you."

The uncomfortable truth was that I missed my wife. Since seeing Nina on the Armajani, I'd been steadily musing about her.

Now I stared into the violinist's eyes. "So tell me, Elizabeth, how long's it been since you stopped caring about your husband and his other women?"

My client didn't like the question. She nearly sneered at me and raised her shoulder in a shrug. "I haven't cared what Perry does for a long time. As I mentioned, I don't allow him to touch me."

"So, it's a marriage of convenience."

"You could say."

"And what exactly do you find convenient about it?"

This time the violinist did sneer at me. "You're certainly very nosy."

"It's my job."

"I suppose. Well, I'll tell you two things I find convenient: I get to play a very fine instrument and my husband is gone a good part of the time."

I nodded.

"You don't think that's enough compensation, do you, Mr. Boyer?"

I enjoyed the violinist mistering me. It came across as a quick spanking.

"You think the payoff should be bigger for living with a philanderer."

"That's none of my business. Let's have a look at the famous closet."

ODEGARD'S CLOSET

After nearly five minutes of fooling around, I finally got the lock to pop with my hook pick. I've got to say, I liked Perry Odegard's taste in clothes far more than I would have suspected. Hard to believe Speedo was a man with a yen for warm, homespun woolens. I had him figured as a cold-blooded dresser, a guy whose closet would be chilled by a flank of sleek Italian suits and patent leather shoes. But along with a beefy row of Harris Tweeds and plaid vests, Odegard's cedar hangers sported a wing of nubby British Isle suits, phantom guards poised to protect their master from just the type of invasion that I intended to make.

I turned toward the violinist, who looked a bit frightened. "Do you buy your husband his clothes?"

"No, no; occasionally a tie, but Perry is a fanatic about choosing what he wears."

"I see." I glanced across at a shelf of laundered shirts, starched pinpoints in French blue and in white, each folded tight and wrapped in a pale blue ribbon from the cleaners. The shirts were monogrammed above the pocket: POF.

"What does the F stand for?"

"Frazier," the violinist said with a grimace.

"Pardon me," I said, "and I'll take a look at what's to see in here."

Parting the sea of woolens, I ducked farther into the closet. After scratching both of my thighs to the point of screaming bliss, I shoved a ruddy brown nailhead left and a black houndstooth right and was nearly overwhelmed by the toasted-heat fragrance of wool, tinged with a twist of cedar. There was only the smallest shadow of light at the back of the closet. I dug in a pocket and pulled out my Mini Laser Flash, a pricey stocking stuffer that Rose found for me at Sharper Image a couple of Christmases ago. I flicked the Laser Flash on low beam and aimed it at the back wall. Up, down. A half-dozen violins, or at least that many cases, were lined up along the base of the wall. The guy had fiddles stashed everywhere.

I stooped to lift the cases one by one, and each bore the weight of a violin. I decided not to examine the violins right then. I aimed the flash to the left and the light bounced back at me from a glass display case filled with guns. I jumped back a step and the rib end of an empty cedar hanger, wedged against the wall, jabbed me in the shoulder. I opened wide to breathe but managed to stay quiet. The gun case wasn't locked. I pulled out a heavy pistol and turned it over a few times before finding a serial number below the barrel and forward of the trigger guard. I repeated the procedure with the other five guns and closed the case.

"Finding anything back there?" The violinist's voice was muffled by the wall of wool between us.

"Yeah, it's a gold mine."

I should have been wary, rooting around in a dark closet without an exit while a woman I couldn't vouch for stood between me and the light of day.

I pointed the flash below the glass so that I was able to make out my own feathery reflection in the gun case. Over the years, I've counted it as a badge of courage to have practiced my trade without carrying a weapon. And yet I've always known it was a foolish choice that would catch up with me. After all, what chance does an unarmed, pothead, existentialist detective have against the genuine existentialists running around with guns in North Minneapolis?

I realized that I was staring at a collection of Lugers. I muttered the words *Kraut guns* under my breath, recalling my childhood epithet for Germans.

"Are you coming out?" the violinist called.

"Not just yet." I thought to invite her to come and have a look at what I was facing, but I wanted a little time to think for myself.

I aimed the Flash to my left and discovered a cedar shelf lined with an orderly stack of books and pamphlets. I ran the light along the spines of a half-dozen gun books: *Brassey's Essential Guide to Military Small Arms; Textbook of Automatic Pistols; Lugers at Random; Axis Pistols; Weimar Lugers,* and even a French title, *La connaissance du Luger.* I wondered whether paging through gun books was an occupational requisite or if Perry Odegard actually got his jollies that way.

The music books began on the right side of the shelf. I shone the flashlight along the spines of two large volumes: *Violins of Cremona* and *Italian Violin Makers.* Next to them was a slender, slipcased volume, its spine stamped with a red swastika and hand-lettered in black ink. I aimed a brighter beam on its cracked spine. It read *Sonderstab Musik: Wien.* I carefully slid the volume from its case. It was a crudely constructed affair, bound in boards, that appeared to be part military report and part cata-log. It couldn't have been much more than eighty pages. Once past the early pages, which were big on numbers and signatures and a few official-looking stamps, it assumed the character of an eccentric catalog. Paired black-and-white photographs of the fronts and back of violins were affixed to each page. Some pages featured sketches of labels from Italian violin makers. I recog-nized the names of some of the makers: Testore, Guadagnini, Gagliano, Goffriller. I flipped through a series of pages that showed outlines of coded violins, rendered in pencil, with care-ful millimeter measurements of the backs, from F holes to soundboards, and so on. A scrawl of comments in German cov-ered the bottom of most pages. Irrational as it might seem, the little book with the swastika on its spine frightened me more than the firearms. I needed to find someone who could help me decipher it. "I'll be right out," I called, slipping the volume under my shirt.

As I slid back between the suits, I gave myself a few good scratches on each leg. Stepping out of the closet, I smiled at my client. "Your husband has a nice collection of German guns back there. Does he go in for target practice?"

"Perry's never shot a gun in his life, Mr. Boyer," the violinist said, sounding as if she were giving a prepared answer. "Perry's terrified of guns."

"And what scares you, Elizabeth?" I asked. "What is it that really scares you?"

The violinist opened her mouth as if she meant to answer, but then thought better of it.

NAZIS AND GNOCCHI

I went back to the office and Googled "Sonderstab Musik." To my surprise, there were a number of websites focused on a Nazi agency with that name. Its charge was to confiscate musical instruments from the countries the Reich invaded. It was a sophisticated effort employing hundreds of German musicologists. They followed invading troops across Europe, looting instruments and determining their value. Hundreds of pianos a week were transported back to Berlin, just from France. Picking violins was a lot easier. The Nazis intended to establish a college in Hitler's hometown of Linz to display the finest instruments and manuscripts from the musical culture of an extinct race.

After a couple of hours of Sonderstab surfing, I'd had a day. I was ready to wilt from malnutrition. I needed to eat and decided to hit Barbette before driving back to Saint Paul. A modest repast would do me. Perhaps a half order of mussels in red curry broth, with a grilled and buttered baguette, a field greens salad, and a pint of Bell's Two Hearted. Anyway, that's how I started out. I took a short break and leafed through the Sonderstab booklet with a second pint of Bell's. Then I ordered the gnocchi with sunburst squash, Fresno chili, and Boucheron chevre. When the final round of food came, I put away the booklet. Clearly, Nazis and gnocchi do not mix.

SURVEILLANCE WITHOUT RISK

The next morning I got to the office early. Sorted through the mail that had been stacking up for the last week and made a few calls on workers' comp cases. I talked with Blossom, filling her in on the Nazi violins and Lugers and asking her to find anything she could on Perry Odegard. Next I called Bobby Sabbatini and asked him to run a check on Odegard's Lugers.

At 10:30 I went down to the street. I thought the violinist might want to take me somewhere else on that fine morning. The red Saab wasn't parked out front, but it was early yet. I climbed up to the Armajani and read the Ashbery poem in each direction.

By the time I got back to the street, the red Saab was parked right where it had been the day before. My client revved her engine at 10:40. Once she pulled out, I followed dutifully in the Mazda. Instead of another destination, however, the violinist headed right back up Lyndale to the office of Jules McCracken, PhD. It was time for me to make an appointment with Dr. McCracken.

Back in my office, I called Lionel Ross, the proprietor of Lion's Stringed Instruments on Tenth and LaSalle. Two blocks from Orchestra Hall, Lion's is a busy establishment, a kind of barbershop for string players, who hang around and gossip on the parquet floors. Some bring their fiddles in to get restrung or their bows to be rehaired. Others come in for appraisals or to check the stock. Once in a while you'll see a bluegrass fiddler, or a smattering of parents with their would-be prodigies, but primarily the shop is the provenance of musicians from the two major orchestras in town.

I met Lionel ten years ago when I wandered into his shop looking for a new cello. After a lapse of many years, almost since college, I'd started playing again. Lion helped me find a decent, nearly affordable instrument—a German-made cello, not twenty years old. It had a surprisingly rich tone for an instrument built on a smallish pattern. After that, I'd hang around Lionel's once in a while, and I ended up working with the man to find a couple of missing fiddles.

I liked going by the shop just after it closed and getting Lion to talk. We'd stand around a workbench for an hour and the old dealer might describe the manner in which a Brescian violin maker carved a scroll. He'd muse about the supple yet bonding quality of a Cremonese varnish. Or paint an image of the way an amber or orangish-red hue was mixed.

A few times in the months after Nina left, Lionel had me out to his house in Saint Louis Park for supper. The dude slow-cooked a righteous pulled pork. I'd pick up a couple of bottles of decent red wine. Together we'd polish off a pot of pork for six, drink too much wine, and wax nostalgic about our lost wives. Lion's had died twenty-five years earlier from lupus. It was odd to see the salty old bastard grow maudlin.

"Lion," I said into the phone, "it's Augie; you have plans for lunch today?"

"Lunch? I got no plans."

"How about a silver-butter-knife steak over at Murray's?"

There was a pause on the end of the line.

"My treat, Lion."

"Augie, I like the sound of that. Give me three-quarters of an hour." Lion lowered his voice. "Claudio's got some cowboy in here looking at expensive fiddles. I don't like the looks of the guy."

"Tell me one thing, Lion," I said, the Sonderstab booklet propped open on the desk in front of me, "what's the market these days on an eighteenth-century Guadagnini?"

"What the hell kind of eighteenth-century Guadagnini you talking about, Augie? They got you working on another stolen fiddle?"

"Could be."

"You working on spec, for crying out loud?"

"Sort of."

"You know, that's really a stupid question, Augie—what's the market on an eighteenth-century Guad? That's like me asking you how much you'd pay for a dark-haired whore with big tits that you haven't laid eyes on."

I took a deep breath and said, "I don't pay for women, Lionel." That was the second time in a couple of days that prostitution and violins had been linked in conversation—a curious alliance.

"Don't play with me, Augie," said Lionel.

"I'm not playing with you."

"All right, Guadagnini. It's a big family, Augie. We've got Joannes Baptista, known as Placentinus, we've got Joannes

Baptista the second, and you can't forget Joannes Antonio, or Josef, or Laurentius, one and two, and, of course, there's the whole shitload of Giuseppes."

I lifted the book to look closely at the label. "All right, Lionel, you tell me. Here's what the label says: 'Joan es B pti ta Guad gn ni Cremonenis fec t Taurini 1777.'"

"You've got to be shitting me, Augie," Lionel said, a bit breathless.

"No, I'm not." It occurred to me for the first time that the label of the fiddle inside Odegard's trunk matched the one in the Sonderstab booklet.

Lion, quite urgently, said, "What color's the varnish, Augie?"

"Huh?"

"The varnish. WHAT COLOR IS THE FUCKING VARNISH?"

I tried to remember. "I can't tell."

"What do you mean, you can't tell? Is it a golden yellow, golden red, deep red, golden orange, or a hard brown?"

"I don't have the violin with me, Lion."

"Is this the instrument you're looking for, Augie? It's a famous instrument. It hasn't been seen since World War Two."

I didn't want to tell Lion any more over the phone. "It's an example."

"An example of what? What are we doing here, looking at pictures in a book?"

"Yeah, but they're black-and-white."

"Aw shit, you're breaking my heart, Augie."

"I'll bring the book with me."

"Why the hell do I need to look in a book? You can't put me on a roller coaster like that. You're gonna pay for that, Augie. I'm ordering the twenty-ounce rib eye on you."

RISK FREE

Before I left for lunch, I checked my phone messages. There was a call from Erica wanting to get together with me that night. A hello from Blossom—she'd found an interesting connection to Perry Odegard. And Detective Sabbatini recited a pacifist poem by William Stafford before mentioning that a check on Odegard's Lugers showed them to be phantom, "at least in this country."

I clicked into my e-mail. A few insurance-related messages that I left for later and something from Rose, which I opened.

> Dad, decided to come home for a few days before Labor Day
> to protest the antiabortion freakout at the state capitol.
> Just wanted to make sure you'll be there.
> —Rosie

I pecked a quick response. Sometimes I marveled at Rose's courage to stand out on a stage and be authentic. She must have gotten her boldness from her mother.

Despite my line of work, I've always carried myself with caution. My nature demands it. I should put a tagline under the name on my business card: Surveillance without risk. Take out an ad to that effect in the yellow pages. People want their detectives daring in the movies, but in real life they want the professional they hire to reflect their own caution. What cuckold wants to think that the dick who's tailing his wife has a bigger prick than he does?

But Rose has never worked for anyone else, just as she's never been the least bit interested in remaining undercover. Although I no longer had the paternal job of protecting Rose above all other creatures on earth, I still worried about the rabid fans and the hate mail that I knew she got. The last time we were together, she said: "Dad, listen: you've got to let Rose be Rose."

THE WINNING OF THE WEST

Lionel let out a happy sigh as the old waiter placed an oversized lunch plate, with a twenty-ounce rib eye, in front of him. It looked to me like a side of beef. I kicked back to check out Lion as he unfolded his napkin. Age had done a funny thing to his skin. Not so much wrinkled it as stretched it out, except where it got tight around his wide snout. The flare of his right nostril had a funny button of skin on it where they'd dug out skin cancers a half-dozen times. It looked as if they weren't done.

Lion tucked his serviette like a bib into the buttoned neck of his short-sleeve white shirt, the underarms of which, years ago, had turned a buttered yellow that the painter Larry Rivers would have been proud of. Lion actually winked at me as his napkin unfurled over his tie—a pastel rendering of old Vienna. I gazed down at my plate of roast chicken, pleased with my sensibleness.

The old waiter squinted at Lion. "Steak sauce?"

"Worcestershire."

As soon as Lionel finished with his first bite, I pulled the

Sonderstab book from my bag. I should have practiced a little more mindfulness and let Lion eat into the heart of his steak.

He angled his fork and knife on the plate, forming an arrow that aimed north of the giant slab of meat to the baked potato. "You're a prick teaser, Augie. You give me one bite of meat and then you pull the fork from my mouth."

"Thought you'd want to see this."

Lionel drew a pair of reading glasses from a protective sleeve in his jacket pocket, rested them low on his nose, and then grabbed the book. As Lion flipped through a couple of stiff pages, his mouth opened into an O. He muttered, "What the hell?" He quickly closed the book and handed it back to me. "Put this away," he said.

"What's the matter, Lion? I thought you'd be interested."

"Where'd you find that thing?"

"It came to me through a client."

"Put it away!" Lion hissed.

A bit confused by Lion's reaction, I slipped the Nazi artifact back into my book bag.

Lionel had another bite of steak and then took a wary look around the room. He bent toward me and whispered, "For Christ's sake, Augie, I've always heard about the Sonderstab project and the fact that catalogs like that existed, but I've never seen one. I don't know anybody who's seen one."

"Well, now you've seen one," I said, stabbing at my chicken, "but you didn't seem very interested in looking at it."

Lion dipped a small slice of steak into a puddle of Worcestershire and chewed on it slowly. "Hey, that little fucker put the fear of God in me, Augie." Lion laid down his fork and leaned so close to me that I was afraid of getting scratched by the cancer patch on his nose. "You know how much a book like that would get from the right buyer?" he said.

"How much?"

"Christ, I don't even want to think about it." Lion regarded his slab of meat again and carved three neat bites.

I cut into my chicken. "So, I suppose if you were able to offer the right buyer one of the prized instruments that's described in the book, along with the book, you could make a real fortune."

"Are you telling me something, Augie?" Lion whispered.

I whispered back. "I think I might know where one of those instruments is."

Lion pulled out the napkin protecting his tie. Old Vienna quaked with the motion. "Let's get out of here," Lionel said, standing.

"What are you talking about? What about your steak, Lion?"

"Let's go."

I stood up and hovered over the table for a moment, considering my plate of roast chicken with hardly a bite taken from it. Then I gazed at the blazoned char marks on Lionel's steak. The mammoth specimen and its companion potato, bursting with sour cream, stood like monuments to the winning of the West.

The black-vested waiter—a trim octogenarian with a boyish grin—approached the table. "Have to leave us so soon, sir?"

I nodded.

"Let me get you a couple of take-out containers and your check."

I glanced around for Lionel, but the man was already out the door.

SWAMPED

When Lionel suggested it, I thought it was the nuttiest idea I'd ever heard. But I have a healthy appreciation for the absurd. I couldn't help being amused by Lion's paranoia and, after we made the arrangements to rent the canoe, I went off to a public bathroom and smoked the rest of a sweet fatty.

It was quite lovely out on the lake. Warm, but with a nice breeze. Lionel loosened the knot of his tie. I pulled off my baseball cap and flipped it to him. "Here you go, maestro, put this on, it's getting hot out here. You ought to have your head covered."

Lionel looked suspiciously at the Seattle Mariners cap I'd grabbed from my cap rack that morning. "What the hell you doing with a Mariners cap, Augie?"

"It's serendipity, Lion; I must have known that we were going to be out at sea today."

"This isn't the sea," Lion grumbled, before slipping on the cap. "This is a fucking pissant lake."

Lion flipped open the double-sized Styrofoam box that held his lunch. "How the hell am I supposed to eat a steak with a plastic fork and knife while I balance a paddle and rock from side to side in this damn canoe?"

"You getting seasick yet, Lion?"

"Go to hell, Augie."

"Hey, it was your idea to come out here. You're the one who wanted to be sure we had some privacy. Like my office or your house in the suburbs wouldn't suffice. The cold war's been over for a while, Lion." Truth be told, I really did love the silliness of it. A paranoid stoner couldn't have come up with a more ridiculous setting for a private meeting.

From his seat in the bow, Lionel turned his Mariners-capped head to face me. Now that he'd loosened his tie, the pastel image of Vienna had been transformed from an orderly European city to a town ravaged by war or natural disaster.

Lion stared at my book bag. "You don't know what you have your hands on there."

I took a peek at the bag parked beside my left foot. "No, but you're going to fill me in."

Lionel turned back to the steak and potato balanced on his lap. He needed a strategy and he knew it.

I paddled through a narrow channel toward the center of the lake. "What the hell; it's a beautiful day, so we might as well enjoy ourselves."

Lionel made an awkward attempt at paddling but his paddle accomplished little more than skittering a shallow, useless trail through the water.

"Put your paddle down, Lion, and eat your lunch. I'll keep us going."

Lionel gave me a skeptical look but finally pulled in his paddle and laid it inside the canoe. I watched him take a deep breath before sticking the plastic fork in his steak. He looked determined if overmatched by the task.

"No sense standing on ceremony; pick it up with your hands, Lion."

Lionel heaved the plastic fork, slid a napkin around a corner of the steak, and lifted it to his mouth.

I watched Lion with his cancered snout gnaw at the steak.

"There you go, Leo. So, when was the last time you were in a canoe?"

Lionel, biting through some gristle, shook his head.

"You've never been in a canoe?! But you wanted to come out here to be safe. Don't you know that a canoe is the tippiest boat in the world?" This little bit of info made Lion flinch. There's nothing as satisfying as watching a person greedy for control end up with less than they started with.

I got out my meal and made dainty work of a chicken thigh. A dark-haired woman paddled past us in a lovely birch canoe. I waved at her and she flashed me a warm smile. Immediately, I wanted to change my life and run away with her, but she didn't need me, she had an Irish setter sitting up tall beside her. I forgot about Lion for a moment and enjoyed the buzz from the weed. It was like a warm heating pad, sensualizing the nerve nodules of my brain.

"That woman's crazy," Lion said, "going out in 'the tippiest boat in the world' with a high-strung dog."

"She looks like she's got it under control," I said. "But I remember the time Rose wrote us from camp. They'd been out on trail for a couple of days in canoes. And she swamped."

"What's swamp?" Lionel asked, looking up from his steak.

"That's when your canoe tips over. It's getting pretty hot out here. Wouldn't feel half bad to do that now."

"Don't get any smart ideas, Augie."

"Don't worry. So, anyway, Rose says in a letter: 'After we swamped I felt like an angel. I went under water, and my pockets filled up with little fish. I thought I was dead, but then I flew up out of the water and resurrected.' You know, she was always a poetic kid." I lifted my paddle out of the water and pointed it toward the shore. "There's Walter Mondale's house."

"He's got a nice view of the lake," Lionel said, and then with a start, "a nice view of us. That's the thing, we're a little conspicuous out here."

"Especially you with that steak. You've got folks in houses up and down the lake with their binoculars trained on you. And everything we say out here echoes to the shore."

Lionel gave me a look.

"I'm only kidding, Lion, but don't you think you overreacted a little bit?"

"You're an asshole, Augie," Lion said in a loud whisper. "Listen, a fool walking around with a Nazi bomb in his book bag isn't going to lecture me about overreacting." He turned and looked at me. "Where the hell did you get that thing?" Lionel put down his napkin-wrapped steak. "And what were you saying about a violin that matched up with a description in the Sonderstab catalog?"

"Remember the Guadagnini I asked you about?"

"Of course. So what's the story with the Guad?"

"You're not going to believe this, Lion, but I saw the Guad in the trunk of a car."

"Oh, fuck." Lionel stamped his feet and the canoe rocked one way and then the other. Lion took a deep breath once the canoe settled. "Was it the same Guad that's described in the book?"

"I think so."

"Oh, Augie, do you know how much the book and the violin would bring together?"

"How much, Lion?"

"I don't want to talk about it. It'd make me sick to my stomach. So you said it's a J. B. Guadagnini, 1777. That's a J. B., the second. I've never seen a J. B. II. I've seen a Placentinus—that's his uncle—but never a J. B. II. You can't remember what color the varnish was?"

"I can't remember."

"Whose car was it in, Augie?!"

"A violin peddler named Odegard."

"What kind of business are you doing with Perry Odegard?"

"You know him, Lion?"

"I know who he is. Dandy with a Jaguar. He's come into my shop. Tries to sell me instruments. Tries to pick my brain. I don't do business like that. I don't deal with gypsies."

"Is he a gypsy?"

"Does he have a shop? What the hell were you doing in his trunk?"

"Just nosing around."

I aimed the canoe toward the bridge and told Lionel to duck his head even though there was plenty of clearance. I tilted my head back as we went under, noting the small, dry-muddied mounds of swallow nests, although I saw no swallows.

Out into the clear of the lake, Lionel asked: "How come Odegard gave you that Nazi catalog?"

"He didn't give it to me."

"You stole it?"

"Borrowed it."

"You're mad, Augie."

"Yes, but that's a given. I did a little research on the Internet."

"Yeah, I know about Sonderstab," Lionel said, turning once more to face me, this time with a sober pinch to his lips. "It was terrible. They had warehouses across Europe. They took every instrument that had any value, every rare manuscript. They took phonographs and phonograph records. Nobody got any of it back. I met people after the war, musicians who had survived, guys with numbers on their arms. They came into my shop. If they weren't looking for their violins, they were looking for something. Maybe the guy doesn't miss his instrument as much as he misses his family, but it's got to ache to know that your precious violin may still be out there somewhere."

"So what's this Odegard character doing with the fiddles and the Sonderstab book, Lion?"

Lionel took several long, hard breaths. "I can't talk about this anymore, Augie; I get too worked up." He tossed a couple of scraps from his steak into the water. In seconds, a good-sized fish rose to the surface with a clean splash and mouthed the fatty gristle. "Carnivorous bastard," the violin dealer said with a chilly chuckle. Lion turned forward and picked up his paddle, dashing it wildly through the water a few times to scare away any other local fish. Satisfied, he snorted and put the paddle down.

We glided quietly for a moment and then I aimed us up the channel toward Cedar Lake.

"How'd you get mixed up with Odegard?" Lionel called over his shoulder.

"His wife's my client. I haven't even met him yet. What do you think he's up to?"

"Hard to say. I've heard about a collector out in White Bear Lake who's interested in acquiring instruments the Nazis had their hands on. You might see if there's a connection."

"Why would somebody . . . ?"

"Some of them think they can pick up good instruments for a bargain because the proper documentation doesn't exist. Then there's another kind of guy," Lionel said, turning back to face me. "You hear about them, I don't know if I've ever met one."

"What are you talking about, Lion?"

"You know, the kind of guy who thinks that anything the Nazis touched has been sanctified. There's plenty of these guys, Augie, whole conventions full of them. And nothing they like more than to collect. That's why that book scares the hell out of me. It'd be like the Holy Grail to these assholes. Plus, it has a utilitarian value. Collectors could use it like a catalog and try to trace the instruments. And if you had your hands on a notable instrument that's documented in the catalog, the sky's the limit. Irrefutable proof that the Nazis had it in their possession."

"Where would you sell it, Lion?"

"It wouldn't even have to be a neo-Nazi you sold it to. Just a run-of-the-mill multimillionaire who hates Jews. There's plenty of folks who qualify. Be quite a conversation piece for some Arab sheikh to have the violin and the Nazi catalog that it's in. I wonder how the hell Odegard got a hold of them."

"You think he's one of them?"

"Nah, the Nazi collectors just represent a stream of money."

Lionel turned forward and tossed the remains of his steak a good distance out into the water. "Fight over it, you ugly carp." Lion pulled out a handkerchief and gingerly dipped it into the lake, cleaning first his lips and then each of his fingers. "Let me have a look at that book once more," Lionel said, rising to his haunches.

I yanked the Nazi booklet out of the book bag, and the violin dealer did a little hop as he reached for it. I could see the small disaster before it happened—one of Lionel's feet stumbled on his paddle, his arthritic hips lurched left and then right to correct his balance, and Lion stumbled against the side of the canoe before we both hit water. Despite the dunking, I managed to hold the Sonderstab booklet aloft. It got splashed a little but not that wet.

As the two of us bobbed through shallow water toward the shore, I called to Lion, the Mariners cap twisted sideways on his head. "Hey, look what I saved for humanity; the Nazi Holy Grail."

"Augie," Lion shouted, "you really are an asshole."

HOW DO YOU DO, MISS ROSE?

I took a long, cool shower after getting home from our dunking in Lake of the Isles. Had a few hits of doobie and lounged in the living room, listening to Dylan's *Blood on the Tracks*. The thing about Dylan is that you can listen to the same music over and over without getting bored. Rose taught me that. I grew up listening to Dylan, but I hadn't paid much attention to him in recent years until Rose put me on a Dylan crash course in advance of our Memphis road trip. Rose had proposed the trip as a way for me to get me out of my funk, just months after Nina left. I was hesitant. I pointed out that Dylan would be appearing in Saint Paul later that summer.

"But I won't be here," Rose said—she'd be back on tour—"and you'll miss out on the rare and wonderful opportunity to take a road trip with me. Who better to show you around Memphis, Dad?"

It was a lovely and diverting trip with plenty of father–daughter bonding. We took our time driving down and spent a couple of nights in funky motels along the river, one night in Keokuk, Iowa, the next in Cape Girardeau, Missouri, towns that Rose seemed to know everything about. In the car, we often broke into song together. We worked out a pretty cool duet on "Like a Rolling Stone." Rose christened the trip the Biscuits and Gravy Tour after I started ordering biscuits everywhere we stopped. She'd point at the white sausage gravy spilling across my plate and say, "That's pig slop you're eating, Dad." I'd smile at her and say, "It's a dirty job . . ." Then I'd watch her eat a baked potato or the organic yogurt she smuggled in from the cooler in the car.

I was surprised by how much Rose confided in me during the trip. She talked about her failed love affairs and about the fear she felt going onstage. She even described the method of self-hypnosis she'd devised to manage the fear.

I, in return, revealed things I'd never told anybody about the period when I went to meetings and was the only doper in a room full of alcoholics. I told her how I'd gotten in touch with some sort of primal shame. How I taught myself to recognize it—like the sound of a dead note on the piano—every time it surfaced, so that the shame no longer resonated like an all-consuming rhapsody. "The trouble," I said, "is that since your mother left, all I'm hearing is dead piano notes, a steady procession of boinking, wooden notes. They've pretty much taken over my internal piano."

Rose nodded and offered a heartbreaking smile. "I know all about shame," she said, without elaborating.

"Yeah," I said, "our sense of shame, even more than opposable thumbs, is what makes us human."

Rose showed me all around Memphis. We went to the Civil Rights Museum and drove up Elvis Presley Boulevard to gawk at the Elvis freaks lined up in front of Graceland. At the Stax Museum, Rose was like a docent, with a host of riffs about Booker T and the MGs, the Bar-Kays, and Otis Redding. People started recognizing her there, despite the shades she was wearing and the Amsterdam Ajax cap with the long brim. She nodded back and said hi, and when a guy and his girl approached her for an autograph, she obliged and said, "Just showing my dad through the history of R & B," and they looked at me as if I were some sort of a celebrity.

The Dylan concert was at the AAA ballpark, and we sat in the grandstands until Willie Nelson came on and Rose talked me into going down onto the field. "Follow me," she said, and we wove through the outer ring of the crowd, where folks stood loosely bunched, drinking beer and smoking grass. It got much denser the closer we got to the stage. People hollered as we tried to slide past them. I suggested that we'd probably gone as far as we should, but Rose said, "I don't usually do this, Dad, but this is Dylan." Finally, somebody recognized Rose and a space cleared for us. We ended up two rows from the stage, people patting us on the backs as we slid by, some hollering "Yo, Rose," and taking photos of her with their phones.

It was a thrill to be down in the pit in the middle of so much energy, seeing Willie Nelson, then Dylan, both aging masters, stir up the crowd. For a flash, I felt as if I had a future.

Just before Dylan launched into his final encore, "All Along the Watchtower," Rose took off her cap and shades and sang out a crystalline, three-note "Hey there, Bob" that cut right through the crowd. She'd met Dylan the summer before, after a concert she'd given in Seattle. Now Dylan, with sweat pouring down his face, raised his neck turtlelike out of his white viceroy coat, spotted her, and intoned, "How do you do, Miss Rose?"

GIRL WITH DEEP POCKETS

What I've always admired in an assistant is an ability to anticipate the holes that I, being such a highly evolved slacker, tend to leave. Blossom covered for me very nicely. She was also a better snoop.

I particularly needed Blossom during this period. Sucking down so much cannabis put me at a decided disadvantage. It fractured my sense of purpose. I'd groove for too long on peripheral curiosities that had nothing to do with the job. Sometimes I'd get blissed with such a bump of benevolence that it was hard for me to imagine evil. I'd stall and lose sight of the fact that, even with the simplest workers' comp jobs, I had to assemble a coherent case. Some assembly required was difficult enough for me in the first place. If Blossom hadn't repeatedly nudged me out of the ether, I'd have been in big trouble.

When the doorbell rang, I was singing along with Dylan's "Buckets of Rain." Blossom stood at the door with her hands on her hips.

"I was just thinking about you, kid."

"Where the hell you been, Augie?"

"Another . . . another misadventure."

I was a bit dumbfounded by the sight of Blossom in a pair of red cargo pants and a black halter top, her nipples standing at attention.

"I've been leaving you messages everywhere," she said, clearly peeved. "I found out some stuff you're gonna want to know, but you don't even call me back."

"Sorry. Like I said, I ran into some trouble today."

"What kind of trouble?"

I shrugged. I strolled by the stereo to turn down the Dylan. Suddenly, the sound of the sputtering air conditioner filled the room.

Blossom took a sniff at the room. "You're like a time warp, Augie—an old doper listening to Dylan on vinyl."

"Yeah, just call me the Dude."

"The Dude." Blossom shook her head and then emptied the contents of her deep pockets onto the coffee table. I'd never seen Blossom carry a purse. But this purging struck me as a curious habit. I wondered if it came from her time in prison, always being forced to come clean. You'd think she'd have gone the other way and become more secretive. I took it as a sign that she trusted me.

Blossom left quite an assortment of items on the table: driver's license and bank card, cell phone, iPod, Swiss Army knife, pad and pencil, key chain, lip gloss, assorted coins, and a silver money clip, with an image of a winking Lucifer, wrapped around a few tens and twenties. But most surprising was a small paperback—*Lunch Poems,* by Frank O'Hara. Sabbatini had been working his poetry mojo on Blossom and she must have figured it was time to let me know.

When she headed to the bathroom, I stole a look at the Top 25 list on her iPod and noticed a number of Rose's songs among the ten most played.

Neko Case and Her Boyfriends—"Mood to Burn Bridges"
Minnesota Rose—"The Yours Truly of the Tale"
The New Pornographers—"Use It"
The Ramones—"I Wanna Be Sedated"

Minnesota Rose—"Razor Wire Rosary"
Minnesota Rose—"Doggerel for Daddy"
Gillian Welch—"The Revelator"
Patti Smith—"Walkin' Blind"
Minnesota Rose—"Ballad of Abu Ghraib"
Prince—"When Doves Cry"

Blossom also had a mass of poets mixed into her artist list. Sabbatini must have loaded them on. There was Ashbery, Bly, Creeley, Robert Duncan. Straight through the alphabet to William Carlos Williams. She must have had fifty poets on there. It cracked me up to think of Blossom walking around listening to Bly read his ghazals.

Blossom's return to the room surprised me. "What are you doing with my iPod?"

"Nada."

"Put it down, Augie."

BORN FREE

A minute later we were sitting across from each other. Blossom crossed her legs in the green wicker chair, while I slumped on Nina's prized Baker sofa, a bit frayed now, my legs stretched across the coffee table near Blossom's unpocketed goods.

"So, what the hell happened to you this afternoon, Augie?"

"I ended up swimming in Lake of the Isles. Me and Lionel Ross."

"That old violin dealer?"

"Yep."

Blossom sipped at her water. "I didn't think Lake of the Isles was a swimming lake."

"It's not. That's why we swam with our clothes on."

"Aw, man, you're really doing too much kumba, Augie."

"Maybe so." I picked a roach out of the ashtray and lit it. "So, what did you find, Blossom?"

"A connection between Odegard and a guy named Frederick Kunz. I asked Bobby to run Odegard's name through the system." Blossom picked up her notepad and flipped through it. "Hey, will you quit smoking that shit, at least while I'm here, Augie?"

"I thought you still liked a little contact high," I said, taking a final hit and then snuffing the roach in the ashtray.

"Okay," Blossom proceeded, all business, "so in 2004, Odegard was sued by a violinist in the Saint Paul Chamber Orchestra. Guy named Heschel claimed that Odegard falsified documents and exaggerated the value of a violin he sold him. The case was thrown out. It's the only record of Odegard, at least under that name, having any dealings with the law."

I pulled my legs off the table and sat up straight. "So where's this Kunz come in?"

"He had quite a hand in clearing up this case and getting it settled out of court."

"Odegard's attorney?"

"Nope."

"Then who is he?"

"Check it out. I did a little research on this joker." Blossom flipped through her notepad. "Frederick Kunz is a leading citizen of Woodbury. Made his money in real estate and got out when the getting was good. Laid a bunch of bread on both the police and fire departments, and in 2002 was named an honorary fire chief by the Woodbury Fire Department, in recognition of all the new equipment he financed. He's got a Little League ball field and a rec center named after him. But that's just the local part. Kunz was one of W.'s elite donors for both presidential campaigns. He became a 'Super Ranger' after rustling up more than a mil in donations for the last campaign. This netted him a White House sleepover."

"Does that mean he got to read W. a bedtime story?" I asked.

"Yeah. Okay, so the guy was offered two ambassadorships, which he declined, and he's also a big contributor to the state and national Republican parties and has been a delegate to the last three Republican National Conventions."

"Cool. So the guy's filthy rich, has friends in high places, and lots of people owe him favors."

"Right. One more thing—he's the regional director of an organization called Born Free."

"What the hell is Born Free? I've heard of that."

"It's a radical antiabortion group."

"That's right; I read about it in Dexter Dunn." I stood up and began pacing. "Born Free. I was hoping it was some kind of save the raptor society."

"No, these are the assholes responsible for all those ugly trucks going around town."

"Yeah, I saw one of those mothers, parked right outside of my office. Made me want to puke."

Blossom nodded and looked down at her hands. "I had one once. I was pretty young." She took a finger and traced the crude tattoo on her left hand. "One of the most unhappy days of my life. It still haunts me. And I don't need some evangelical motherfuckers reminding me of it when I walk down the street."

"I'm sorry." I rested my hand on Blossom's arm.

She turned her head away. "Anyway, I think these pricks are involved with the Labor Day rally on the capitol grounds."

"Yeah, Dexter had all that. Apparently, the governor's behind the whole thing. Dexter sees it as part of Holsom's Machiavellian scheme to get the VP nod."

Blossom picked up her chain of keys and began jingling them.

"And Rose is coming to town to play the antirally or something."

"Rose is coming?" Blossom asked with delight.

"Yeah, it's next weekend already. So why's Kunz bailing out a putz like Odegard?"

Blossom flipped open her notebook again. "In standing up for Odegard, Kunz claimed he had purchased thirteen rare Italian violins from the dealer since 2001. He said he was satisfied with the values the guy put on the instruments."

"Thirteen. That's a lot of fiddles." I did a little pacing. "Kunz must be the Nazi collector."

"Nazi collector?"

"Yeah, Lionel told me about a guy—I thought he said White Bear Lake—who's into violins that were confiscated by the Nazis."

"That's fucked up."

I pulled a handkerchief from my pocket and wiped a ribbon of sweat from my forehead.

"Your air conditioner is for shit, Augie. So what have you found on the violinist?"

"Not much yet. I tracked her to her shrink's the last couple of mornings. She made a point of leading me there. I'm going to make an appointment for myself with the guy, see what I can find out. Otherwise, the lady's husband's off to Prague, probably picking up more fiddles. I went through the guy's closet yesterday. Fucking clotheshorse. Besides the violins, he has a nice collection of Lugers that, according to Sabbatini, aren't registered."

Blossom applied a couple of stripes of gloss to her lips. "Why do these boys like playing with guns so much?" Standing, she gathered her things back into her pockets. "All right, I'm out of here."

I walked Blossom to the door.

"So, Augie, when I couldn't get in touch with you today, I took a ride out to Woodbury. Kunz has a mansion on a fucking hilltop. And guess what he's got out front—two giant Snoopy sculptures flanking his front door. I figure he's got security cameras inside them and that they do their own snooping."

"Two Snoops," I said with a laugh. "That's a nice touch, not something every Nazi would think of."

WAXING NOSTALGIC

Not long after Blossom left, I was surprised by a call from Nina. A bit ripped still, I said, "Ah, my estranged wife."

"Don't call me that."

"All right, my strange wife."

Nina ignored my variation. "How are you, Augie?"

"I'm swell, and you?"

"I've been better."

"I didn't say I haven't been."

"No, you're swell, Augie."

"Your point?"

"Don't have one, but I've been wanting to get in touch since I saw you on the bridge."

"And here we are."

"If you'd rather not talk now . . ."

"I can talk."

"Actually," she said, "I was wondering if we could get together. No big thing. Maybe for coffee."

"What's up?"

"I'd rather tell you in person."

"You getting married again, Nina?"

"Hardly."

"Good, because you need to get divorced first."

"Thanks for the reminder."

We agreed to meet for coffee the next day at the Dunn Bros. in Loring Park. But five minutes later, Nina called back, wondering if we could meet at the Institute of Arts.

"Why there?"

"I don't know, I always liked looking at paintings with you."

"Are you going soft, Nina? You waxing nostalgic in your old age?"

"Yeah, it's creeping up on me."

"Well, it seems to me that your nostalgia and my nostalgia should be going separate ways."

"Look, Augie, I won't take more than a half hour of your time."

I wanted to ask her again what this was all about, but I flashed on the possibility of some dark reality. Maybe she was going to tell me that she'd been diagnosed with pancreatic cancer. "Hey, Nina," I said, "you can have a full hour of my time."

FIRED AND REHIRED

The next day, a little after noon, Elizabeth Odegard paid an unannounced visit to my office. She'd gone home and changed clothes since getting back from her visit to Dr. McCracken. It was the third day in a row that I'd followed her there. She'd dressed for the doctor in a red silk ensemble and a pair of matching shoes. Now she was in designer jeans, a man's blue-striped dress shirt, and a pair of clogs. She stood just inside the door, her mouth slightly open, a little fear in her eyes. I'd be lying if I said she didn't look appealing.

"Perry's home from Prague," she said, looking at me with a bit of panic in her eyes. "He's furious. He accused me of stealing some book from his closet."

"A book?" I led the violinist over to the teak sofa. My prick suddenly went hard. For Christ's sake, I thought, this is not the time I needed a hard-on. I scooted around my desk and sat behind it.

The violinist didn't seem to notice. "I don't know what he's talking about," she said. "Some instrument catalog from Germany. You didn't see anything like that when you were in there, did you?"

I shook my head. "No, I don't remember anything like that. I saw a number of books on guns and two or three big, glossy books on violins." The woman was still standing. "Why don't you have a seat?"

Protected by my desk, I watched the violinist fold herself in half and sit on the edge of the teak frame. "What's your husband think you're up to?"

"I don't know."

"What *are* you up to, Ms. Odegard?"

"I don't know what you mean," she said, raising her eyebrows.

"Why have you hired me?"

"I told you. To find out what my husband is doing."

I caught the violinist's eyes. "I think you already know all you want to know about your husband. What's going on with Jules McCracken, PhD?"

"How do you know about Dr. McCracken?"

"Come on, you've led me to McCracken's every morning this week. You park right outside my office."

"I haven't led you anywhere." The violinist opened her mouth and licked her upper lip slowly.

I wondered if she could possibly know that I was sitting behind my desk with a prodigious boner.

"I had no idea you were following me," she said. "I like to park there and meditate, looking out at the lake."

I offered the violinist a sweet smile. "You can't see the lake from that spot, Ms. Odegard."

"But I know it's there."

"How often do you see Dr. McCracken?"

The violinist shrugged. "Quite often lately."

"How often is that?"

"On weekdays."

"Every weekday?"

"Yes."

"That must get rather expensive."

The violinist had crossed her legs and was holding her arms

folded over her breasts as if she were determined not to let any more of herself out.

"So, Dr. McCracken is your shrink?"

"I guess you could say that."

I fixed my eyes on the violinist's moist lips. "What does he help you with, Ms. Odegard?"

"That's personal," she said, putting a hand in front of her mouth.

"You seem rather uncomfortable talking about yourself."

"Well, I didn't come here to talk about me." The violinist stretched out her long neck. It was quite a lovely neck and I wondered how it would look adorned with a string of beads.

My prick was still man-sized. I took a second to discreetly scratch my left thigh. "All right, let's talk about your husband then. His specialty seems to be trading in instruments that were once possessed by the Nazis."

The violinist's eyes rose in alarm and she pinched her lips together.

"Instruments confiscated from Jews," I said. "But that much you already knew."

"I didn't know about the Jews."

"No? You knew about the Nazis and you knew that the instruments had been stolen. You just weren't sure who the Nazis stole the instruments from?"

"Right."

"That seems unlikely."

The violinist sat back on the sofa, trying to affect a casual disinterest.

"Are you Jewish, Ms. Odegard?"

"No."

"I didn't think so. I'm not, either. But my wife is. I should say my former wife. But that makes my daughter Jewish, you see. So I figure the Nazis could have walked right into our home and waltzed off with my cello, all my quartet music, my records of Pablo Casals, my tuner, my turntable, my CD player, and my iPod, if it happened to be lying around. What else? They'd have taken our piano, dead keys and all. They'd probably have taken my daughter's guitar, the original manuscripts of her first songs, and so on. And then someday it would all end up in the hands of a guy like your husband, who'd try to sell the lot for a premium to a tycoon who wears a silk swastika T-shirt under his suit and believes that anything touched by the Nazis has been blessed by God."

The violinist had turned pale. She bit her lower lip. "That's very shocking, Mr. Boyer. I don't know what to say."

"I'd like you to tell me everything you know."

"I already have."

My prick finally under control, I stood and walked around the desk. I faced the violinist, whose hands were folded in her lap. With her mouth slightly open and her head tilted to the side, she looked as if she was straining to hear a message.

"Are you hearing voices, Ms. Odegard?" I asked with a jokey laugh.

I could see that my client hadn't taken it as a joke. "What are you talking about?"

"Oh, nothing, it was just the way you had your head tilted. Like you were listening for instructions."

I boosted myself onto my desk and dangled my legs for a moment. The violinist scooted farther back on the sofa. A little blood had gone out of her face.

"So, do you know a man named Frederick Kunz?"

My client gulped for air, and then shook her head no.

"I thought you might know him, Ms. Odegard."

"Who is he? Why should I know him? What does he do?"

"Your husband does business with him."

"Well, perhaps I've met him, but I don't recall his name."

Clearly, Elizabeth Odegard was lying, but there didn't seem any point in pushing her on it right now. I pulled a tin of Altoids out of my pocket and shook it. "It sounds to me like there are about seven of them in there. What would be your guess?" I held the tin out toward my client and flipped the lid. I was surprised that she actually looked into the tin with me. I nodded my head as I counted. "What do you know—seven. Isn't that something? Except for the fact that I cheated—I already knew how many were there."

I held my hands open in an aw-shucks gesture, then plucked out three Altoids and dropped them onto my tongue. I smiled at the violinist, who appeared a little dazzled by my bit of low-grade flimflam. I remained seated atop the desk and watched her stand.

"Mr. Boyer," she said in a slow, even tone, "maybe there isn't anything more you can do for me. I don't think I need your services anymore. I trust the retainer will cover your expenses up to now."

"I haven't accomplished anything for you, ma'am. I'm happy to return your retainer."

The violinist shook her head. "That won't be necessary."

"It's really not my policy to take money from confused young women whom I've been unable to help." I said that with a bit of bite. I was pissed to have wasted the time. "Hey, this won't be the first time I've been fired without having a clear idea of why I was hired." But there was something going on there that I didn't want to give up. "Listen, Elizabeth, why don't you consider keeping me through the week? I might find out something useful for you. Tell me one thing. Who is it you're afraid of? Your husband?"

The violinist shook her head. "Perry doesn't frighten me. He's very predictable."

"So it must be somebody else. Dr. McCracken?"

"Of course not."

"You do seem worried." I could almost smell her fear. I sniffed the air and got a whiff of her fragrance. I couldn't place it, but was glad that she'd switched from Ysatis. This one had a note of honeysuckle. I guessed Annick Goutal's Le Chèvrefeuille, a fragrance Nina also wore, but in the old days.

The violinist was hiding her eyes. I wondered how much of her fear came from self-induced paranoia. Suddenly, she looked up at me for a long, unguarded moment. For the first time, I saw the frightened girl, small freckles and all, break out of the put-together woman's face. Her eyes grew very large and she whispered: "Frederick Kunz."

BLIND MAN'S BLUFF

I planned to get to the museum early so that I could spot Nina before she saw me. But she was standing in front of the Max Beckmann triptych, the appointed spot, watching me amble toward her. She flashed me a full-faced version of the girlish smile she had when I first knew her.

In her mid-forties, Nina was still a handsome woman. She

had a long, slender face with full lips, cheekbones like those of a stylish girl from Prague, and a pair of big brown eyes that she could work to her advantage. Now, however, her eyes were shaded with anxiety. She'd hoped I'd give her a kiss, a little peck on the cheek, but I stayed at a safe distance. I watched her eyes narrow as she took in my distance with a nod.

"I saw you coming up the stairs, Augie."

Beat at my own game. "You came early."

"Yeah, I was done with my last client at two."

As if on cue, we both turned to face the huge Beckmann with its lush palette and half-naked creatures sprawled across the canvas. I've always admired the painting. The texture is a thing of beauty, like a late Braque with sand mixed in the paint. Beckmann titled it *Blind Man's Bluff.* I had no trouble identifying with the dude in the blindfold—the poor, unseeing man, the object of all shame. Beckmann, a German exile living in Holland, painted it toward the end of World War II. I counted nineteen distinct characters, if you included the figure in the donkey head and tuxedo. There's a cross-eyed woman playing a lovely harp. A joker with sticks and a conga. A couple of slackers in togas playing conical flutes. The large, spiky leaves of a sansevieria give the crazed cabaret a blush of the tropics.

Nina laughed, nodding at the Beckmann. "It's just like my life."

"What, one long party?"

"Chaos, is what I was thinking. No rhyme or reason to the way things turn out."

I glared at her. "I'm sure there was plenty of rhyme and reason when you left me."

"I can understand why you'd still be angry."

"Of course. You're the anger specialist, after all."

"Don't be mean, Augie."

Nina looked back at the giant Beckmann. "I used to love looking at paintings with you. All the things you saw. The questions you'd raise. I loved the way you included me in your speculations. You'd say: 'Doesn't it seem like that single dark line suggests the whole mountain's in shadow?' or 'Do you think he instinctively worked the clouds to go against the grain of the mountain? Is he striving for a sense of turbulence or a pastoral mood with a bit of foreboding on the horizon?'"

"It was all bullshit, Nina."

"Don't say that."

"You were easy to bullshit, so that's what I did."

Nina wasn't having it, but I didn't want to find out what had brought on her rush of nostalgia.

Nina turned away from the Beckmann. "I remember the day when it occurred to me that anybody who responded to a painting with such sensitivity would make a good lover. We were standing in the Hans Hofmann room in the Berkeley Museum. I didn't care for Hofmann's paintings, and there was a roomful of them. I told you that they looked wooden to me. Downright stiff, like exercises in abstraction. Do you remember what you said, Augie?"

"Of course not. That was years ago. Anyway, whatever I said, I was bullshitting."

"I don't think you were. You said: 'I didn't like the Hofmanns at first, either, but then I made an effort to look at them one at a time and, after that, to see just a small section of a painting at a time.' You pointed to one of the canvases. 'Look at what he does with that swell of blue growing out of the ground. Isn't it glorious?' I couldn't say if it was glorious, but you'd begun to seem so. Do you remember Professor Myeroff's course?"

"Sure."

We'd met in Herter Myeroff's Modern Art History, a two-quarter course at Berkeley. I was auditing the class. I'd already graduated and had been wasting time working hack jobs before taking the LSATs. Nina was only a sophomore. Professor Myeroff, a lovely, old-world gent, had actually known a number of the painters we discussed in the second quarter of the course, people like Kokoschka and Beckmann. The most modest of authorities, Myeroff invited students to weigh in with their impressions of particular paintings. His manner had quite an influence on me.

I sat in the row behind Nina. I noticed her the first day and wanted to get her attention. I commented fairly often about the paintings. Professor Myeroff was fond of my comments, not because they offered global insights but because I zeroed in on small sections and expressed awe at a particular effect the painter had created. It was only thoughtful jive, my specialty.

"One day you said something about a painting of William Blake's."

I recalled the painting. It was Blake's *Oberon, Titania and Puck with Fairies Dancing*. I wasn't going to let Nina know that I remembered.

"I don't remember the painting," Nina said, "but I remember your saying something about Blake's deftness in setting the fairies in motion, how the lightness of his touch gave the fairies a quality that made them seem imaginary. You asked if that was the artist's intention. Do you remember what happened next, Augie? I turned around and answered you. It was absolutely spontaneous. I turned and said yes. It was the first time I'd looked directly into your face. You were so cute. You looked like you hadn't even shaved yet. I felt myself blush when you smiled back."

LUCRETIA

We strolled through the Matisse room, not speaking to each other, two once-married souls wandering past paintings we were both familiar with. I watched Nina a moment as she stood in front of Matisse's *Boy with the Butterfly Net*. Her head tilted to the side as if she were trying to become the boy. It looked as if Nina had just had her hair cut—a shoulder-length bob at her $150-a-cut salon. She liked the put-together look. She needed the illusion.

I walked on through the room, starting to get impatient. Why the hell did Nina want to meet me? What was her damn secret? Or was all that just a ruse to get together with me and play with my head? The queen of discreet anger, mind-fucking me in the museum.

I thought of sneaking off to find a couple of my favorite paintings. Rembrandt's *Lucretia* wasn't far off. God, I loved that painting. It was the painter's second version, capturing the poor, dishonored woman the moment after she plunged the knife into her heart, her white tunic bruised with blood. Lucretia, in the muted heart of her resignation, is more striking than any Madonna I know. Facing her squarely makes you tender.

I needed some irony and stepped into the surrealist room. Nina followed close behind. I had little interest in the paintings, but I had a perverse desire to hear Nina explain how her life was like a surrealist painting. I took a breath and told myself to chill. The woman was obviously troubled. I turned to look at a nifty little masterpiece by Magritte, all seamless surface. A little too coy for my taste.

Nina sidled up beside me. "Isn't it wonderful?" she said, smiling at the Magritte.

Yes, wonderful, I thought. You walk out on me after nearly twenty-five years to be with another man, another therapist, for God's sake. A tall, rumpled Brit named Manny who came to a party at our house once and stayed too long.

I wandered out into the broad hall and, again, Nina followed.

"Did you hear that Rosie's coming to town?" I said.

Nina looked directly at me. "No, I hadn't heard."

"Yeah," I said, as casually as I could, "something about the pro-life rally at the state capitol. She's going to play at a counter-rally."

I took some sicko satisfaction in the fact that Rose had cut her mother off. It was crueler than any response I could fashion. I sensed the vastness of Nina's isolation. Like someone who'd collaborated with the enemy. After the separation, our mutual friends rallied around me, but I went into hiding. Quite a few of them fell away. I doubt many returned to Nina.

I gazed at my longtime wife. "Rosie will probably be all wrapped up in the rally and not have time to see anyone."

"Oh, I'm sure she'll make time to see you, Augie."

We wandered into a room of Dutch paintings. I took in the porcelain perfection of a Franz Hals. The portrait of a rosy-cheeked man in middle age, smoking a pipe. He reminded me of myself, toking on a fat reefer. But it was hard to imagine this gent's wife cheating on him.

NINA'S NEWS

We moved into a room with a few Turners, a Constable, and a couple of horsey Gainsboroughs. It was time to get on with it. I took hold of Nina's arm.

"So what's up?"

She shrugged. "I don't know."

"Come on, you didn't call me because you missed me."

"That's where you're wrong."

"Well, that's too bad," I said. "You don't get to miss me."

"That's not fair."

"You want to talk about fair?"

Nina shook her head. "I'm in trouble, Augie."

"What kind of trouble?"

"I can't talk here."

"What's the matter with here?" I said, sitting down on a polished bench. "There's nobody around."

Nina sat down beside me. Across from us was a portrait of a lady by Constable. She was even more put together than Nina. I noticed a book peeking out of the pocket of Nina's big handbag.

"What are you reading?"

She pulled out the book and flashed the spine at me. *The Human Condition,* by Hannah Arendt.

"Sounds like some nice light reading," I said.

"I have a client who's an Arendt scholar."

"Isn't Arendt the one who came up with 'the banality of evil'?"

"Yes," Nina said. "She was talking about Eichmann."

I wondered if the phrase could be applied to the Bushies, and decided that for them I'd stick with plain evil. I smiled at Nina. "So, how's your soul?"

"What kind of question is that?" She raised her eyebrows at me. "You expect me to be some kind of guilt-ridden wretch?"

I winked at her.

"Screw you, Augie."

I turned slightly so I could see one of the Turners, a dark and frothy seascape that suggested the end of the world. "By the way, there's something I've been meaning to ask you—do you know a shrink named McCracken?"

"Julie McCracken?"

"Yeah, Jules McCracken; he's got an office out on Lyndale."

"I used to know him. We had offices in the same building on Snelling."

"But you didn't sleep with him?"

"Fuck you, Augie."

"I'm sorry."

Nina patted her eyes with a tissue. "Why do you have to be such a bastard?"

"It just comes naturally. What can you tell me about McCracken?"

"Are you looking for a shrink?"

"No, a client of mine's been seeing him."

Nina turned to the side and blew her nose. "Julie McCracken was a sweet man. He had a terrible tragedy. His son got involved with a satanic cult in college in Madison and took his own life. After that, Julie made a name for himself doing interventions."

"Interventions?"

"Mostly kids who had gotten themselves swallowed up by cults. Moonies and devil worshippers. Things like that. The families would pay huge sums to get their children back. It takes a lot of deprogramming."

"And that's McCracken's specialty?"

"Right. I'm surprised you've never worked on anything like that."

"No, never have," I said, trying to figure how McCracken's specialty matched up with my prodigy. I took a deep breath and shifted my attention back to Nina. "So, you told me you were in some kind of trouble. Is it of the existential variety?"

"I wish it were."

I fought my instinct to turn back to the Turner. I wasn't ready to hear Nina's bad news. "So, what kind of trouble?"

"The worst kind."

"Are you sick?"

Nina pursed her lips together tightly, then let them relax. "I'm pregnant."

"Oh, my."

Nina wiped tears from the corner of her eyes. "What a funny thing to say."

"Funny?"

"I mean it doesn't sound like something you would say, Augie."

"Well, I'm full of surprises. They just happen to be little surprises compared with yours."

Nina's eye makeup was smudged. She pulled out her compact and took a quick look at herself. "I must present quite the comic picture."

"Why's that?"

"A pregnant old lady who's made a mess of herself. I'm old enough to be a grandmother."

"You're not an old lady, Nina."

"I feel like one sometimes."

"Are you thinking of having the baby?"

"Of course not."

"You could become the mature Juno."

"Shut up, Augie."

"What's Manny say?"

"The relationship with Manny is for shit."

"I'm sorry to hear that."

"Why would you be sorry?"

"I don't know. I've made my peace, Nina. I'm trying to move on."

"I don't believe you."

I shrugged.

"Well, then you're a more evolved character than I am, Augie."

I flashed her a wide smile. "We both have known that for a long time, Nina."

We shared a smile.

"So, do you have someone to go with you?"

"Of course," she said.

"That's good," I said, "because I don't think I'm big enough for that."

"Nobody is."

"Oh, I'm sure there's some fool out there." I watched Nina's eyes fill with tears. She sniffled, and I handed her a handkerchief. Then she blew her nose and threw back her head, trying to pull herself together.

"You know," she said sniffling, "I had . . . I had a really curious reaction when I found out. It was strange . . . I mean, I couldn't believe it. I met with a nurse practitioner at HealthPartners and she talked a little about nutrition and gave me a prescription for prenatal vitamins. She said something about setting up a next appointment and how I'd want to think about an amniocentesis, given my age. And I just nodded. Then I sat in the parking lot for a while. I turned the rearview mirror so I could see myself. And I had this glow. This crazy kind of happiness. A kind of wonder, you know, that I could have a baby. I mean, twenty-four years after having Rose. Just the biological wonder of it—a baby, at my age. It was so strange. I began singing, singing a little song to myself. Reality hadn't set in yet. That came soon enough.

"Do you know what I did last Saturday, after I saw you on the bridge? I dressed in a slouchy sweat suit and drove over to Cecil's Deli in Saint Paul. I ordered chopped liver. I think it was the thought of the liver that brought me to Cecil's. It was a genuine craving. For a few weeks I'd had some nausea and went through a couple of boxes of gingersnaps. But that's passed now. I actually found the smell of the liver restorative."

"You're a better man than me, Nina."

"I thought of my mother. I wanted my mother. I remembered her face, making chopped liver. She had a kind of peasant glee as she pushed the shiny livers through the hand grinder." Nina dabbed her eyes.

"When I finished at Cecil's, I drove around the corner to the Planned Parenthood on Ford Parkway. It was late Saturday afternoon and the place was closed. I knew it would be closed. I don't know, I just wanted to commune there for a moment. But there were protesters with absurd signs out front. One woman actually held a sign that read: JEWISH ABORTION DOCTORS = JEWISH MURDERERS. I parked my car and got out and started arguing with the protesters."

I put a hand on her shoulder. "Nina, this isn't a good time for you to take this on."

"I know. But I couldn't believe what happened. I started arguing with the Jewish-murderer woman, and another woman got on her cell phone. Within five minutes a truck drove up. The damn thing was plastered with pictures of dead fetuses. All bloody and ugly. I started sobbing right in front of those damn women. I was so ashamed of myself for letting them see me cry. God damn them," Nina said, and she began crying again.

I held her for a few minutes and she gradually pulled herself together.

"Nina," I said, "you need to take care of yourself. You know how to take care of yourself."

"Of course." She nodded.

"You're going to be okay." I glanced at one of the Turners. The wild seascape seemed like a picture of Nina's terror. Poor woman. I stood up slowly. "Look, it was good to see you." I could see Nina's eyes turning anxious. "I'm in the middle of some business that's getting hot. I've got to get going."

There was a hint of pleading in Nina's large brown eyes.

"You're going to be fine."

She nodded and handed me back my handkerchief.

"Stay in touch," I said, and the absurdity of the phrase haunted me down the hallway.

MUTUAL HUMILIATION

Late that evening, after eating one of my rare but virtuous diet dinners—a salad of romaine hearts with a small, broiled tuna steak—I got out my cello and played a bit of Hindemith's

Sonata for Cello Alone. As I played, I wondered if it was natural for a man to feel concern for a woman who'd cuckolded him. I was worried for Nina. It had been an odd feeling to hold her when she fell apart at the museum, and now, once I played through the Hindemith, I put down the bow and stretched both of my arms around the cello.

A bright-pitched sound wave raised me out of my reverie. Then I remembered the device planted in Odegard's Jaguar. I rushed to the monitor on the hall table, hoping that the beeping icon wouldn't be aimed out 394. I wasn't eager to make another trip to the western suburbs. But I was in luck—Odegard was heading east. He'd just passed the Walker Art Center and was heading to the on-ramp to 94 East. Nice to have the skanky dealer coming my way.

I guessed that Odegard was heading directly to Woodbury and a visit with Herr Kunz. Would young Elizabeth be sitting beside her husband in the Jag? I strapped the monitor on my wrist like a big watch. Then I grabbed my book bag and gathered a few more items for the road: cell phone, minicamera, iPod, and a can of Diet Coke. What else could a middle-aged spy need?

According to the device, a Magellan Meridian, Odegard was just crossing the Mississippi into Saint Paul. I dialed through my iPod looking for something appropriate for a violin adventure. When Bach's Sonata no. 1 in G Minor, played by Arthur Grumiaux, kicked on, I grinned at myself in the rearview mirror. As a confirmed technophobe, I especially adored all the technology at my command. Here I was, perched in my purring Mazda, listening through earbuds to a fabled French violinist on a recording made fifty years ago in Berlin as I watched a blip on a screen that represented a Jaguar traveling due east, the numeric coordinates above the blinking blip incapable of even a hint of irony.

By the time the Mazda squirted onto 94 at Dale, Odegard's Jag was only a half-dozen cars ahead of me. I actually spotted the creamy SJ8, just before the Marion exit, but my view was too obscured to tell whether Odegard had company in the front seat. I decided to slow down a little. No need to crowd the dude. It was still nine miles to Woodbury, and the beauty of the device was that it would track my mark within ten meters of his location, so even if he tucked his Jag into a garage, I had him. With Bach streaming directly into my ears and my wrist map blinking, I luxuriated in the heaven of geeks.

The first time I'd worn the monitor, back in June, I could hardly take my eyes off the backlit color map as I drove. The insurance company had sent somebody out to bug the Impala of a do-ragged gent named Rasheed Rouse. I tracked him from his apartment on North James in Minneapolis to a softball game in Brooklyn Park. The dummy's headfirst slide into second base, which I captured on camera, did little to support his disability claim. Nasty work, that. But, in this economy, I accepted what was offered. Although I hated the business that the insurance companies tossed my way, I'd also grown to despise the frauds, especially the ones with so little respect for the enemy.

I had no idea what I'd find in Woodbury. I reminded myself that I was on the way to the house of a neo-Nazi, not that I'd been invited. It seemed a far more dangerous destination than one of my insurance runs through North Minneapolis. As a white guy driving around a black neighborhood, I wasn't the most popular character around. But the idea of peeking into the pad of a guy who believed that Hitler had had a good plan seemed a little more chilling. I pictured a massive security gate and a phalanx of Rottweilers surrounding the house, even though Blossom hadn't mentioned the presence of anything like that.

After all, she got close enough to see the two Snoopys in the front yard.

To my surprise, Odegard shot north onto 35E at Spaghetti Junction and I had to scramble to get over in time to make the exit. Forget about Woodbury. I stayed pretty close to the violin dealer when he merged onto 694, then followed him off the Century exit and west along Wildwood toward White Bear Lake. Maybe Lionel had it right and Kunz kept his instruments warehoused out there.

I tracked the dealer through Mahtomedi and down along the lake. Odegard turned off Oak Street, into a lane that wasn't marked, save for coordinates, on the monitor. I gave Odegard a minute's lead, then parked in a spot partly hidden in the brush, fifty yards behind the Jaguar. There was no house in sight, but I spotted a mailbox labeled F. A. Kunz. I shone a light into the passenger-side window of the Jaguar but saw no dimple in the leather seat. A dirt road wove through a quarter mile of woods, past a few outbuildings. The path was still damp from a late afternoon shower and I could make out a single set of fresh foot-prints. Size eight and a half, I guessed. Odegard in his prim Ital-ian loafers. The violin dealer had arrived alone.

I decided to take a peek at the outbuildings. I didn't expect farm machinery—they sure as hell weren't growing corn out there—or boats, as I figured a boathouse would be closer to the shore. My light disturbed a gray squirrel in a yellow barn-turned-garage. The furry rodent scampered from the driver's seat of a snowmobile. Like most of the natives in this crazy state, he must have been longing for winter. Beside the Arctic Cat was a World War II–era Mercedes, a nicely waxed black behemoth that may have been some sort of limo in its day. It looked to be in fine running condition. I pointed my flashlight at the fat trunk of the touring car. Instead of a single license plate, it boasted three: a Minnesota collector plate; a long, narrow German plate; and a vanity nameplate like the kind you pick up in tourists' shops. The blue vanity plate read "Ludwig." I jotted down the number of the Minnesota plate.

I aimed the light around the corners of the barn garage, expecting to find a colony of freaked squirrels. Then I scanned the rafters, wondering if bats were hanging up there. Instead I saw three Nazi flags, each suspended from its own pole. The one on the left, in green and white, featured a small swastika under the crest of an eagle. I tried to read the circling letters on the middle flag but could only make out the word *Sozialistische*. The SS flag on the right was a stark black and white with stylized letters and a death's head in the top left corner.

I peeked quickly into the second building, a large, contemporary garage fifty yards up the road. It housed a Porsche from the late sixties with a vanity plate that read "Tristan"; a late-model BMW coupe with plates I couldn't see; and a Hummer the color of hot mustard.

From a distance, the house didn't appear particularly welcoming. It was a brick monstrosity that looked more like a Gothic orphanage than a lake home. The dude hadn't brought any Snoopy sculptures out to this joint. Coming closer to the house, I expected to be greeted by frothing Rottweilers, but it was nearly quiet. I held my breath and could hear the faint strains of a violin playing a crisp, cut-time march. It wasn't Sousa; more likely a German military ditty. I wondered if I'd spot Perry Odegard marching inside. I tiptoed around to the back of the house, hoping not to trip a hidden motion detector. Thankfully, the householders must have mistaken the woods for security; either that or they were tired of having squirrels and raccoons set off their halogens.

Through a gap between the curtains, I could make out an empty kitchen divided by track lighting into a series of bright vectors. Somebody had prepared a plate of cheese and pâté. The leavings, along with the cores of a couple of apples and a fancy tin of crackers, sat on a butcher block at the center of the room. I noticed a cocktail shaker and a couple of bottles of rum on a side counter. The violin music stopped. A man coughed. A new military march began. I tried to guess how many people were inside the house.

The curtains weren't drawn at all in the next room. A dozen folding chairs were set up in two rows. There was a podium up front and a small film screen. I wondered what kind of flicks the good folks watched. Nazi highlight reels? Aryan hygiene flicks? Off to the right side was a large flip chart with some sort of list that I couldn't make out. I zoomed in with my Sony mini but still couldn't make out the words. I took a few shots of the chart and the rest of the seminar room.

After slipping the camera back into my pocket, I went flat against the house sliding down to the next room, a formal dining room with a brass chandelier, dimmed to atmospheric. The room's mullioned windows were uncovered. Nobody appeared to be in the dining room, either. I saw a painting on the far wall. It had a little switched-on lamp affixed to the top of the frame. The wholesome family portrait—blond peasants gathered around a harvest table—looked like Aryan art. I edged myself slowly toward the front of the house, stumbling over a drainpipe but managing to keep my balance.

It was through the windows of the parlor, which spilled off the living room, that I had my first sighting of Perry Odegard. The violin dealer wasn't marching, but down on his knees, butt-naked, as they say, taking an oversized brunette on all fours from behind. He couldn't have been in the house much longer than ten minutes. So much for foreplay. I squinted for a moment, trying to make sense of what I was seeing. The woman being pleasured reminded me of the mother in the Nazi family portrait, give or take a hundred pounds of apple dumplings and the color of her hair.

It's hard to account for another man's tastes—that's something I'd learned in the years on the job. And yet I had a distinct sense that this bit of coupling wasn't Odegard's choice, but part of his job. Call him a full-service violin dealer.

I couldn't figure where the fiddle playing was coming from. It sounded much closer than before. I assumed that the male cougher and the violinist were one and the same, and that, though I couldn't see him, he, too, was witnessing the randy act. I pulled out my miniature Sony again, engaged the zoom, and snapped a dozen pictures of the couple on the floor and then flicked it to video, just to get a little hunk of it on the record.

I never particularly cared for these jobs when they turned pornographic, but the parlor sideshow was something out of the ordinary, so I stayed more tuned in than usual. The large woman, her massive breasts swinging beneath her, began heaving toward climax.

A man's authoritative voice said something I wasn't able to understand, and Perry Odegard pulled himself away from the throbbing mound of woman. The violin lit into a new march, more sprightly than the ones before. The speaking voice issued some more instructions and Odegard turned the brunette over and dove in, missionary style.

At this point, a man entered the room. He was a tall fellow in his sixties who looked more like a gracefully aging corporate CEO than a Nazi. So this was Herr Kunz. He wore a knit shirt with some sort of nautical logo and a pair of tan linen trousers. Instead of black SS boots, he stepped daintily in a pair of penny loafers. What amazed me was that the man kept playing his violin, his bow arm not faltering in the least, as he walked deeper into the room. The dapper Nazi had quite a bit of facility on the fiddle, though I didn't particularly care for his taste in music. The closer he got to the couple, the more he ramped up the tempo. Odegard, I realized, was trying to screw to the rhythm, but he was having trouble matching the tempo.

I turned away for a minute. Sometimes the mind can only absorb so much dissonance. Was the woman Kunz's wife? Was the fiddle player really Kunz? I'd heard about men who got their jollies watching their wife getting screwed, but this was over the top. The whole enterprise seemed an exercise in mutual humiliation.

Now at the parlor window, I wondered why on a nice night like this when I could have been enjoying Erica's company, or sitting at home listening to Bach with a glass of good Malbec and a gentle reefer, I was peeking through a window at obscenities that made me ill. There had to be an easier way to make a living. With that thought, one of my feet slipped from under me and my head bumped against the window frame.

The violin stopped playing its march and I ducked below window level. I heard a couple of intense voices, but couldn't make out the words. I expected barking dogs and a flood of lights. Instead, everything grew quiet and the lights went dim. It was as if the folks in the house were expecting a blitz. I huddled under the parlor window. Counted to sixty. Did it again. I heard a door open. Close. Footsteps. Quiet. A lamp came on in the parlor. I counted again to sixty and, looking up from my crouch, saw a pair of eyes staring at me. I gasped for a breath and noticed another pair. Ringed eyes. It was all I could do not to scream at the sight of two fat raccoons poised a few feet from my face. I stood in a hurry and could see the man with the violin—Kunz?—sitting at a small library table, typing a speedy message on his laptop. By the time I reached my Mazda, Odegard's Jaguar was gone.

THE MIRACLE MAKER

The next morning I slept in. I hadn't meant to. I'd forgotten to set the alarm. It was the first time in years that I awoke to the smell of brewing coffee. It was as if I'd slept for so long that I'd returned to an earlier time, to the bosom of married life, with Nina rising a half hour earlier than me and engaging the Braun coffeemaker. I lay back dreamily, scratching at my right thigh.

Meanwhile, the coffee was coming toward me in a mug. "So you decided to wake up, Augie."

I propped myself up against the headboard and looked at Blossom Reese, her lips drawn in a wide smile, her red hair freshly spiked with gel.

"What are you doing here, Blossom?"

"That's a question I've been asking myself. I couldn't rouse you any other way, so I came over. The door wasn't locked. The rest is history."

"What time is it?"

"Nine forty-five."

"I've got to get going."

"You're catching on. Have a hit of coffee first." She handed me the mug. I swilled it down in a hurry, burning my gullet, and handed back the mug. Blossom perched on the edge of an over-stuffed chair spilling over with dirty clothes.

"Come on, Blossom, I need to take a shower."

"What, are you in the raw?"

"Yeah. You going to just sit there?"

Blossom puckered her lips. "I didn't realize you were so modest, Augie."

"I'm not."

"Tell me something," she said and aimed her eyes at me sideways. "Have you ever wanted to fuck me, Augie?" It wasn't so much a come-on as a straight question.

"I never thought it was mine to want," I said, but I couldn't keep from nodding my head.

"I just never knew if you found me sexy."

"You're Bobby's girl and I'm loyal to both of you."

"Nice job of skirting the question."

"What would you have preferred me to say?"

"That you think of me night and day."

"You wouldn't want that."

"How do you know what I want, Augie?"

"Okay, I'm gonna dash for the shower now." I threw the covers back—let the chips fall where they may—and scampered toward the bathroom.

"Let me know when you're in the shower," Blossom called. "I got some more on Kunz."

I looked after my business, then ran the hot water. Once I'd stood under the fat showerhead for a few minutes, I hollered for Blossom. It took her a minute of twirling the knob before she burst into the bathroom.

"Fucking steam bath in here, Augie. Who takes a steam bath on a hot day?"

I stuck my head out from behind the shower curtain. "Have a seat on the toilet, Blossom, and quit playing with my head."

"Get your ass behind the curtain," she said. "Okay, that conversation we just had? Let's forget we had it."

"Fine," I said, holding my hard prick under the shower.

"So, you ready for a little more on Frederick Kunz? Not only does he hang out on the pro-life websites, he's a major presence on the Holocaust denial sites. He's a guy who likes to express his opinion. He's got editorials on a couple of the most wigged-out sites, and he posts frequently on others. Goes by F. A. Kunz."

"Same as with the White Bear letterbox. What's the A stand for?"

"Adolph, I'm guessing. He's an arrogant guy, Augie. Thinks he's above the law and beyond detection. Chastises the other pro-life fucks for not putting their money where their mouth is. Fighting baby killers doesn't come cheap. He says that the end justifies the means when the issue is the lives of millions of babies. I think he's planning something big."

"What makes you say that, Blossom?" I asked as I tried to rub away the shampoo I'd gotten in my eyes.

"He keeps mentioning this Labor Day Miracle bullshit."

"You think he's the miracle maker?"

"Could be. Listen, I know this guy, Trevor. Trevor's a pretty accomplished hacker. He could get us into Kunz's e-mail."

I stuck my head out into the steamy room. "Can you get me together with Trevor today?"

"When?"

"Noon."

"That's in two hours, Augie."

"I know when it is. Now, quit flirting with me and get out of the bathroom."

HAND WASHING

I parked across Lyndale from McCracken's office. The three days that I'd tracked the violinist she'd come out sometime between 11:45 and 11:50. I figured that McCracken ran a forty-five-minute hour. At 11:40, I picked the lock to the bathroom around the corner from McCracken's office. I had a little time to stall. I washed my hands carefully. If I could wash my hands of anything, I wondered what it would be. That was a big question. I'd need a good blast of bash and a couple of hours of leisure to figure that one out. I tried to imagine being one of those obsessive fucks who washed his hands fifty times a day. What were those poor souls trying to wash away? You could never convince me that it was only the fear of germs. I checked my watch. The violinist should just be leaving.

In McCracken's waiting room a young woman, a tightly wound creature in her late twenties, sat with her hands folded in her lap. I gave her a quick smile as I sat across from her. She smelled of Baby Magic. Maybe she washed her hands fifty times a day and applied lotion after each washing. I must have picked up her vibe in the bathroom. Things were weird in McCrackenville. I wondered if the great man could free someone from the cult of compulsive hand-washing. I checked my watch: a minute before the hour. I wondered what McCracken did with himself between appointments. Maybe he had a sink in there. At twelve on the dot, McCracken, a husky man in his fifties with a swarthy complexion and a shaved head, opened his office door.

He did a start at the sight of me. "May I help you, sir?" he said in a surprisingly high-pitched voice.

I walked toward McCracken with my hand extended. My father's first name came out of my mouth, followed by a bastardization of his last name. "Robinson Boyd. I was referred to you . . ."

"Yes, but you must call for an appointment, sir."

"It's a very pressing matter." I stared directly into McCracken's watery brown eyes. "It's time-sensitive."

McCracken averted his eyes. "Yes, but as you can see, I have an appointment waiting."

"If I could have just two minutes of your time." I turned toward the woman whose time I was stealing. "I'm so sorry to interrupt." She was clearly agitated, rubbing her hands together in a ritual hand-washing, without soap or water.

McCracken craned his neck around me. "Jennifer, will you excuse me for a minute?" Peeved, he led me into his office and closed the door. "What can I do for you?"

"Robinson Boyd; may I sit?"

"Yes, but make it brief."

I sat across from McCracken in an overstuffed chair. "It's about my daughter, who I believe . . ."

"Hold on, who referred you to me?"

"Nina Gordon."

McCracken spread his hairy hands, each of which sported a pinkie ring, over his knees. "Nina Gordon. Do you see her professionally?"

"I have in the past."

"Anger issues?"

"Yes," I said, spiking my voice with an edge of aggression, "but I've taken care of that."

"So, your daughter."

I pushed my breath in and out very rapidly. "I believe my daughter is being forced to commit a crime."

"What kind of crime?"

I continued my rapid breathing. "Murder."

The word seemed to amuse McCracken. "Do you know who is behind this supposed crime?" he asked, holding a steady, patronizing smile.

"Yes." Here came the gamble. I fixed my eyes now on McCracken's right pinkie, which was poised on his knee. "A man named Kunz."

"Kunz?" McCracken said, his pinkie twitching.

"Yes, Frederick Kunz. Wealthy businessman, lives in Woodbury. Nazi sympathizer. Pro-life freak."

Beads of sweat broke across McCracken's forehead. "Never heard of him."

"You're sure?"

McCracken stood and wiped his forehead with a handkerchief. "Mr. Boyd, my twelve o'clock is waiting for me."

I stretched my legs out in front of me. "By the way, my daughter has a friend named Elizabeth Odegard, whom you're helping."

"Get out of here." McCracken went to the phone on his desk.

"Who you calling?"

"The police."

"Good. I have a lot of friends down there." I pulled out my wallet and flashed my private investigator badge.

McCracken put down the phone. "You have no right coming in here."

"Tell me this, Dr. McCracken," I said, standing, "are you as good at programming as you are at deprogramming?"

"I have no idea what you're talking about." McCracken narrowed his dark eyes.

"Doctor, are you working for Kunz?"

"Get out of here," McCracken hollered.

I pulled a business card out of my wallet and tossed it onto the shrink's desk. "Give me a call, Dr. McCracken, if you feel like washing your hands of this business. Just don't wait until it's too late."

COMEDY TEAM

Blossom and her hacker buddy, Trevor, were sitting in my office when I got back. Trevor, a lanky guy in his mid-twenties, wore bleached jeans and a Thelonious Monk T-shirt.

I shook the hacker's hand. "Thanks for coming over, Trevor."

"No worries, man."

"I wish it were true, but suddenly I've got a shitload of worries." I sat on the end of my desk. "I'm worried about this Nazi, Kunz, that Blossom's told you about, and there's a shrink named Jules McCracken that's really got me freaked. I think the two of them have a little something going on."

"Jules McCracken," Trevor repeated, writing the name on his left hand.

"You get to meet McCracken?" Blossom asked.

"Yeah, I met him." I looked at her directly but she wouldn't face me. I figured she was still feeling embarrassed from our earlier conversation. I turned to Trevor. "The guy specializes in deprogramming, but I think they've got him brainwashing my client. I just don't know what they're trying to get her to do."

Blossom, looking at one of her tattoos, said, "Trevor can get inside anything."

"Anything except Blossom's pants," the hacker said with a smirk.

"I didn't know you were interested." Blossom's face turned bright red.

"Look," I said, "everybody's interested. But what do you say we leave Blossom's pants out of it for right now?"

"For sure, man."

"First of all, I need you to get into Kunz's e-mail."

"No worries. Blossom's going to give me a list of some of the sites he visits, and I'll do a little port scanning and get into the dude's car pool lanes, grab his e-mail accounts, and paste myself like invisible ink into his bcc folders. Then, when I'm on his recipient lists, I'll get every e-mail he sends."

"Great," I said.

"We need it fast, Trevor," Blossom said with a silly grin on her face.

"I'll work tonight."

"Then we'll worry about McCracken."

"Kunz and McCracken," Trevor said. "Sounds like a comedy team."

"Yeah," I said, standing. "Let's just make sure that the joke's not on us."

MAN ENOUGH

I got up early the next morning and took my time whipping up the lather for my shave. After showering, I regarded myself warily in the fogged mirror. Something was bothering me, a certain apprehension I couldn't put my finger on. It had been days since I'd stopped spreading the testosterone over my belly. I'd have to be man enough without the steroid. I flexed my biceps and laughed at myself. I recited a dozen fresh lines from McGrath's poem, lines about working long hours in the field at the age of nine, the boy doing his best to impersonate a man. At fifty years old, I was rallying myself toward a similar goal.

First thing at the office, I checked my e-mail. Still nothing from Trevor. I hoped the dude wasn't a bust. We'd need some actual evidence to get the police interested. I clicked Rose's site to see if she'd left any clue about her arrival in Minnesota. No word on the band's schedule page, so I clicked into her blog.

MINNESOTA ROSE

SCHEDULE   PRESS   GALLERY   LYRICS   BLOG   ACTION

August 28, 2008

I'm heading home to Saint Paul over Labor Day to play a pro-life rally at the capitol. Of course, I'm performing in the counterrally. The governor and a mass of evangelicals are planning a huge antiabortion bash on the capitol grounds. Apparently the guv hosted a Christian revival there a few years back. So much for the separation of church and state. An organization called Born Free is behind this rally and they're bringing in their troops from across the country.

Everybody thinks this is just a little sideshow to energize the Republi-cans. They kick off their national convention the same day. I'm thinking it may be remembered as the sideshow that steals the show. The nuts run-ning this thing think Labor Day should really celebrate women in labor. They're mobilizing tents and medical crews and pregnant women about to deliver, for a mass birth-in on the capitol grounds.

Watch our action link, because I'll be posting details and a call for par-ticipation if you're in the Midwest or want to caravan out to support our rights. I'm pretty certain that we'll end up joining one of the many protests that are already gearing up for the convention itself. The whole world will be watching.

I was a bit shocked by Rose's entry. She'd clearly been thinking things through, connecting the dots. Which was a lot more than could be said for her old man.

Deciding to get my ass in gear, I called Elizabeth Odegard and told her I wanted to come over.

"When?" she said.

"Right now."

"But I have an appointment."

"Yeah, you have an eleven o'clock with McCracken. It's eight thirty now. With any luck, we'll be able to get you down to Dr. McCracken's on time."

"But Perry's here."

"Good. I'd like to meet him."

"He's exercising."

"Great, I'll bring him a PowerBar."

A LOT OF YEARS OF BAD LUCK

The violinist wasn't happy to see me at the door. Although the temperature had hit eighty-five degrees by 8:00 A.M., she'd dressed for winter in a turtleneck, a wool blazer, and a tweed skirt. Her lips quivered for a moment as she stood in the open doorway. "I don't know why you had to come here."

"Things are getting out of hand," I said, taking off my Kansas City Monarchs cap. "I want to talk with you and your husband about Frederick Kunz." I wasn't sure she was going to invite me in.

The violinist narrowed her eyes. "Aren't you working for me?"

"That's what I'm doing."

The violinist pulled back the door. "We don't usually have company at nine in the morning."

"Don't think of me as company."

She led me into the foyer. The heavy green curtains in the living room were drawn back from the wall of windows looking out on Loring Park. One step into the room and I understood the violinist's winter garb—the air conditioner was revved up like in a cold storage unit. I was glad I'd worn a sport coat.

Perry Odegard was stretched out under the window on a recumbent bike. The little stud had a small blister on his lip, just below his milky-blond mustache. A herpes souvenir, no doubt.

Odegard was engaged in quite the executive workout—his short legs pedaled as he sipped coffee from an Aztec-patterned mug and read the morning paper. The dude even had a convenient table for his mug. He raised his flaxen head, with its platinum highlights, in an antinod toward me. It wasn't hard to see that the violin dealer, decked out in a baby blue velour suit, was pissed.

"This is August Boyer," the violinist said, walking me toward the recumbent bike. "Perry Odegard."

The prince lifted his mug and had another sip of coffee.

I smiled at each of them. "You guys like it cool in here."

"Perry likes it cool when he exercises."

"What can I do for you, Mr. Boyer?" Perry Odegard asked. The man's voice was deeper than I'd expected—he sounded as if he'd spent half a semester at some cut-rate broadcasting school.

"I'd like to talk to you about Frederick Kunz."

"Yeah, and you can kiss my ass."

"Hey, asshole," I said, deciding to match Odegard's attitude, no matter my testosterone level, "let's not get off on the wrong foot."

"We're not getting off on any foot."

"Perry," the violinist whispered.

"Shut up," Odegard said to her with a glare. I watched his face turn red. He didn't know how to play this one.

It would have been nice to flatten the little punk before he got off his Schwinn. But I decided to chill and watch him self-destruct.

He wasn't done hollering at his wife. "Why the hell did you bring this guy into our house?" He turned to me. "Who the fuck are you, anyway? My wife hired you for something? What did she hire you for? To spy on me, right? You drive a little Mazda? You're the dummy with the Mazda, right? Right?" Odegard shouted, the bike wheel spinning furiously.

"I wouldn't characterize myself as a dummy," I said, "but I do drive a Mazda. Zoom-zoom. So now that we've established our primal antipathy, Mr. Odegard, you mind if I sit?"

"Suit yourself," the violin dealer said. He slowed his pedaling and lifted his Aztec cup for a sip of coffee.

The violinist led me to the creamy leather sofa across the room, but she remained standing. Odegard climbed off the bike, gripped his crotch, and gave it a little hello, how are you before strolling over to the leather chair across from me. After he plopped into the chair and swiveled back and forth a few times, he lifted his chin toward his wife. "Don't you have something to do, Liz?"

"I'd like to speak with both of you," I said.

"Who the fuck do you think you are?" Odegard hollered.

I ignored him and turned to the violinist. "Why don't you sit down, Ms. Odegard?"

The violinist glanced at her husband but didn't budge.

Odegard boosted himself out of the swivel chair and stood with his hands on his hips, his head tilted in a pose of indifference.

It's hard to scare somebody off the scent when you stink as much as Odegard. I did a quick breathing exercise. Flicked on a bit of mindfulness. Counted the violin dealer's front teeth. It would have been nice to knock out two or three of them with one shot. Instead, I whispered out a long breath and collected another. I caught Odegard's eye. "Look, you want me to go to the police, dude? Tell 'em about the Nazi violins you've been trading?"

Odegard stepped closer to me. Put on his thinking cap. "Bull-shit," he bluffed.

I kicked back on the couch. "They're already interested in you."

The silent violinist, who'd been standing behind the sofa,

stepped back farther. Oddly, I was the only one in the room sitting.

Odegard's forehead was a scrunch of worry. Then he turned to his wife and did something with the herpes side of his lip that terrorized her.

I smiled up at Odegard. I felt like pouring it on. "I can also tell them about your collection of Nazi-era Lugers, which aren't registered. And then there's all that I've learned about Frederick Kunz. The fact that he's the guy who got you off your last rap links the two of you inextricably. I'll tell them about the Nazi estate in White Bear Lake. About the guy's impressive collection of Third Reich paraphernalia. And maybe, just to tease their prurient interest, I'll offer some details of the little party you had the other night with Kunz and the big brunette."

Odegard nearly lost his balance at the mention of the fat lady. "There's nothing illegal there."

I smiled at the violin dealer, who dropped his hands into the pockets of his velour pants.

"Anyway," I said, "that's just the tip of the iceberg."

Odegard took a deep breath. "Would you like a cup of coffee, Mr. Boyer? Could you get Mr. Boyer a cup of coffee, Liz?"

"I don't want coffee. I want you two to sit down." I stood up and stepped clear of the sofa, indicating where I wanted them to sit. I perched across from them in the matching swivel chair.

"Okay, Ms. Odegard, why don't you tell me your history with Frederick Kunz."

The violinist took a sideways glance at her husband.

"Go ahead, tell him whatever you want," Odegard said, wiggling his lip at his wife.

The violinist cleared her throat. "Frederick Kunz is my uncle."

"Is that right? Uncle Fred." Now I was pissed at both of them. Why was the prodigy leading me around in circles?

"He's my father's brother," she said. "Both my parents are deceased. I lived with my aunt and uncle from the time I was twelve."

The violinist scooted back on the sofa, folding her hands in her lap. I thought she was going to kick her legs back and forth like a little girl.

"Tell me some more about your uncle."

"Well, he bought a violin for me when . . ." She paused and looked at her husband again. "When I got into Oberlin. I think that's what got him started with collecting. He plays a little bit himself."

"I know; I've heard him."

I tried to hold her eyes. "Is your uncle the person who introduced you to your husband?"

The violinist glanced toward her feet. "Yes."

"And when did you first become aware of your uncle's taste for Nazi paraphernalia?"

"I never knew," she said, taking a look at her closely clipped fingernails.

"Never?"

"Not until . . . not until I moved back out here after I left Oberlin. I . . . Perry and I would go over to his house."

"Which house?"

"Well, we went to both."

"What did you make of that stuff?"

"I thought it was creepy. He said it was just a collection, a good investment, really, because the value of Nazi things appreciates so much."

"Just like good violins."

"Right. He said that it had nothing to do with any ideology."

"And you believed that?"

"Not really," she said, unbuttoning her blazer and letting it fall open.

I found myself noticing the shape of the violinist's breasts, blooming under her tight turtleneck. My mindfulness kicking in. I averted my eyes. Ordinarily, I wouldn't stop myself from a little discreet ogling, but there was something amiss with Elizabeth Odegard.

"So tell me, does your uncle have you play the violins he's interested in buying, try them out for him?"

The violinist glanced quickly at her husband. "Sometimes."

"So these fiddles were instruments that your husband located on his trips to Prague and Vienna?"

"She doesn't know about any of this," Odegard shouted. Then he turned to his wife and told her to pull her blazer together.

I watched her button it, with a blush of modesty. "How about your uncle's political views? Does he ever discuss them with you?"

"Not really."

I turned away from the Mrs. and fixed my eye on her husband. "How about you? Does it ever give you qualms trading these instruments?"

Odegard cleared his throat. "I'm a businessman, Mr. Boyer. A client's interested in a certain type of instrument, it's my job to try and find it."

"No questions asked."

"Sure, I ask questions."

"Not just how much he's willing to pay?"

Odegard unzipped his loungewear a bit at the neck. "Hey, I'm not a moralist, Mr. Boyer. I don't sit in judgment of another man's harmless hobby."

"You sure it's harmless?"

The violin dealer crossed his legs. "Look, the guy's a collector. What's so hard to understand about that?"

"And you don't give a damn where the violins came from?"

"Let me explain something to you, Mr. Boyer. A fine Italian violin has both a pedigree and a fate. A master made it three hundred years ago and it's passed through quite a few hands by now."

I wanted to tell Odegard to take his pedigree and fate and shove it up his herpesed asshole, but another breathing exercise brought me to Gandhi Land. "So, it doesn't offend your sensibility, Mr. Odegard, that these instruments have been stolen?"

"I have no information about that."

"What are you talking about?" I said, standing, sending Gandhi for a snooze. "What the hell were you using that fucking Sonderstab catalog for? It's a goddamn checklist of prime instruments confiscated by the Nazis, isn't it?"

"I want that back, Boyer."

"You can kiss my ass, Odegard. Now, how about the big brunette? How does she figure into the package?"

"She's not germane. I'd rather leave her out of this."

"I bet you would."

"Hey, I don't have to listen to this. I'm sitting here trying to be cooperative, asshole." Odegard's nostrils flared. He was genuinely ticked off.

"So, is the brunette Kunz's wife?"

"Hell no. The wife never goes to White Bear Lake. She stays in Woodbury."

"Okay, let's leave out the fat woman you were screwing, for a minute." I turned to the violinist, who was clearly agitated. "Has your uncle Fred ever discussed his views on abortion?"

"Not . . . not in my presence," she said. Then she clenched her teeth and I watched her cheeks turn a quick, fevered rose.

"You shouldn't play poker, Ms. Odegard."

I turned toward the violin dealer. "How about you, Odegard? Have you heard Kunz talk about abortion?"

"Absolutely," he said, glad, perhaps, to have the attention shift away from the Nazi fiddles and the fat brunette. "Kunz is a real hothead about that issue."

"What do you mean?"

"Well, you know, the guy's got some rather extreme views on the subject."

"Like what?"

"Perry," the violinist said.

"You don't have to worry about protecting your uncle, Ms. Odegard. And for that matter, you don't need to worry about protecting your husband. They both seem like men who know how to take care of themselves."

Odegard took this last bit as a compliment and flashed his pretty-boy smile. He shifted his neck sharply to the left and a bone in his back cracked, satisfying him.

"Okay, Odegard," I said, "tell me about Kunz's views on abortion. Do you share them?"

"No way. The guy becomes a madman on the subject."

"What's he say?"

"Hey, I don't want to get anybody in trouble." Odegard folded his hands in his lap and did his mum's-the-word routine.

I turned to face the violinist. She moved her lips without speaking. "My uncle has . . . he has a theory," she said, finding her voice, and then nibbling on the nub of her thumbnail.

Odegard sneered at his wife. "You don't have to tell him any-thing, Liz."

"Shut up, Odegard," I hollered.

The violinist turned away.

"Elizabeth," I said, trying to bring her back.

Odegard was wiggling his lip at her.

"You were saying your uncle had a theory."

"It's none of your business, Boyer," Odegard said.

"It is my business, asshole, because your wife's hired me."

"I've had enough of this." Odegard stood up and flipped me off. "You know, you're not the first one she's hired," he said, and walked out of the room.

I swiveled in my chair to watch Odegard head down the hall-way and disappear into the bedroom suite. Maybe the guy would console himself with a stroll through his wardrobe. More likely he'd be on the phone with Herr Kunz. I turned toward the violinist.

"What's going on here?" I asked.

"I don't know what you mean."

"What's this about you hiring other investigators?"

My client fidgeted. "That was a long time ago."

"Tell me about it."

"I'd rather not."

"Do you want me to help you? What's with your husband doing his mind-control number?"

The prodigy answered with a blank stare. I felt as if I was talk-ing with somebody whose grasp of English was limited.

"You were saying that your uncle had a theory."

"Yes."

"What kind of a theory?"

The violinist nibbled on her nubbed thumbnails. "He believes that all abortion doctors are Jewish and that they're using abortion as a tool to eliminate Gentiles."

"Really. What else does he say?"

"He says that Jewish women don't have abortions themselves, that they're under orders to breed as many babies as possible. He says that's what they do in the Zionist state."

"The Zionist state?"

"That's what he calls it. He thinks that if abortion isn't stopped now, the Jews will end up winning a war of attrition in this country."

I scratched my head. "That's an interesting notion. I read somewhere that Jews account for less than 3 percent of the U.S. population. Do you know how long this war of attrition would take? Let's just say we'll all be globally warmed out of existence before that."

The violinist nodded.

"Have you heard him mention any action he plans on taking? Has your uncle expressed a wish?"

"Well, I suppose if my uncle had a wish . . ."

"Yes?"

"It would be to eliminate abortion altogether."

"And how would he do that?"

The violinist folded her hands together. "Eliminate the clinics."

"And short of that?"

"Eliminate the abortion doctors."

"Does he use the word *eliminate*?"

The violinist drew her head down, turtle-style, closer to her shoulders.

I wondered if she'd ever had an abortion. The woman was hard to read. A blank slate. I'd heard about certain child prodigies who grew up to be emotional dwarfs. Spent eight hours a day practicing, could play Paganini at six, but never developed a genuine personality.

"Has your uncle mentioned his activities with Born Free or the national Mother-Child Labor Day rally on the capitol grounds?"

She met my gaze but didn't answer.

"Are you aware of any of your uncle's plans for the rally? Are you trying to protect him?"

The violinist had shut down, but I didn't stop asking questions.

"Is this why you hired me, Ms. Odegard, to find out about your uncle? Is that why you've hired others? How does McCracken fit in? Does he work for your uncle?"

The violinist stood and strolled over to the window.

"Do you think your husband is involved with any of this antiabortion business?"

With her back turned to me, my reluctant client spoke again. "Perry has no ideology. He has no ideas. He's all about merchandise. He's all about buying and selling."

I stood. "And what are you all about, Ms. Odegard?"

"I don't know," the violinist said sadly. She turned to face me.

"So, you're just a victim of circumstances?"

She looked blankly at me.

"I want you to take me to meet your uncle."

"I don't know that I can do that. My uncle is a very busy man."

"You can do it. I'll be with you."

"When?"

"Today."

"What if he's not available?"

"We'll try our luck."

I heard Odegard padding down the hall. He'd dressed in a gray houndstooth suit with a rosy silk square ruffling out of his breast pocket. The suit fit him beautifully, except for the fact that his right coat pocket was bulging with a Luger that his small hand couldn't quite cover.

"You ever thought about becoming a model, Odegard?"

"Get up, Boyer."

I remained seated. "Pardon me, but I'm a guest of your wife." I smiled over at the violinist.

"The party's over, Boyer."

I reached into my pocket for my tin of Altoids. Nothing like playing chicken with a stolen-violin-dealing, Luger-packing, Nazi-trading fop. I opened the tin and saw I'd pulled out the wrong one. I admired the tight little joint I'd twisted that morning. I wanted to take it out, have a couple of tokes, pass it around the room, but I feared that might be pushing it. I shoved the tin back into my pocket.

"Get up, Boyer." Odegard drew the gun.

"What are you doing, Perry?" the violinist screamed.

"Shut up, Liz."

"That thing's not even loaded," I said, on a hunch.

"Want me to try it out on you, asshole?"

I stood, thinking about how long Odegard had been down the hall. Had it taken him that long to change into his suit? Or was he figuring out how to load the gun? As a parlor game, chicken isn't all it's made out to be. I thought of my former client Gregory Sands, whose eyes were shot out in this very building because he offended the pride of a couple of imbeciles.

Odegard waved the long pistol back and forth. "Get out of here. I don't want to see your tired ass again, Boyer, or I'll blow your brains out."

I nodded agreeably to the violin dealer, and then pulled my cell phone from my pocket and punched Blossom's number on my speed dial.

"What the fuck do you think you're doing?" Odegard hollered, moving toward me now. Did the guy intend to shoot me point-blank? Luckily, Blossom answered the first ring. "I'm at the Odegards' in Loring Park," I blurted.

"Put that down," Odegard shouted.

"One fifteen Willow. Le Palais. The guy's holding a Luger on me and making threats."

"Put it down!"

I nodded and dropped the phone back into my pocket. "That was my assistant, Blossom. I like to keep her up to speed."

"Get out of here, Boyer," Odegard said, waving the gun again.

I'd pushed the guy as far as I should. But I had to push him just a little further. "Come on, Elizabeth, you're coming with me."

"The fuck she is," Odegard shouted.

I spoke directly to the violinist. "I can't leave you here with this madman. Come on."

"I'm going to blow your brains out."

"You already said that, Odegard." I took a deep breath and thought of a brown pebble dropping into a deep river. "Listen," I said, "the cops are on their way. Unless you want to spend the rest of your life in Stillwater as the candy-ass for a gang of hard guys, I'd put the gun down."

I stepped slowly toward the violinist, keeping my eye on Odegard, then grabbed hold of the violinist's arm and led her toward the door.

"You'd better not," Odegard shouted. He held out his arm with the gun.

"Let go of me," the violinist shouted. "He's going to shoot."

The crazy shit aimed above my head and pulled the trigger. The blast lifted me off the ground. The violinist screamed. Half the known world shattered. Or so it sounded when the floor-to-ceiling hall mirror exploded in a bright metallic shower of glass.

"See, it's loaded," Odegard shouted, in awe.

The dude had created his own Kristallnacht in the middle of the morning. As I opened the front door and yanked my sobbing client into the hall and down the stairway, I hollered, "That's gonna bring a lot of years of bad luck, asshole."

THE MINNESOTA MARTYRS

"Perry's not coming after us," the violinist said as soon as we hit the street.

"What makes you say that?" I asked, leading her across to the park.

"I know what he's doing."

"What's that?"

"Sweeping up the glass. If there's one thing Perry hates, it's a mess."

"Well, he's certainly made himself a nice one."

The violinist pulled a handkerchief from her blazer pocket and patted her forehead. "God, it's hot out here," she said.

"You're dressed for winter."

She unbuttoned her blazer and slipped out of it.

I checked my watch. "It's hard to believe, but you still have time to get to McCracken's. Seemed like your husband was holding a gun on me for a couple of days."

As we approached Harmon Place, I led her out of the park. It seemed safer to be on the sidewalk with other people.

"You shouldn't have pushed Perry like that," the violinist said.

"I shouldn't have pushed him? Your asshole husband shouldn't have held a loaded gun on me. That wasn't my idea of fun."

I opened the yellow passenger door of my forest green Mazda for the violinist.

"This is your car?" she said.

"In all its glory."

Once the prodigy was buckled in, I drove up Lyndale and made a U-turn a couple of blocks north of McCracken's, in front of Vera's, home of the caffeinated happy hour. I pulled a ten-dollar bill from my wallet.

"Elizabeth, would you mind running in and getting me a large Americano? Get yourself whatever you'd like. I'll be right here."

The violinist took the ten—she seemed to like the assign-ment—and said, "Anything you want with the Americano? A muffin, a scone?"

"No, just the coffee."

I pulled out my phone and punched in Blossom's number.

"You okay?" Blossom asked.

"Yeah."

"I didn't call Bobby. He'd have had a squad car over there and it sounded like you had things under control."

"I wouldn't go that far." I took a deep breath. "Asshole shot up a mirror. Scared the hell out of me. You don't want a guy like that holding a gun on you. I've got the violinist with me now. Going to take her visiting. Can you get over to my office?"

"Sure."

"We won't be there. I've got the code grabber in my book bag.

It'll get you into Odegard's garage. I'd like you to see if the asshole's still stowing violins in his trunk. I'm tempted to take one of them for safekeeping."

"Which one?"

"The Guadagnini. But don't you do it."

"Wouldn't think of it."

"Any word from Trevor?" I asked.

"Yeah, I just heard from him. He hacked into Kunz's e-mails. There's a $50,000 offer out for each hit. Three abortion docs in the Twin Cities, two men and a woman, and they each have a Jewish name."

"Aw, shit."

"Kunz has been circulating a hit list with the names and addresses on it."

"Oh, God. Is this for real?"

"The communications are coming from Kunz's various e-mail accounts."

"Is there a timetable?" I asked.

Blossom spoke so quickly it was hard to keep up with her. "They're hoping to bag all three docs by Labor Day. It's perfect timing. There's a shitload of extra law enforcement in town, but it's all tied to the Republican convention. It's the perfect storm, the way they see it. Kunz and his people have been doing their scouting. They know that the police are completely distracted, all wigged out about anarchists and left-wing demonstrators. There's going to be huge protests outside of the convention center by Women Against Military Madness, the Anti-War Committee, and the Iraq Peace Action Coalition. Plus there's an anarchist group called the RNC Welcoming Committee that has the police totally freaked. And if these wackos nail an abortion doc or two, they're going to be thrilled to have all the media. The fuckers are certain that they're right and that history will see them as heroes."

"Just like W."

"Right. God is on their side."

"And we know who the devil is," I said.

"Damn right. It's holy week in Minnesota. The killers will be known as the Minnesota Martyrs."

I zipped down my window and spit onto the street.

"I think we better go to the FBI, Augie."

"We don't have time for the FBI. They're reactive. They like to unravel shit after the damage is done. To the FBI, abortion docs rank pretty low in the hierarchy of terror targets. They're not essential to homeland security."

"But we've got particular threats, Augie; we've got actual targets with names and addresses spelled out."

I watched the violinist come out of Vera's carrying a tray of coffee and a pastry sack.

"What are we going to do, Augie?" Blossom asked.

"I'm going out to see Kunz right now and try to nip this sucker in the bud."

WHERE'S MCCRACKEN?

"First we're heading to Dr. McCracken's," I said.

"I don't want to go to Dr. McCracken's," the violinist said.

"Why's that?"

The violinist pulled a Danish from a sack and, taking a bite, pretended she hadn't heard my question.

I glanced at her as I backed out of my spot and spun another U-turn on Lyndale. "You see Dr. McCracken five days a week; you must have plenty to talk about."

"What happens between Dr. McCracken and me is confidential."

"Did somebody tell you that you can't talk about it?"

"It's understood," the violinist said, taking another bite of her Danish.

"I don't understand it." I smiled at my client and tried to get her to smile back at me. She wouldn't.

"Do you know what McCracken's specialty is?"

"He has a specialty?" The prodigy wiped the corners of her mouth with a napkin.

"Yes, brainwashing."

"What are you talking about?"

"The clinical term is deprogramming. He specializes in helping people who have been members of cults get free. That's pretty intensive work, and it would stand to reason that he'd see this type of patient, like he sees you, every day of the week. Do you know what a cult is, Elizabeth?"

She nodded.

"Have you been a member of a cult?"

"I have not," she said, making a show of being offended by my question.

"But I figure a guy with a talent for deprogramming could just as easily . . ."

"If you must know," the violinist said, "Dr. McCracken helps me with my playing."

"But you don't bring your violin."

She pointed to her head. "It's all up here. I struggle with confidence."

It was a plausible line, but I didn't buy it. I pulled up across from the building where McCracken had his office and I looked at my watch. "You'll be right on time."

"Are you going to wait for me?"

"I'll be here."

I waited a few minutes for the violinist to get across the street and into McCracken's office. Then I followed. At first, I didn't know what to make of the sight of her standing tall in front of McCracken's outer door and knocking three times. She didn't notice me watching. She waited a few seconds and knocked again thrice. She was beginning to get anxious.

"Isn't the doctor there?" I called, from down the hall.

"The door's locked. I'm sure he left a message at the house." A little terror had crept into her voice. "He must have had an emergency."

GUESS WHO

I wanted to believe that my little showdown with McCracken the day before had scared off the quack. In any case, I decided not to say anything more about the shrink unless the violinist raised the subject. She seemed to be getting more nervous by the moment. Once I pulled away from the curb, she turned down the passenger-side visor and studied herself in the mirror. She took a tube of lipstick from her small clutch, spread it amply, flattened her lips together, and then turned her head to examine the effect.

"I suppose you want to look just right for your uncle."

The violinist shrugged, then narrowed her eyes and took a long look into the mirror. In a moment, she folded away the visor and turned her head toward me, forcing a smile.

"My uncle won't be very happy about this, if he's even there."

I waited a beat before responding. "I'm not concerned with your uncle's happiness. I'm worried about the damage he's trying to do." I turned to face the violinist directly. "How much do you know about his plans?" I demanded.

The prodigy turned her head and looked out the side window. "I'm sure you know more about my uncle's plans than I do."

It was time to take another wild leap. "Tell me, Elizabeth, have you ever had an abortion?"

"That's none of your business."

I kept my eyes on the road and quietly asked: "How old were you?"

"I told you, that's none of your business." She began tearing up.

I decided that a little banter was in order. "I've known a lot of women who've had abortions and I think it's been hard for all of them, in one way or another. I really don't know what I think of abortion. I can understand how some people see it as murder. I don't see it that way, but I'm hardly in favor of it. I don't know if anybody is in favor of abortion. I do believe that it should be a woman's right. And that's the law."

The violinist was sobbing, her face nearly glued to the side window.

"I bet you were quite young."

"Sixteen," she said, surprising me.

"Still in high school."

"I was in the conservatory at Oberlin."

"You got in early."

The violinist nodded, still facing the side window.

"You must have been quite the prodigy."

"For better or worse."

I felt as if this was my last chance to get my client to talk. A single misstep and I'd lose her. "Did someone go with you?" I asked, as casually as I could.

The violinist didn't answer.

I turned toward her. "What about your boyfriend?"

"I didn't have one," the violinist said, her voice far away.

I puzzled over this a moment. "You didn't have a boyfriend?"

"My uncle. When I came home over winter break. . . . It wasn't . . . it wasn't the first time."

"Your uncle?" Suddenly, I knew.

WRAPPED SNOOPY

Heading up the long driveway to her uncle's mansion, Elizabeth Odegard snapped to. "Pull up to the far end of the circle. You can leave your car there." She caught my eye and held it a moment. What she'd told me was a piece of sealed business. I nodded my agreement, tossed my baseball cap into the backseat, then stepped out into the warm day, a strong breeze giving my thinning scraps of hair a tousle.

I'd forgotten about the giant Snoopy sculptures that Blossom had mentioned. At the base of the mansion's graduated stairway was a deadbeat Snoop, crafted of faux gumballs. Poor dude looked as if he'd contracted some rare canine leprosy. Across the stairs, a pensive Snoopy, sprawled across the roof of his house, was wondering how the fuck he'd ended up at Kunz's.

I turned toward the violinist and asked her how she liked Snoopy art.

She gave me a pinched smile. "I don't much care for it. It's not really art at all."

I nodded and tried to draw the prodigy into a conspiratorial smile. Finally, she relented.

Frederick Kunz had been watching us awhile. He stood at the open front door. When I spied on Kunz at the White Bear Lake place, I hadn't noticed that he parted his hair in the middle or that he had milky-blue eyes. The eyes of a child molester.

The dude was dressed in pleated gray slacks and a yellow broadcloth shirt with the sleeves folded neatly to the elbow. He sported a witty bow tie in a pattern of miniature red and yellow hearts. I wondered if he had one with peace signs. The man was long and lean. So was his nose. So were his fingers.

"Hello, Liz," he said, sounding surprisingly human as he greeted his niece with a kiss. "Listen, before I forget, your aunt Katherine wants to see you." Kunz extended his hand toward me. "How do you do, Mr. Boyer? I watched you drive up from a window upstairs."

"I'm glad we didn't catch you by surprise."

Kunz showed me his amused smile. "No, a little bird told me you might be making a visit."

I looked at Kunz's long, beautifully manicured fingers and thought of him touching his niece when she was still a girl. The violinist had tucked herself into a zone and would no longer meet my eye. Meanwhile, Kunz seemed in no hurry to welcome us into his house.

"I saw you admiring my Snoopys." Kunz motioned toward the two monstrosities standing directly in front of us. "Nothing more American than *Peanuts*. Matter of fact, I've been trying my damnedest to purchase one other Snoopy. Maybe you've heard of it. A Snoopy doghouse wrapped by Christo. You know who Christo is?"

"Of course," I said. "As a matter of fact, your niece and I were talking about Christo on the drive out here." I'm not sure why I said that, but I've always enjoyed the way that making someone else complicit in your bullshit quickens the blood.

I smiled at the violinist and watched her swallow her surprise. "As I was telling your niece, I happened to be in New York a few years ago when *The Gates* was unfurled in Central Park. Quite ravishing."

Kunz didn't want to hear about *The Gates,* which is just as well because I didn't see it. The molester inhaled deeply through his thin nostrils. "Did you realize that in the late seventies, Schulz created a comic strip that paid homage to Christo?"

"I must have missed it."

"I can re-create it for you," Kunz said, drawing with his hand in the air. "First panel: Snoopy leans against a rock, musing, 'I remember when Christo created the *Valley Curtain* in Colorado.' Next panel: 'I loved the *Wrapped Walkways* in Kansas City and the *Running Fence* in California.' Third panel, with Snoopy walking now: 'I wonder what he'll wrap next.' Fourth and final panel . . ."

"It's Snoopy's doghouse," I said, killing his punch line.

"Right. Oh, the expression on Snoopy's face when he sees his house wrapped like that."

I couldn't believe we were having this conversation.

"Christo's response to the strip was to actually wrap a Snoopy-style doghouse. It's in the Schulz Museum in Santa Rosa, California. I've offered them much more than it's worth, enough money to build a new wing for their damn museum, but they won't sell it. I've made appeals on the basis of Schulz being a native of Minnesota, a Saint Paul boy, for God's sake. I've stressed that Christo's doghouse belongs here. They're impervious to reason. I keep upping my offer."

I looked into Frederick Kunz's milky blues. "Some things don't have a price on them."

Kunz grinned. "I don't believe that."

"Well," I said, "you must have enjoyed the miracle-wrapped buses in the Twin Cities." It seemed clear to me that Kunz paid for the wrapping.

"Indeed," Kunz said with a broad smile. "I like a creative approach. Like creation itself, it's often taken for granted."

"It must seem like a nice bit of intelligent design to you."

"I don't go in for semantics, Mr. Boyer. But take a look at the world," he said, spreading his hands across his estate, "could you call its design anything other than intelligent? Sadly, life has been cheapened all around us, Mr. Boyer. People just need some help to see its value. The miracle that it is."

"And you're here to help."

"Absolutely. Once they get our message, everybody will be cheering."

"Just like the folks in Baghdad."

Kunz turned away and took his niece's arm. He led us into the house and down a paneled hallway to a large library. I gazed at the half mile of walnut bookcases carved into the walls. There were many leather-bound matching sets, no doubt picked up in antiquarian bookstores but never read.

"Here's my consolation prize." Kunz led me to wall with a Christo litho of Snoopy's wrapped house, scraps of fabric and twine attached to its surface. "This thing cost a pretty penny and makes me angry every time I see it."

"Because you can't get your hands on the original?" I said, with a bit of taunt, before regarding the lithograph again. "It's quite handsome."

"You like it, Mr. Boyer?"

"Yes, quite a bit." In his enhanced sketch, Christo gave Snoopy's abode the majesty of a carriage house.

"You know something about art, don't you, Mr. Boyer?"

"Not much. I was an art history minor in college. But that was a lifetime ago."

"I'm sure you're being modest." Kunz lifted the framed dog-house off its hook. "I'd like you to have this."

"What do you mean?"

"It's my gift to you," Kunz said with a grin.

"I couldn't take that."

"Sure you can. I'll have my girl Galina wrap it up." Kunz leaned the framed piece against the wall on which it had just hung.

He crossed to the other side of the room and talked into an intercom. "Galina, would you please come down to the library with coffee and that rhubarb pie from last night? And let Katherine know that Elizabeth is here, will you?"

Kunz turned back to me. "So, again, Mr. Boyer, I'm offering you this lithograph as a gesture of friendship."

"But we're not friends."

Kunz put two fingers over his lips. "In the South there's a certain custom that I appreciate."

"Are you from the South, Mr. Kunz?"

"No, but I'll adopt good ideas from any place. And there's much to aspire to in Southern manners. If a man comes by your house while you're eating, you offer him a plate of food. He's expected to decline the offer. That way you save face in case you're short. But if you make a second offer, it tells your guest that you've got plenty and you expect him to dine with you. But if your guest declines that second offer, he's seriously offended you. I've made my offer twice, Mr. Boyer. You don't want to offend me."

"What I have to say to you may more than offend you."

"Oh, I doubt that. I don't take these things personally. It's easy enough to see that you're trapped in an ideology, Mr. Boyer, that's had its day. You went to Berkeley, didn't you?"

I nodded. The creep had been checking up on me.

"What did they used to call it?"

"I can't remember—Sodom or Gomorrah?"

"Berserkley. Women used to walk the streets wearing intrauterine contraceptive devices as earrings."

"That's not the only place they wore them."

"You come from a world that has little respect for human life, Mr. Boyer. But human life is regaining its value. It never really lost it. Only the deluded did. Only those who see life as chaos. Only those who don't accept our purity."

A tall woman in a silk pantsuit stepped carefully into the library.

"Katherine," Kunz said, acknowledging his wife.

"Hello, Liz," she said, giving her niece a polite hug. "It's so good to see you."

After being introduced, I studied Katherine Kunz. She was a striking woman, with a swath of white hair like Susan Sontag's and high cheekbones worthy of a model. But Mrs. Kunz didn't look to be in good shape. Sixty years old going on seventy-five. She had blanketed her face with powder, but I could still see a number of spirited capillaries bursting in patches over her cheeks and attached barnacle-like to the sides of her nostrils. I guessed she had a taste for vodka, equal parts Absolut and grapefruit juice—a quart of each before dinner. She probably reserved a decent cognac for winding down in the evenings.

Mrs. Kunz was making plans with my client. "Liz, why don't we go upstairs and catch up? Wouldn't that be nice? We'll call for tea and cookies."

I watched the prodigy walk off, arms linked, with her aunt. Both her aunt and uncle talked to her as if she were still a child.

"My wife has had some serious health problems," Kunz volunteered.

"I'm sorry to hear that."

"She's coming along, thank you, coming along. Please, sit, Mr. Boyer."

I took a seat in one of the mission chairs while Kunz eased himself down on the long sofa.

"Mr. Kunz, tell me about your relationship to the antiabortion organization Born Free."

"I'm a card-carrying member, Mr. Boyer."

"And your involvement with the Labor Day rally slated for the state capitol grounds?"

"We don't call it a rally, but a celebration. A celebration of life. That's what our organization is about—life. We celebrate women and children. We celebrate the family. We celebrate diversity. We're a very positive organization. We don't dwell on the ruthless murder of innocent children. Our motto is 'Choose Life.' There will be women enduring the pains of labor and giving birth at our Labor Day celebration. By the way, Mr. Boyer, I understand that your daughter is going to be present at the state capitol grounds. Performing, no less. She shares your ideology, doesn't she?"

I smiled at Kunz; I wasn't about to discuss Rose with the molester.

A large, uniformed woman wheeled a wooden serving tray into the room.

"Oh, good, Galina." Kunz stood and walked over to the cart. "What do we have here? Coffee. Some of your rhubarb pie. How do you like your coffee, Mr. Boyer?"

"Black."

"Fine, that's how I like it." Kunz poured the coffee himself from a silver pot.

I took a long look at Galina. Bent over the cart, slicing huge wedges of pie, she appeared familiar to me. She leaned toward me and handed me a plate of pie and I remembered where I had seen her. I looked into Galina's round face. She was clearly the oversized brunette whom Perry Odegard had been taking from behind.

"Mr. Kunz," she said in a thick Russian accent as she handed her boss a slice of pie.

"Oh, Galina, one more thing," Kunz said. "That piece of art leaning against the wall down there—would you wrap it up in something that will protect it? Mr. Boyer is going to take it with him."

"Yes, sir."

"She's quite an addition to the house," Kunz said after Galina left the room with the framed Christo. "She's very willing. I found her at the Jewish Community Center in Saint Paul. They have a lot of immigrants from Russia coming through, including some solid women looking to work. She still has family over there. I'm helping her to get them over here, sponsoring them. My wife didn't like the idea of having Galina work here at first. Katherine said, 'Are you sure you want a Jewish woman working in this house?' And I told her, 'I have nothing against Jews.'"

"Would you excuse me for a moment?" I said, standing. "Could you point me in the direction of the bathroom?"

"Yes, straight up the hallway, third door on the left."

I figured I had two, three minutes, tops. I closed the bathroom door and punched Blossom's speed-dial button.

"Guess what?" she said, answering.

"What?"

"I got the violin."

"What violin?"

"The Guadagnini."

"What do you mean, you got it?"

"I took it from Odegard's trunk."

"You weren't s'posed to do that! I just wanted to know if it was there. Where'd you put it?"

"It's in your office."

"Get it out of there. Take it over to Lionel's. Tell him to stash it somewhere. Listen, have Sabbatini and Trevor meet me over at my office at three o'clock. We've got to come up with a plan."

"Where are you, Augie?"

"At Kunz's. Gotta go." I flushed the toilet without using it. When I stepped back into the hall, I was surprised to see Kunz standing there.

"You didn't wash your hands, Mr. Boyer."

"I must have forgotten."

"You had other things on your mind. Just like that invert Larry Craig, who forgot to flush the toilet at the airport."

"I can assure you, Mr. Kunz, I wasn't tapping my feet."

"Of course not. Since we're up this way, I'd like to show you my collection of instruments. I understand you're an amateur cellist."

I nodded and followed Kunz through a narrow doorway. We took a circular staircase down to a sunken wing that had no natural light. I can't say this was my first choice for recreation: being led into a bunker by a Nazi who'd raped his niece.

"Got any lights down here?"

"Of course," Kunz said with a snappy, sadistic laugh. He hit a switch and a track of soft lights illuminated a large Gothic room with marble floors and dark wood paneling. There were two grand pianos squared off against each other in the center of the room. Running along the perimeter were glass display cases filled with violins. I noticed a small case of gauges, measuring temperature and humidity and who knows what else. I breathed for a minute. Long. Deep. I considered how much better these instruments were being looked after than their former owners had been.

Kunz walked me by the display case closest to the door. Two violins were propped on stands. I read the labels. "Pietro Giacomo, Brescia, 1707. Bruges, 1943." The other label read "Ferdinand Gagliano, Napoli, 1759. Lyon, 1942."

"Two of the violins you're proudest of?" I asked.

"Well, these two are quite important examples of their periods."

"Does the second date refer to the date of confiscation by the Nazis?"

"Allegedly. Allegedly," Kunz said with a stout laugh. "But that's just a bit of fiction to go along with the many others. The Nazi Party had no interest in musical instruments. They were fighting for their lives. Do you really think they had time for musical instruments, Mr. Boyer?"

"So it's the fiction of these instruments' theft that gives them their special value?"

"You could say that if you like."

"Were all these instruments allegedly confiscated by the Nazis?"

"Yes. You see, it's just a harmless hobby. A little like stamp collecting; you're never quite satisfied until your collection is complete."

"You don't happen to have any violins from Vienna, do you?" I asked, remembering the "Wien" stamped on the spine of the Sonderstab booklet.

Kunz inhaled sharply through his nose, but didn't answer.

"You see, I once knew a man who alleged that his father's violin was confiscated by the Nazis in Vienna."

"In any case," Kunz said, plowing ahead, "I'm hosting some friends, in town this weekend for the convention, who will appreciate the collection."

"Will the president be coming by?"

"No, I'm afraid not," Kunz said, clearly flattered. "But he has been here."

"I wouldn't doubt it. But if we could change the subject for a moment, I want to talk about abortion."

"My pleasure, Mr. Boyer." Kunz motioned to his instrument collection. "As you can see, I'm an open book. I've got nothing to hide. I'm probably not a lot of fun for you investigative types. But that's part of my philosophy—keep everything in the open, absolutely transparent and aboveboard. Then there are no unpleasant mysteries."

"Good," I said, "let's have a nice open discussion. Tell me how and when you plan to have the three abortion doctors in the Twin Cities killed."

Kunz folded his arms in front of him. "I don't know what you're talking about, Mr. Boyer."

"You know, the three Jewish docs. I have evidence connecting you to them, evidence that you've offered $50,000 apiece to have them assassinated."

Kunz stiffened and stood taller.

"By the way, that sounds like you're getting a very fair price. Fifty grand a life, sounds like a bargain to me. I know how much you value life. Yes, fifty grand is a real bargain. Especially when you consider what those fiddles are worth, or the money you've raised for George W."

"This is nonsense."

"It's not nonsense." I stepped around so that I was standing face-to-face with Kunz. "The police are looking at the evidence right now."

Kunz smirked. "That's all a fantasy somebody dreamed up. I'm against abortion, Mr. Boyer. Most of the people in this country are."

"That's not even true."

"Of course it is. And pro-life groups like Born Free are working quite effectively, within the system, mind you, to change it. Soon abortion will be illegal across the land."

"Look, Kunz, we're onto you and we're going to stop you."

"You'd be far better off, Mr. Boyer, putting your fantasy life to bed." Kunz bowed his head. "Listen," he said, suddenly humble, "I have personal reasons for despising abortion." Kunz's milky eyes began to tear. "My wife and I tried for years to conceive a child. I've talked with hardly anybody about this, you understand, but we did everything we could possibly do. Spent a fortune on fertility experts. Finally, after years of trying, my wife got pregnant. We weren't young anymore. A miracle had taken place in the house. You know what I'm talking about, Mr. Boyer; you have a child. My wife walked around with a glow on her face. A kind of happiness was building that I'd never experienced before. We decided not to tell anyone until she got through the first trimester. So, it was just our blessed secret."

Kunz pulled a handkerchief from his pocket and dabbed at his eyes.

"Around eight weeks, Katherine lost the baby. I don't know that she's ever fully recovered, and it's been quite a few years now." Kunz made a show of blowing his nose. "I've been told that many women have their abortions at around that time, six to eight weeks. It's so unfair. How much we wanted that baby, and these others willfully destroy God's gift."

I couldn't abide this sentimental recital. How was a man who'd been trying to contract three murders capable of such mood making?

"And then there's Elizabeth's story," Kunz said between sniffles.

"Yes, tell me what you did to her," I said, facing the Nazi with my hands on my hips.

"I don't know what you're talking about. The poor woman had an abortion when she was quite young and now she can no longer have children."

"And who got her pregnant?"

Kunz shifted his weight from one foot to the other. "Listen, I don't know what my niece told you, but as you may have noticed, she's not well."

"Nobody around you seems to be very well."

"My niece is heavily medicated. She imagines things."

"Right, and the Holocaust never happened."

"I don't know what you're talking about, Mr. Boyer. My niece is bipolar and quite paranoid. What they used to call paranoid schizophrenic. If she takes her medication, she can function. If not, she might say and do anything. That's why she came to you, and believe me, you're not the first one."

"Tell me about Dr. McCracken."

"Who? Dr. McCracken," Kunz said with a laugh, "I've never heard of a Dr. McCracken."

"What do you have him programming Elizabeth to do?"

Kunz took a cigarette out of his coat pocket and shot a high flame from a lighter at the tip of his cigarette. "You know, I'm tired of all your ridiculous accusations, Mr. Boyer. I'd like you to leave right now."

"Fine." I looked directly at Kunz. "Get your niece down here and we'll leave."

Kunz blew smoke out through his nostrils and strolled toward a marble-top library table. He flicked his cigarette in an ashtray shaped like a grand piano with its lid propped up. Then he opened a small drawer and pulled out a gun.

"I don't think my niece is safe with you, Mr. Boyer. She stays. You leave right now. I'm happy to walk you to the door."

OFFICE PARTY

When I walked into my office, Bobby Sabbatini hollered, "Where the hell you been, Augie? I broke my ass to get free. Do you know what's going on out there? There's a bunch of black-garbed anarchists all over downtown Saint Paul, with hoods over their fucking heads, measuring the diameters of manhole covers. We got Republican delegates pouring into town, antiwar protesters of every stripe, not to speak of the pregnant born-agains, everywhere but in the hospital. The press has arrived from all corners of the globe, looking like they've just awakened from an eight-year slumber. And then there's this little plot to knock off three abortion docs. But nobody knows where the hell you're at."

"Fuck off, Bobby. I was in a secret location memorizing poems." I coughed for a moment and took in the scene. Blossom sat upright on the leathered teak sofa. Trevor, the hacker, in an iconic Dexter Gordon T-shirt, leaned against the wall beside Dylan's calendar image. Sabbatini was perched atop my desk, with his leather bomber slung over a file cabinet, and his service revolver bulging out of his shoulder harness. I wondered how many more guns I'd have to face before the day was over.

"Yeah," Blossom said, "don't you believe in checking in?"

I looked at my watch. "I told you three o'clock, so I'm fifteen minutes late."

Bobby rolled up the sleeves of his yellow shirt. "She was worried about you."

"That's sweet, Blossom," I said.

"Screw you, Augie." Blossom flipped me off for good measure. "You don't check in. You turn off your cell phone."

"Look, I needed to chill for a little."

Trevor, who found all this amusing, gave off a stuttering laugh.

"Yeah, Blossom," Bobby said, "the Augster needed to chill."

"Which means he got high," Blossom said. "He thinks he's the Big Lebowski."

Trevor smiled at me. "Dude."

Bobby pointed to the window air conditioner. "No way you can chill in here, not with that weak-ass unit."

"He's got one to match it at his house," Blossom volunteered.

"Fuck you all," I hollered. "Enough with the office party. Get off my desk, Bobby."

Bobby stood and tugged on his linen trousers. "Now he's giving orders."

"Dude," Trevor said, laughing again. His head nudged the

calendar so that Dylan swung side to side for a moment, appearing to grin. "Hey, I like the cap, dude," Trevor said. "Kansas City Monarchs—Negro Leagues. Very hip."

I faced the smiling hacker and shouted, "Shut the fuck up, Trevor! You fucking geek."

The room grew quiet for a moment. Everything except the fan on the old air conditioner. I walked around to my desk chair.

Sabbatini winked at me. "So this is where the ex-wife got the inspiration for her anger books."

I did a little breathing and sat down at my desk. "Look, I had two assholes pull guns on me today."

Sabbatini grinned. "And the day's still young."

"I'm not in the mood for you jokers."

Sabbatini said nothing to this and sat down beside Blossom on the leather teak. He put his arm around her and she tucked in snug beside him.

I offered a weak smile, trying to lighten the room a little. "Plus, I have dinner company tonight."

"What are you making for her?" Blossom asked.

"Chicken with forty cloves of garlic."

"What? Is she an ethnic chick?" Sabbatini asked, with a wink. We had a quick laugh at that.

"So, it didn't go so well with Kunz?" Blossom asked.

"Hell, no. I don't know what I expected. I took the prodigy out there with me. And, of course, that fucker Kunz denied connection to any of it. He was all benevolence and bullshit. A bunch of Aryan, pro-life banter, until he pulled a gun on me." I stood up and began to pace. "These fuckers like Kunz think they can get away with anything. This asshole has a spread in Woodbury with a small museum of stolen violins. Worst of all, he wouldn't let me bring his niece back."

"He kept her out there?" Blossom asked.

I nodded. "Yeah, with a gun on me. I've had enough for one day. You know what I blame all this on?" I said, standing still on a spot in the middle of the room. "This lawlessness, this fucking arrogance? I blame it on the Bushies."

"Let's not get off into politics, Augie," Sabbatini said.

"Who's getting off?" I shouted, pacing the floor again. "I'm not getting off. I'm just saying that this goddamn adventurism isn't coming out of nowhere. We've got a fucking real estate developer putting out a contract on three abortion docs. Where does this asshole get his cojones from? The fish rots from the head, is what I'm saying, which is why this country stinks so much. And one more thing, this business about anger—that we're not supposed to express it anymore—that's bullshit. America has ended up lobotomized. We should be angry. Not at each other, but at our fucking government. It screws us in the ass against our wishes and we disassociate. I think we should be livid.

"And this fucking W., this fucking wastrel just goes on. He's bleeding us right down to the wire. We're eating his shit, and we're going to be eating it for a long time still. And he'll be out there for another thirty years, dusting his legacy. The man's looking forward to the lecture circuit, did you hear? Got to refill the coffers, he says. Just like Clinton has. The Bush grin goes on. Here comes Eddie Haskell, the former leader of the free world."

"Right on," Trevor hooted, throwing a fist in the air. "I've never heard a cop talk like that."

"I'm not a cop," I said. "And the reason they're trying to pull off this shit now is they think they can get away with it just like Bush and Cheney have."

"Plus," Blossom said, "our man Kunz is well connected; he's

slept in the White House. He's already bought his presidential pardon."

"And this Labor Day bullshit on the capitol grounds," Trevor chimed in, "is like totally sanctioned by the governor."

"Sanctioned nothing," I said. "It's been blessed by the motherfucker."

"I hear there's a new protest group out there," Sabbatini said. "The Phony Soldiers."

"Who are the phonies, again?" I asked.

"According to Rush, those are the vets willing to acknowledge the disaster."

"That's right," I said, "and the denialists are the genuine soldiers. I've been doing my best to ignore the news, but it still creeps in. I hear Al Franken's hit a rough patch with his Senate race."

Sabbatini nodded. "The guy's having trouble proving that he's not funny."

"But have you heard his October surprise?" Blossom asked, giving the three of us a sly smile.

"I saw he challenged Coleman to release his SAT scores," Sabbatini said.

"What's the surprise?" Trevor asked, jumping up and down in his Skechers.

Blossom pushed out her lips in a little tease. "Al's getting bar mitzvahed again."

"Where'd you hear that?" I asked.

"Dexter's column."

"Oh yeah, I saw that," Sabbatini said. "Apparently, he missed his Haftorah portion in May, and he's had to learn a whole bunch of new shit. Word is Al's bar mitzvah's a hot ticket. It's being billed as the freshest new entertainment since before the writers' strike."

"Yeah," I said, "but I don't get the bar mitzvah. So, Al out-Jews Norm Coleman."

"Oh, it's a lot more than that," Sabbatini said. "He shows he's serious. Coleman keeps calling him a funny man. And he brings a little ceremony back to the office, a little dignity. This was Paul Wellstone's seat. Dexter says that Al's prepping extra portions of the Torah. You have to memorize that stuff because it's got no vowels. The man's developing serious skills, Augie." Sabbatini took a deep breath and flashed his most handsome smile. "I'm gonna get to Al before he's elected. Watch, he'll be bringing a lot of poems with him to Washington."

"Don't count your chickens," Blossom said. "Coleman'll try something radical to get his ass reelected."

Sabbatini grinned. "What can he do? Clearly, he's proven himself a master of change."

"And change is the buzzword of the season," Blossom said.

"But Coleman's exhausted his options," Sabbatini said. "The dude's already converted from Jew to Christian, and from Democrat to Republican. The only option he's got left is a sex change. I'm sure he's checked it out. I mean, he might not look bad with boobs."

"Go, Ms. Coleman," Trevor hooted, in a spot-on Sean Penn Spicoli. "Maybe Coleman can rip off Obama's motto for his own use," Trevor said in his normal voice. "Change you can't believe in."

"I guess it's emblematic," I said, "of the Republicans' situation. They've finally run out of tricks. Mission accomplished."

"Hear, hear," Sabbatini said, a big grin on his face. "You know, I think a short poem is in order."

"No, Bobby," Blossom said.

Sabbatini's eyes sparkled. "It's starting to get to her, Augie. This is the last resistance before the conversion sets in. Pretty soon, Blossom'll be bringing us poems."

"The hell."

"Here's something from Louis Jenkins," Sabbatini said, "the master of Duluth. It's called 'Squirrel.'"

> *"The squirrel makes a split-second decision and acts on it immediately—headlong across the street as fast as he can go. Sure, it's fraught with danger, sure there's a car coming, sure it's reckless and totally unnecessary, but the squirrel is committed. He will stay the course."*

PONTCHARTRAIN POOTIE

A moment later there was a knock on my office door.

"Who the fuck is that?" I asked. "They sure as hell better not be packing a gun." Before I could get to the door, Conrad, my gangly, seventy-year-old marijuana connection, walked in.

"Got your Pontchartrain Pootie, Augie." Conrad's eyes darted around a little crazily as he spotted the others in the room. "Pardon me," he said, nodding obsequiously.

"Excuse me for a moment," I said, and walked Conrad back down the stairs.

"You didn't tell me you gonna be entertaining, Augie."

"You didn't tell me you were coming."

"Who's that dude wearing a gun? Who's that, Augie?"

"A Saint Paul police detective."

"I thought I recognized him. You setting me up, Augie?"

"Hell no."

"Better not be," Conrad said as we reached the bottom of the stairs. "Last thing I need is some Saint Paul detective on my ass."

We were standing just inside the street door of the Beamish Building.

"Like I say, I got your Pontchartrain Pootie."

"What's Pontchartrain Pootie?" I asked.

"You haven't heard of it yet? You got a treat ahead of you. Well, you know when New Orleans was destroyed and they let it rot except for the Quarter, brothers had to get resourceful, so they be growing smokable by the swamps of Lake Pontchartrain. Hence its melodious moniker."

"A new appellation, huh?"

"Yes, sir, and those motherfuckin' Cajuns know their *terroir*. You smoke this shit through a clean pipe and I guarantee you'll pick up hints of chicory."

"I don't understand the Pootie."

"I didn't expect you would. Well, some things you not meant to understand, Augie. And I ain't gonna explain 'em to you." Conrad nodded his head toward my hat. "Hey, I like your cap, Satch. Kansas City Monarchs, huh? When did you go and become an honorary Negro?"

"How much do I owe you, Conrad?"

"It's $275 for the half ounce."

"Isn't that a little steep?"

"Hey, we're not talking no funky leaf here, Augie. This ain't no shaggy shake. This shit's not gonna burn up your throat like some peckerwood poison oak. This is a half ounce of beauteous bud. It's $250 for the lake effect, as I call it, and $25 for delivery."

"I didn't ask for delivery."

"I can't be in the come-and-get-it business anymore, Augie, not with all the heat they've brought to Saint Paul. Motherfucking convention. So my customers got to absorb my transportation costs." Conrad pointed through the glass door to the Blue and White cab idling on the street.

I wrote a check and handed to him.

"That ain't gonna go rubber on me, now, is it, Augie?"

"Have I ever bounced a check, Conrad?"

Conrad shook his head and reached into a pocket of his cargos and pulled out a fat baggie of buds. "May the lake effect bury you in pleasure, Augie."

"Spoken like a true minister, Conrad."

THE GREAT MOTIVATOR

Sabbatini had a big grin on his face when I walked back into the office. "What the hell's Pontchartrain Pootie, Augie? Is it a hooker or some kind of herb? Are you smoking Cajun herb these days, Augie?"

"Dude," Trevor said.

The others started laughing.

I walked behind my desk. I was pissed. With everything that happened to me that day, I had to explain Pontchartrain Pootie. "Let's cut this bullshit right now," I said. I faced everybody in the room. "I want to talk about the abortion doctors. I think they're in real danger."

Sabbatini snapped to attention. "I've got protection lined up for all of them beginning tomorrow."

"The weekend begins tonight," I said.

Sabbatini shrugged. "My hunch is that they're not going to try anything big until Monday. Labor Day."

I shook my head. "Your hunch isn't good enough, Bobby."

"Listen, I'm pulling every favor I've got with both the Minneapolis and Saint Paul forces. Couldn't be a worse time. City cops are spoken for. Plus we got extra cops coming in from Saint Cloud, Duluth, Rochester. It's nuts, Augie."

"Do we know when these Born Free nuts are coming to town?" I asked.

"Best we can tell," Blossom said, "the big rendezvous is tomorrow."

Sabbatini shook his head. "They're already here, Blossom. You should see the number of crucifix-wielding pregos, with babies about to drop, walking through downtown Saint Paul."

I turned toward the hacker. "Trevor, have you been able to track e-mail responses to Kunz's $50,000-a-hit offer?"

Trevor snapped his head back and his long hair flew behind him. "Nah, sorry, man. It's like everything went black. The system figured out it'd been hacked. It self-destructed. It sucked the digital cyanide. It went disappearo, man."

"Just like the White House e-mails," Blossom said. "Just like the CIA videotapes."

"Trevor, thanks for your work. Let Blossom know how much we owe you."

"Like, do you want me to split, dude?"

"Yeah, but keep working on it. And as soon as we get a hold of Kunz's computers, we'll call you."

After Trevor left the office, I faced Sabbatini. "So, as far as we know, the assassins are already in place?"

Sabbatini shrugged. "I really don't see anything happening

until Monday, Augie. This may be an assassination plot, but it's also theater. They want to have everybody in the house, including all the convention folks and press, before they stage their play."

"That's one theory."

"Hey, I can try and get protection beginning tonight, Augie."

"Do it. You know anybody on the Woodbury police force, Bobby?"

"I know a couple of detectives." Sabbatini scratched his head as if he was trying to remember a name.

I stood and walked out from behind my desk. "I figure Kunz probably owns the Woodbury police, given how much he's donated to the city." I paced back and forth in front of Blossom and Sabbatini.

"How about the FBI?" Blossom asked.

"I know an agent," Sabbatini said. "A good man. Francis Synge."

I couldn't make sense of the name. "Francis, sing? It sounds like a command."

"It's Synge. S-Y-N-G-E. He's black Irish. Goes by Frankie. I might be able to get him interested. He's the guy I was telling you about. Got quite the mind for poetry."

"No, Bobby, this isn't the time for another poetry freak."

"Oh, I think you'd be pretty impressed with Frankie Synge."

"All right, get him. Get him in a hurry, Bobby." I stopped pacing and stood in front of them. "What we need to do is get over to Kunz's by tomorrow morning with some law enforcement and a search warrant."

Sabbatini shook his head. "That's a tall order, Augie. It's already Friday night. Labor Day weekend."

"How about the governor's office?" I asked.

Sabbatini stood. "What about it?"

"The governor's on the hook for this fucking antiabortion carnival. Everybody knows that it wouldn't be happening without him. He's not going to want to have a couple of doctors knocked off, especially with his designs on the convention."

Blossom jumped up. "I know some people at the governor's office. Let me get down to the capitol and see what I can scare up before everybody leaves for the weekend."

Sabbatini buttoned his shirt cuffs. "I'll track Synge and get him interested."

I nodded to Blossom and Sabbatini, both of them charged and ready for action. Suddenly, I'd become the great motivator.

SHRIEK

I didn't hear the door open, and I don't believe Erica heard it, either. We had Van Morrison blasting through the living room speakers. Erica had left Ritchie at home with a neighbor and brought her bong over instead. I should have known better. The lake effect from the Pontchartrain Pootie was formidable, and a good high has a way of making Erica impossibly sexy. We made love after we put the chicken in the oven and it was all I could do to keep up with Erica. She'd peeled a fat clove of garlic, sliced it in perfect halves, and rubbed the halves back and forth over my erect cock until most of the garlic became a part of me. Apparently, there is no end to the ways that garlic can be absorbed.

My plan was to do a light cleanup in the kitchen after we ate, but Erica filled the bong again and, before I knew it, she was sitting naked on top of the kitchen counter, eating a small container of Nance's organic yogurt.

She called over to me at the sink. "Leave the water running and get over here."

"I will not," I said, and turned off the faucet.

"You need to be more obedient," she said. "Get over here." She spread her legs open and I was supposed to be her servant. "Don't forget your duty," she said.

There are times when I really don't mind serving, but I would never have chosen to have my grown daughter walk in on me when my face was planted between the legs of a woman closer to her age than mine. But these things happen. Rose's shriek grew hair on my back that I'm sure I'll have for the rest of my life.

We recouped very quickly, largely because Erica, unlike me, is not a creature of shame. As soon as Rose's shriek echoed off the refrigerator, Erica said, "Caught in the act." She took a final spoonful of yogurt, pushed the majestic brass bong to the side, jumped off the counter, handed me her empty yogurt container, and, naked as a jaybird, gave Rose a hearty handshake. Erica walked out of the kitchen at a normal pace, perhaps to give Rose a chance to admire the lovely flower tattoo just north of her ass.

It took a little while to break the ice once Erica returned, fully clothed, to the kitchen, but I could see that Rose had taken a shine to her. After Rose made herself a small pot of green tea, we shifted the party to the living room. I brought out a pricey bottle of Ridge zinfandel and a couple of fresh glasses. After uncorking the bottle, I filled glasses for Erica and myself with a bit of flourish.

"Isn't he gallant?" Rose said.

"He sure can be," Erica said with a wink.

"I suppose I don't live up to my potential in that regard."

Rose chuckled. "Yeah, you're a bit of an underachiever, Dad."

Erica sipped her wine. "I'm actually quite pleased with his achievements."

Rose started laughing, then pointed to me. "Look, he's blushing."

I tried without much success to shift the focus. "I got to say, Rosie, I've never heard you scream like that."

"Yeah, and I've never seen you, you know . . ."

The three of us rattled out some nervous laughter.

"I never thought I could do anything to shock Rose," I said.

Rose scrunched up her face like a puppet. "You wanna know what the weirdest part was?"

"I'm not sure," I said.

"Well, as soon as I figured out what I was seeing, I looked at the place Erica was sitting and thought, that's the same spot where Mom cut the grapefruits every morning."

"That's awkward," Erica said.

"Hey, I'm over it. We're all grown-ups here. So, like how long have you guys been . . ."

"Been an item?" Erica said.

"Yeah."

I smiled at Erica. "Are we an item?"

"Well, I'm not sure what constitutes an item," Erica said, "but we've been seeing each other a little more than five months."

"God, you don't tell me anything, Dad."

"Maybe he only tells you what's really important."

"Erica," I said sharply.

"I like to tease him," Erica confided, "because a lot of times he doesn't know that I'm teasing."

"I know what you mean." Rose turned to Erica. "Can I ask you something?"

"Sure."

"Your tattoo."

"It's a branch of lilacs."

"It's so awesome."

"Thanks. I think your dad was puzzled by it at first," she said, smiling over at me. Erica leaned toward Rose. "It's a generation thing. I think he's a bit freaked out that I'm younger than him. But he's really a sweetheart."

"He is a sweetheart," Rose said.

"Hey, am I here?" I grumbled.

"Yeah, and we just happen to be talking about you," said Erica. "He's a what-you-see-is-what-you-get kind of guy."

"My agent," I said, a bit exasperated, holding my hand out toward Rose.

Rose turned toward Erica. "Did you get your tattoo done here?"

"Yeah, Steady Tattooing and Piercing in Stadium Village."

"I know that place."

Erica grinned. "Yeah, it's upstairs from a Ben and Jerry's, and I had my friend Rosemary come with me and spoon me little tiny bites of Cherry Garcia while the guy was working on me. I'm lying on my belly, just barely opening my mouth like a fish for the ice cream, and the guy keeps saying, 'Don't move, don't move now, it's your ass.'"

I must have had a pout on my face because Erica said, "Oh, look who's feeling neglected." She scooted over toward me on the sofa and gave me a kiss on the nose.

"Hey, Rose," Erica said, "I've got one of your CDs, and I picked it up even before I knew your dad."

"Yeah? Which one."

"*The Yours Truly of the Tale.* I really like it. My favorite is

'Rosette.' I sing along with that one. And I get a real kick out of your Schwarzenegger song, 'Girlie Boy Meets Girlie Girl.'"

"Rosie," I said, "speaking of steroid-laced governors, you should tell Erica what happened to you on your sixteenth birthday."

"Oh, yeah."

"What happened?" Erica asked.

"Well, my dad thinks this is more amazing than I do."

"It was amazing."

Rose sat up straight. "Okay, so I'm with my parents on my sixteenth birthday. They're taking me out for dinner. We're at Frost's, waiting to be seated and I'm like daydreaming about what kind of kiddie cocktail I'm going to order. Then my dad nudges me. I look up and here comes this group of suits and this beaming behemoth, who kind of rocks side to side as he walks."

"Jesse?" Erica shouts, excited.

"Yes."

"Oh my God."

"And he's really sick-looking up close; his skin's kind of scaly. He's like a cross between an old Hell's Angel and, I don't know, a dung farmer. And then he kind of brushes past me as he goes by."

"You touched him?" Erica exclaims.

"No, he . . ."

"He touched you? Gross."

"You voted for him, Erica," I said.

Erica shrugged. "But I never wanted to be touched by him."

"He didn't exactly touch me. He just sort of brushed by. But that was gross enough. I mean the guy just sort of oozes testosterone."

"Gross," Erica agreed.

I sat there wondering if I'd ever oozed testosterone.

"And then he apologizes to me. He like turns his giant head and goes, 'Sorry about that, miss.'" Rose managed a decent imitation of Jesse's steroid voice. "But here comes the really sad part—I answer him. I go, 'No problem,' just like some suburban nerd. Meanwhile, my dad is going nuts. He goes, 'The governor told you he's sorry. The governor told you he's sorry on your sixteenth birthday.'"

Erica shook her head. "I can't believe you touched him. The man's feral."

"And you voted for him," I said.

"Who else was I going to vote for? Norm Coleman, that slimeball? Skip Humphrey? At least he's better than the asshole we've got now."

"Really," Rose agreed.

I winked at her. "So how long are you in town, Rosie?"

"Well, you know, I'm here through Monday to do the Labor Day protest gig, and I may stay through the week for the convention. There's supposed to be some righteous protests going on. Is it cool if I crash here?"

"It's your home."

Erica stood. "Look, I gotta go. The babysitter beckons. Sorry to leave you with the dishes, Augie."

"I'll help him," Rose said, jumping up with a burst of girlish energy.

Erica gave her a warm smile. "So nice to meet you. Sorry for the shock."

ZOMBIE

"Where are you?" I asked the violinist when I finally got her on the phone.

"I'm at home," she said.

"Been trying you all day. You okay?"

"I'm fine. I stayed and had dinner with my aunt and uncle, then they had someone drive me home."

I propped myself up against one of the fat arms of my mohair easy chair. "What's going on with you and your uncle, Elizabeth? What's he trying to make you do?"

"Nothing," the violinist said, her voice sounding far away, drugged like a zombie.

"Did your uncle give you any medication?"

"No."

"You didn't take anything?"

"No."

"Tell me about your uncle and Dr. McCracken."

The violinist didn't answer.

I began pacing. "Who pays your therapy bills, Elizabeth?"

"I do."

"For five sessions a week?"

"Yes."

"Was there a message for you from McCracken?"

"No, but I remember him saying something about having to take off today."

The woman was lying to me. "What's it like with Perry?"

"He's gone." Her voice was flat and unemotional.

"What do you mean he's gone?"

"He took both of his large Tuscany suitcases. He didn't leave a note."

"He just split?"

"Well, he swept up all the glass from the mirror."

"How about his closet?"

"The closet's locked."

"Where do you think he went?"

"I don't know, but his car's gone."

For some reason, I'd left the GPS monitor on top of my bureau all day. "Listen, I'm going to be over to your place in twenty minutes. I don't think you're safe there."

"I'm safe," she said, distant again. "I feel very safe."

"That's great, but I don't like the way people have started to disappear. I don't want you to be next."

I ran upstairs and picked up the device. Odegard's Jag was parked at the airport. I found Rose sitting in a contorted yoga position in the middle of the living room. She smiled at me.

"Got to run out for something," I said.

"Trouble?"

"Preventative."

THE T-WORD

Sabbatini got me on the cell while I was waiting to pay for a scorched black coffee at SuperAmerica.

"You're working late," I said.

"Yeah, I managed to get Agent Synge interested and he's finding us a couple of guys from the terrorist unit to work on it. They're going to inspire the Saint Paul and Woodbury police departments."

"Sweet," I said, sounding to myself like Rose.

"Yeah, the only way to get any attention these days is to use the T-word. But it is terrorism, Augie."

"Just like the war in Iraq. Just like Abu Ghraib. Just like Guantánamo Bay." Now I was really sounding like Rose.

"I've got to agree with you, Augie."

"Does the department know you've become a left-wing freak?"

"They're more freaked about the poetry. I've got a few others memorizing. Detective Rossi, a two-hundred-pound lass from Coon Rapids, is all over Anne Sexton. And Lieutenant Bosco, from Boston, is working on Olson's Maximus poems."

"You're crazy, Bobby. You may become the first cop ever tossed off a force for agitating with poetry."

"It's a revolutionary movement, Augie. Once you get a cop to memorize a poem, it becomes part of his marrow. One poem leads to another. His mind's more supple. Once the mind opens, the heart is next."

"I gotta go, Bobby."

"Sure. So Synge's looking for a search warrant tomorrow morning, and Blossom got us somebody in the governor's office. You were right, Augie; they don't want trouble."

I put my money down on the counter. "Gotta go, Bobby. I found the violinist and have to collect her for safekeeping."

"Hey, is it true what I hear, Augie? That she's a looker?"

"She's not my type, Bobby."

BOYER, YOU'RE FUCKED

In the car, after a few painful sips of coffee, I hit Blossom's number. It was a lot to ask, and I felt almost sorry that Blossom answered.

"Hey, Blossom, I hear you did some good work over at the governor's office."

"That what Bobby said?"

"Yeah, he's proud of you. I'm proud of you, too. Listen. I found the violinist and I'm on my way over to fetch her now. I think they've either drugged her or womped her with some mind control. I have a big favor to ask you. Can she bunk with you tonight? She can't stay alone."

"Oh, Christ, man, are you kidding? My place is a fucking mess. I made myself a gumbo and I haven't cleaned up."

"Don't bother with that."

"I don't intend to. All right, she can have the futon. It's a little ratty, but she's not getting my bed."

"Keep your bed, Blossom. Hey, I'll owe you."

"Augie, it's gonna take you a lifetime to pay back all the shit you owe me for."

***

After talking the violinist into packing a bag for the weekend, I picked the lock on Perry Odegard's fabled closet. It looked light—a suit or two, maybe a sport coat, and a short stack of laundered shirts. Wading through the woolens, I wasn't surprised to find the valuable goods gone. There was nothing left on the shelves except a motley bunch of books on violins and Lugers. I wondered where the dude stashed his guns. They wouldn't have made it through security. Probably in the trunk of his Jag.

Only a single violin case remained in the closet. I lifted it and, as I expected, it was empty. Still, I felt compelled to unzip the canvas cover and unlatch the case. I did it carefully as if I were handling something potentially explosive. As if I knew how to handle something explosive.

There was nothing inside the velvet-lined case. Not even a bow. I unlatched a frog to the lid of the resin pocket. Had the dude even taken his cake of resin with him? When I lifted the lid I saw my name—Boyer—written in blue ink on a folded piece of yellow-lined paper. I unfolded it quickly. Three words were scrawled: "Boyer, you're fucked."

STRANGE BEDFELLOWS

Blossom's Lowertown loft, a large, high-ceilinged warehouse of a room with a kitchen nook piled with crusty dishes, was getting blasted by loud music from a neighbor's pad.

"I don't even hear it anymore," Blossom said, shaking the violinist's hand. "That's the price you pay living in one of these artist lofts." Blossom smiled at the violinist and took her small suitcase. "Come on in, Elizabeth; it's not exactly luxury living, and the appointments are a little raw, but we'll make you up a cozy spot."

"It's nothing against your place," the violinist said, looking back and forth between Blossom and me, "but I don't see why I have to stay here."

"You're not safe at home, Elizabeth," I said, speaking slowly, as if to a child. "Your uncle has made some very serious threats, and your husband is acting crazy."

The violinist nodded and put her instrument down beside the suitcase.

"Why don't you sit?" Blossom said, motioning to the futon, which was covered in a heavy cotton print—a noble safari scene featuring elephants and giraffes.

I watched the violinist sit. I figured the futon couldn't be any less comfortable than my teak sofa. Still, I decided to remain standing. I didn't plan to hang out.

Blossom sat down beside the violinist. I was amused to see the two women together. Strange bedfellows. The one with spiked red hair and tattooed hands, the other a prim, blond virtuoso.

The violinist glanced around the big room, and said, "I like your place."

Blossom laughed. "Why, thank you."

It had been a long time since I'd been there. I took a quick look around. A Victorian plant stand, with a huge succulent growing out of a coffee can, sat between a pair of orange molded-plastic chairs from the sixties. Behind the chairs, a bank of windows was adorned with a couple of dozen prisms suspended by fishing line from the ceiling. I was surprised to see a framed poster of Rose from *The Yours Truly of the Tale* across the room, in the middle of a wall of musician portraits. Rose, her hair beautifully braided, sat on a bench above the Mississippi.

"Hey, Blossom, Rose just popped into town this evening."

"You better get that girl to call me."

"I'll do what I can." I thought about Rose walking in on Erica and me that evening. I'd never forget her scream, or watching Erica take a final spoonful of yogurt before climbing off the kitchen counter.

Meanwhile, the violinist stood up and walked toward her violin. It almost seemed as if there were a magnet pulling her toward the instrument.

Once she lifted the case, she turned to Blossom. "Do you mind if I play?"

"Of course not."

"It might help settle me down. You guys don't have to listen."

"I just hope you'll be able to hear yourself," Blossom said, "with all the racket."

My client went through a series of preparations with her bow and her chin pad before tuning the instrument. She strolled with her tuned fiddle toward the bank of windows. I wondered how the sound vibrations would affect the hanging prisms.

Then, with her back to us, the violinist raised her instrument and dove into the Sarabande from Bach's Partita no. 1 in B Minor. I knew it well from the Arthur Grumiaux performances I'd listened to so often on my iPod. But this was something else. I couldn't believe the crispness of the violinist's attack. The first chord rang in the air at the instant the bow hit the strings. Absolute authority. It reminded me of how baseball announcers described certain hitters—the ball just jumps off his bat. I was amazed at the ease with which she managed the double stops, fingering the multiple strings with both precision and flair. Her bow arm worked as a fluid mechanism, at once supple and powerful.

I closed my eyes as I listened. As a nonbeliever, I rarely use the descriptor *godlike,* but it's the only way to convey the richness of the violinist's tone and the purity of her intonation. With my eyes closed, it was easier to appreciate the architectural perfection of the Bach. Had I ever heard it played with such ringing clarity? When I opened my eyes, Blossom smiled at me, and I let out an audible sigh of appreciation for what I was hearing.

After all the fiddles in trunks and closets, and the absurdity of their dollar values, it was easy to forget that violins were made to be played. How good to finally hear one, especially one played with such majesty. Maybe every hundred years, a violin like Elizabeth's is lucky enough to end up in the hands of someone so talented.

I wondered for a moment if the violinist was fully there or if she was only present in the playing, as technique and habit, muscle memory and nerves. But the sound of the violin had a warmth at its center, a resonance within its ringing, and I knew that she was playing with everything she had.

When she finished, Blossom and I applauded. Elizabeth bowed a little shyly and slipped the violin back in its case. The electronic hash and the pounding of the bass drum from Blossom's neighbors filled the loft again. The three of us were quiet.

SMOKING BUDDIES

When I got home, I was surprised to see Rose still up.

"I'm a night owl, Dad, and I'm on West Coast time."

We stayed up late talking. I told her a little about the threats to the abortion doctors, but not about the violinist. I didn't want to think about the violinist. For a few hours, at least, she was in Blossom's hands.

"I don't like you being a part of this rally," I said. "Not with all these kooks running around."

"I'll be safe, Dad; all I'm doing is singing a song or two."

"Let's see how it goes. If things don't cool off, I'm going to ask you not to sing."

"That's exactly when I should be singing."

"Not when your safety's at issue."

We sat together in the living room sipping a "rare" jasmine tea that Rose had brought with her from LA.

"You must get a lot of rare things in LA, Rosie."

"Hey, you can make fun of LA really easy, Dad. I do all the time. The thing about LA is that the people truly surprise you. There's a lot of good people out there. I'm seeing positive changes. People are getting more political. They're starting to come around on animal rights."

Rose stretched out on the Persian carpet that her mother left behind. I watched her contort her lithe body into a half-dozen yoga postures. Then I got down on the floor beside her and rolled a fresh joint of Pontchartrain Pootie. Rose and I had smoked a little bit together on the Memphis trip. She claimed not to be scandalized that time. "I always knew you were an old doper, Dad."

Now the joint went back and forth and it seemed as if we'd been smoking buddies for years.

"Hey," I said, "you talked to your mother?"

Rose shook her head in the negative.

"I had coffee with her the other day," I said, and filled my lungs with Pootie.

Rose grinned at me. "So are you guys entering a period of détente?"

I shrugged and watched Rose draw on the doobie. "Your mother has some big news."

Rose blew out her smoke in a hurry. "What? Is she getting married?"

"That's what I thought," I said.

"Tell me," she demanded, passing the fatty to me.

"She should tell you, Rosie."

"Come on, Dad. You can't do that."

I put a clip on the roach and handed it to Rose. "She's pregnant."

Rose's face went blank. She opened her mouth and looked as if she might catch a fly. "She's not going to have the baby," Rose said, finally.

"No, but she's pretty upset about the whole thing."

"Who cares?" Rose got a mean look on her face, the kind she wore as a teenager, when she was on the lip of spitting rage. Now her eyes opened wide with concern. "How about you, Dad? How's it make you feel?"

"Hey, it's life in the big city," I said, a little too glibly. "Your mother's got a new life and so do I." I flashed Rose a big show smile.

"It's good," she said, taking a final toke, "to see you happy, Dad."

Was I happy? I wouldn't go that far. I didn't even know if being happy was the goal. More than anything, I wanted not to be bothered, to hold the world at arm's length. Why not move to the suburbs, dude?

"Erica seems so cool," my daughter said with a grin.

"Yeah, she's a good egg. How about you, honey? Are you happy?"

"Am I happy? I don't know. I get wound up. I spend a lot of time spinning my wheels. Dad, I want to be relevant, but I don't know how."

"You're very relevant, honey," I said.

Rose smiled at me. "And I'm clueless about men. I had this thing with our bass player. I guess it wasn't very smart of me to get involved with him. You know, we've been on the road together for quite a while now, and he's like ten years older than me, and about as laid back as I'm wired. But a few months ago he started acting—I don't know—very courtly toward me, and the next thing you know I'm all dreamy about him and his beautiful green eyes. Funny, the way your mind runs away with you," she said, tilting her head back. She rubbed at her eyes as they started tearing. "Next thing you know, he's cheating on you."

"I'm so sorry, honey."

She nodded to me. "Guess you know all about that."

I didn't say anything.

Rose gave me a bright smile. "Well, you sure have a nice thing going with Erica."

"I'm afraid she's too young for me. She'll come to her senses sooner or later."

"She adores you, Dad."

"She's fond of me. I treat her well." I took a final hit of the joint and blew the smoke out slowly, then dropped the dead joint in a cup filled with empty pistachio shells. "I'm just a safe harbor for her, a temporary berth. Ultimately, she's going to want a more fiery relationship. She just doesn't know that yet."

"That's very patronizing of you," Rose said.

"I don't mean to be patronizing."

My daughter shot me a serious look. The eyes lasered, the small nostrils flared—an earnest question was on its way.

"Are you in love with her, Dad?"

It was a question that deserved repeating. "Am I in love with her? I'd say I love her, but I'm not in love with her."

As soon as I saw the disappointment creep onto Rose's face, I wished I had lied.

THE BEAT GOES ON

Rather than wait at home for Sabbatini's call, I headed down to the office. Another of the ugly abortion trucks was parked outside of the Beamish Building. I wondered if the damn thing had been parked there all night. A little gift from Kunz? With any luck, I'd soon be returning the favor.

There were three messages on my office machine. The first was from an attorney named Ralph Quilacy, of Ford, Walker, Lowenstein and Quilacy, representing Frederick Kunz, asking for the name of my attorney or a preferred address for serving a summons. So now Kunz was going to sue me?

The next message was from Lionel. "What's the matter with you? I call, you don't answer. First, your friend Odegard comes in, wanting to liquidate a few Nazi violins at bargain basement prices. I told him I'm not buying, but, Christ's sake, I could have made a bundle. Next thing, you send in this punk dame with the Guadagnini we were talking about. You trying to give me a coronary, Augie? This is a famous instrument. Nobody in the legit world knows it still exists. I walked into the back room with that Guad and started to cry. Such a beautiful instrument. So, what the hell am I s'posed to do with it?"

Finally, a message from Nina. "Good seeing you at the museum.

Hey, I remembered something else about Julie McCracken that I don't think I mentioned. He got into trouble nine or ten years ago. A group of parents had hired him. They claimed that a 'feminist' therapist had coached their children to believe that they were victims of incest. Apparently, Julie went overboard deprogramming the kids. Anyway, for what that's worth. Take care."

I barely had time to scratch my head and think about that one before my cell started ringing. Erica kicked things off. "I'm so embarrassed about last night. Rose walking in on us like that."

"You sure seemed cool last night," I said.

"What do you mean by that?" she asked, sullen.

"I mean, it didn't seem to bother you." I'd thought, at the time, that it was only Rose and me who were embarrassed.

"I'm just like the next person, Augie; I know how to put on a good act. But now I've had time to think about it. It's like waking up in the morning after being horribly drunk and all you can think about is what a fool you've made of yourself."

"But you weren't drunk."

"But I was stoned out of my head and I was coming on your kitchen counter."

The words made me want to laugh, but then I remembered myself, kneeling, with my head between Erica's legs.

"Augie," she said, "I'm worried about us."

"Why's that?" I didn't want to have that conversation. Not then. Maybe never. I slid open my desk drawer. If only it were big enough for me to hide in.

"Something's wrong."

"Oh, Erica, you worry too much." I rummaged around inside the open drawer.

"I don't know where you are."

"I'm right here," I said, pulling out a postcard Rose had sent me the year before from the Grand Ole Opry.

"I don't know if I can trust you. I feel like you wouldn't be above leaving me naked on the kitchen counter."

I didn't respond to this. I had no desire to go round and round with Erica. I picked up the postcard from the Grand Ole Opry and turned it over. "Wish you were here," Rose had written. I wished so, too. "Can you imagine seeing Patsy Cline here?" I actually could.

"I want you to come over tonight," Erica said, as firmly as a school principal. Suddenly, the *beep-beep* of the call-waiting added to my anxiety.

"What time?" I said, hoping to close out quickly enough to catch the other call.

"I know Rose has just got into town, but we need this, Augie. I'll cook a nice dinner and have somebody take Ritchie for the night."

"What time?" I asked again.

"Oh, I don't know. Let's do it early. How about six?"

"Fine," I said, "I'll bring wine. See you then."

I lost the waiting call, but in a moment the phone rang again. It was Bobby, talking in a squad car with a two-way radio blaring behind him. "Did you just try me?" I asked.

"No. Listen, I think they have a Saint Paul judge willing to come in at eleven."

"You think?"

"Augie, there seems to be some problem with jurisdiction. Whose jurisdiction does this fall into?"

"Bullshit, Bobby. The rally's taking place in Saint Paul."

"Yeah, but Kunz's offers were made via e-mail. Whose jurisdiction is that? Plus, the e-mails may not be permissible in court."

"They're just passing the buck."

"Look, Augie, I've talked to Saint Paul, I've talked to Ramsey County, and I'm hearing the same thing."

"For Christ's sake, we've got an enormous disaster about to happen and we can't get anybody's attention."

"Relax, Augie. We've got a judge coming in at eleven."

"You think. So, what's your FBI buddy's take on this e-mail jurisdiction bullshit? Aren't the feds reading everybody's e-mail anyway?"

"Yeah, but they don't have to bother with jurisdiction. As long it's got a pimple of terrorism on its face, the feds can do any damn thing they please."

"But this is terrorism!" I shouted. "You said it yourself. I don't understand you, Sabbatini. Last night you're talking like Abbie Hoffman and today you sound like a government witness."

"Hey, Augie, it was you who was talking like Abbie Hoffman." Sabbatini slipped into his cop-on-the-street voice. "You're going to have to calm down, Augie. You are going to have to calm down. Understand?"

"Yeah."

"Listen, in other news, we've got all the security in place for the abortion docs. Which was no small task. But everything's going to be okay. Just fine. Dandy. Do me a favor, Augie. Chill. Just a little, not too much. I like you with an edge. But I can't have you eating me alive, man. Are we copacetic on this, Augie?"

"Yeah."

"Cool. And when this Born Free lunacy's over and the Republicans have coronated McCain right before he's admitted to the old people's home, and after the delegates have gone on their last, good-riddance shopping sprees to the Mall of America, and taken their final tour of Larry Craig's bathroom stall at the airport, how's about we get together and play some quartets? Call up those fiddle-playing pharmacists again. A little Haydn might be what the doctor ordered."

"Sure, Bobby. First thing. But I gotta run. Let me know when something breaks."

I wasn't feeling good about the way things were unfolding. Things were slack. And pretty soon I'd have to figure out what to do with Elizabeth Odegard. I couldn't ask Blossom to babysit the prodigy all weekend.

DISAPPEARO

Blossom had an uncanny way of knowing when I was thinking of her.

"I've been trying to reach you," she said, her phone voice tense. "I don't know what happened. She disappeared."

"What are you talking about?"

"She left."

"Elizabeth? What do you mean? She's not there?"

"She walked out. Took her violin and her suitcase and left."

"Oh, for God's sake." I banged my fist against the desk. "How the hell could that happen?"

"I'm sorry, Augie. I didn't realize that I was supposed to hold her captive."

"What time . . . ?"

"I don't know. We . . . we went to bed and then she wasn't there in the morning."

"Where the hell is she?" I shouted into the phone, before hanging up.

❄ ❄ ❄

I began by calling the violinist's numbers. No dice. I drove over to the Odegard condo. No answer to the buzzer. I popped the lock on the front door easily enough, but the door to the unit was a bitch. After twenty minutes of steady jimmying, and with sweat rising across my forehead, I finally popped the deadbolt and stepped inside the apartment. I checked the bathroom first, figuring that after a night on Blossom's sofa the violinist would take a shower first thing. But none of the towels were damp and, given that there was no whiff of perfume in the apartment, I figured that she hadn't been there. As for Odegard, the GPS had his Jag still at the airport. In the kitchen, I hit pay dirt: a list of frequently called numbers that included two each for McCracken and Kunz.

For caller ID purposes, I decided to dial from the condo. When McCracken answered, I closed my eyes and threw my voice as deeply into the cellar as I could.

"Hello, McCracken."

"Mr. Odegard?" McCracken said. "Kunz told me you were out of town."

"I was," I said, trying to approximate Odegard's faux broadcaster voice. "Have you seen Liz?"

"Not for two days. She called me this morning."

"From where?"

"She didn't say." McCracken sounded impatient.

"How's her treatment going?"

"You know I can't discuss that with you."

"But I'm her husband."

"Please, Mr. Odegard," McCracken said. "we are very close. Don't do anything to upset her now."

"Close to what?" I asked, slipping back into my own voice.

McCracken heard my slip and hung up the phone.

I left the apartment and walked for a few minutes around the small lake in Loring Park, trying to understand what the conversation with McCracken meant. Obviously, Kunz and Odegard were complicit in a plan to brainwash the violinist, and Kunz was running the show. What were they doing to her? What was the "treatment" meant to accomplish? She'd come to me to reveal her uncle's plot, but now she was missing and time was running out.

I drove over to McCracken's office on Lyndale. I figured that the building itself would be locked on Saturday, but in fact it was open. There was a sign posted on McCracken's door: "Due to a family emergency, Dr. McCracken will be out of the office this week and next. He's made every effort to contact each of his clients."

I was back to square one.

A little after noon, Sabbatini called. "The judge hasn't issued the search warrant yet."

"What do you mean, 'yet'?" I asked.

"He wants to spend some time reviewing the materials."

"Bullshit. Now's the time."

"Anyway," Sabbatini said, "Frankie Synge and I have decided to pay an informal visit to Kunz. Sometimes all you have to do is flash a badge or two at these creeps and they'll fold their cards."

"I want to come along."

"Can you stay cool, Augie?"

"I think I can."

POETRY AGENT

Agent Francis Synge was a smiling gent with a sensible potbelly and a full shock of curly white hair. He had a rubbery Irish face that contorted into a dozen nuanced expressions, from amusement to indifference. But he was mostly amused. Sabbatini and I drove out to Woodbury with him in his Beemer. Bobby sat shotgun while I slunk in the back beside Synge's Panama hat, which had a seat of its own.

As soon as we hit the road, I told them both about the violinist going missing and asked Sabbatini if he'd spoken to Blossom.

Sabbatini shook his head. "Blossom? No, no. Haven't spoken with her since last night."

It was funny the way Sabbatini answered, as if he wasn't telling something. Synge noticed as well. I watched his lips thin out and stretch into Jack Nicholson wonder. He shot me a wink in the rearview mirror. "Hey, Bobby, you got something going with this Blossom?"

"She's my girlfriend."

Synge winked at me with the corner of his mouth. "So let me get this straight. Your assistant is his girlfriend. We're bordering on the incestuous here."

"And," I said, "it goes on. Blossom's not only Bobby's girl and my assistant, she's also friends with my daughter."

Sabbatini, sitting quietly in the front seat, looked as if he wanted this conversation to go away.

Synge opened wide and flashed some Curious George delight. "Minnesota Rose," he said. "She's something special. I've got her on my iPod, 'The Yours Truly of the Tale.'"

"She must have quite an FBI file."

Synge shrugged up through his eyebrows. "I haven't seen it. I just know her music. I even saw her back a few years ago at First Avenue."

"You really get around," I said.

Synge winked at me in the mirror. "I need to keep up with the venues. It's how I work. I'm a regular at First Avenue and the Fine Line. But you'll find me sitting on the rail at the Turf Club and tossing the big ball with a Bloody at the Bryant-Lake Bowl. I'm like Casper the Friendly Ghost, Augie. I'm there but I'm not. Over the years, I've learned how to project an aura of invisibility. I'm only visible to those I want. It works out. I'm nice to them and they tell me things. Mostly bullshit, but you'd be surprised the way truth oozes its way out, the tiniest pearl in the middle of a giant turd."

Synge wrinkled up his forehead. "So, gentlemen, here's what I'm seeing in the near future, a song by Minnesota Rose called 'Blossom.'" Synge broke into a madcap silent smile that cracked me up. Sabbatini tried to laugh along.

"I can't wait for the lyrics. You both might be in it."

Sabbatini turned and winked at me. "Hey, Augie, did I tell you that Frankie's reading poetry?"

"Glad to hear it," I said.

"Yeah, Bobby's got me memorizing it," Synge said, his expression in the mirror mimicking that of a memorizing man.

"You're the guy he had doing the Black Mountain poets."

"Yes, it's a good starting point, and the revolutionary theories of these poets are not lost on me. Now I'm studying Olson's 'Projective Verse.' What a subversive theory. The man advocates for projecting language into the atmosphere like missiles, like improvised explosive devices."

"It's a theory of poetics," Sabbatini said.

"I prefer a holistic approach," Agent Synge said with a wink. "But now I'm narrowing my field. Staying local. After all, Minnesota has a quite a treasure of fine poets with seditious streaks."

I smiled at Synge in the mirror. "So you're keeping tabs on poets plotting conspiracies close to home."

"You laugh, Augie, but we've got files on most of them."

"I wonder how poets would feel about having an FBI agent memorizing their poems."

"They should be honored," Synge said. "Just as I'm honored to memorize their work. You know, Minnesota's got its share of subversive poets. You've got the history of Bly and McGrath."

I was thrilled to hear my man's name.

"And poetry has penetrated deeply into the Minnesota church. Think of all the Lutherans who go to bed at night and dream of being Unitarian Universalists. And Garrison projects a fresh poem every day on the radio. In those UU congregations, poetry has become the scripture. Believe me, a striking percentage of the population eats Powdermilk Biscuits and memorizes poems."

Sabbatini grinned. "And to think that I've been carrying on undercover. So what are you committing to memory these days, Frankie?" Sabbatini asked.

"Bill Holm's *Boxelder Bug Variations*. It's a seminal work."

"Good choice, Francis," Sabbatini said.

"He approves," Synge said, wrinkling into his wry smile. "But I've been really reading around. Poetry is a place where a man can afford to be promiscuous."

Sabbatini turned and grinned at me, then shot Synge one of his handsome man smiles. "Hey, Frankie, I'm thrilled that you're embracing the poem, but I thought FBI agents were supposed to devote their desk time to editing Wikipedia articles."

"No, we leave Wikipedia to our comrades at the CIA. The poetry's more than a hobby for me, Bobby. I began my career at the bureau as a cryptologist. Did a lot of work with ciphers and code systems and published a few articles in forensic science journals. Here's the deal—as cryptologists become more sophisticated, criminals have to invent new methods of communication. I see poetry as the next frontier. We've found terrorists transmitting messages through poems. It's epidemic at Guantánamo Bay. Now the first anthology of poems from Gitmo is a bestseller. Are people aware of what's being disseminated? National security has been breached. It won't be long before the bureau has an office of metaphorics. I'm teaching myself the code right now."

Sabbatini forced a laugh. "You're pulling our legs, Frankie."

Synge drooped the corner of his mouth into a smirk. "Believe what you want, Bobby."

THE LADY OF THE HOUSE

Agent Frankie Synge looked like another man with his Panama on. Give him a fake mustache and, even with the Irish mug, he'd look like a Spanish don.

Synge stood at the base of the stairway. "So these are the famous Snoopys."

Sabbatini knocked up and down the stretched-out Snoop's long body a few times as if he were playing the timpani. "We should send these to the lab. He might have something besides security cameras stashed inside."

"A real treat," I said, "for the guys down at the lab."

Synge gave off a hoarse laugh.

Finally, we climbed the stairs. After Synge pushed the bell for the third time, Katherine Kunz came to the door. She looked at the three of us standing in front of her and shook her head. "I'm sorry, my husband isn't here."

I stepped forward and held out my hand. "August Boyer, Ms. Kunz; I was here yesterday with your niece."

"Oh, yes."

I looked into her eyes, which were red and watery, and I could tell that she'd been drinking. She couldn't wait to get rid of us and back to her vodka grapefruit. "This is Detective Sabbatini from the Saint Paul Police Department and Agent Synge from the FBI."

Synge took off his Panama and said, "How do you do, ma'am?" Without his hat, Synge's shock of white hair was just that.

The lady of the house's eyes grew large as she shook each of our hands. "I'd invite you gentlemen in, but our housekeeper is off today. . . ."

"No need, ma'am," Sabbatini said. "Though it'd be great to have a quick word with you."

"Is anything wrong?"

"We're not sure yet," Synge said, smiling. "But I've got to tell you, if you don't mind my saying, I love the gray streak in your hair."

"Thank you," she said, looking away.

Synge wasn't done. He knew a pickled, charm-starved woman when he saw one. "Me, I turned white all over at forty. My mother wanted me to dye my hair. My own mother. But yours, yours is quite a beautiful look. Natural, too, isn't it?"

"It's just the way it grows," Mrs. Kunz said. "Would you gentlemen like to come in?"

"That'd be nice," I said. "We'll only stay a moment."

"I can run and make tea."

"Don't bother," Sabbatini said. "We just had tea before we came out."

Synge pushed it a little further. "But I don't think we'd mind a sip of sherry, ma'am."

Katherine Kunz returned a moment later with a tray holding four glasses and a bottle of Tio Pepe. She led us into the same large library where her husband had brought me.

"Maybe you'll each pour yourself what you want," she said.

"Absolutely." I stood beside her and looked at her hands. There was no way they'd be steady enough to fill sherry glasses. "May I pour you a glass, ma'am?"

"Yes, that would be nice. I'm not supposed to have people in," she said, sitting and taking great pains to smooth out her skirt.

"Why's that?" Synge asked innocently.

"Oh, my husband's funny that way. He likes to have control over things."

"In what way?" Synge asked, furrowing his brow.

"Well," she said, sipping her sherry, "I used to say that if Fred were in politics, he'd only participate if the votes were guaranteed before they were cast."

"That sounds like smart politics," Synge said.

My phone started ringing and I turned it off. Synge nodded to us, and Sabbatini and I sat back, happy to let the FBI agent lead the interview. He was fun to watch. He reminded me of

Tony Bouza, the former Minneapolis chief of police, a cop with an intellect whom I once saw at a Francisco Clemente opening at the Walker. The chief was the most elegant creature in the room. Synge was a larger man, but he still moved like a cat.

"Why do you think we've come out here today, Mrs. Kunz?" Synge asked, freshening the lady's sherry glass in a flash.

"I suppose you gentlemen want to talk with Fred about the Born Free rally this weekend."

"How did you know?" Synge's face went bright with wonder.

"Well, he doesn't talk with me about it, but I hear things."

"Like what?"

Mrs. Kunz finished her sherry in a gulp and floated a hand over the Sontag gray streak at her temple. "Like who he's going to have lunch with this afternoon and where."

"You know that?" Synge said with a mischievous smile, refilling her glass again.

She nodded. "Well, I don't really know the men, but I know that they have something to do with the Born Free rally."

"And you know where they're meeting for lunch?"

Mrs. Kunz looked away. She knew she was about to cross a line. She turned back and gave Synge a naughty smile. "You didn't hear it from me."

"Of course not."

"They're having lunch at Cecil's in Saint Paul."

"The Jewish deli? Why there?"

"Oh, Fred loves their Russian Reubens and the matzo ball soup. He used to take me there, but that was many years ago. Plus, it's just a few blocks from the Planned Parenthood on Ford Parkway. There's a big protest in front, all weekend."

"Of course," Synge said.

Sabbatini stood. "We'll be good to our word, Mrs. Kunz, and not take any more of your time." Synge and I stood as well.

"One more thing," I asked, as Katherine Kunz led us up the long hallway to the front door. "Do you happen to know Dr. Jules McCracken?"

"No, I don't," she answered too quickly.

"Are you sure you don't know of him, Mrs. Kunz?" I asked. "Dr. Jules McCracken?"

Although it was me asking the question, Mrs. Kunz grabbed hold of Frankie Synge's arm. "It brings back a very difficult period in my life. I spent some time in Dr. McCracken's Saint Paul clinic."

"He has a clinic in Saint Paul?" I asked.

"Yes. It's very small; you wouldn't know it was there. Two-forty-five North Snelling. It's behind a used-bicycle store and a drive-through coffee booth."

"That's in my backyard," I said, smiling at Mrs. Kunz.

She smiled back. "What do you know?"

A TASTE FOR PASTRAMI

As Synge powered his Beemer down Snelling Avenue, I pointed out the low building behind Java Jive that must have served as McCracken's clinic.

"You want me to drop you off?" Synge asked.

Sabbatini overruled the idea. "Nah, you stick with us, Augie; we'll come back and visit the good doctor."

Synge shot down Snelling, catching the lights all the way to

Ford Parkway. A mile west, the block surrounding Planned Parenthood was swollen with protesters. The street had been closed off.

"Did you know they were closing the street, Bobby?" Synge asked.

"How would I know? I can't keep up with all this bullshit."

We drove as close as we could to the barricades. Two of the ugly antiabortion trucks flanked a street party of protesters.

"Recognize anyone, Augie?" Synge asked.

"Bunch of cretins," I said, looking out over the crowd. "Let's get over to Cecil's."

"Sure," Synge said, "I've got a taste for pastrami."

I spotted Kunz sitting with three men at the rear of the restaurant. "There he is, guy in the back, in the tan sport coat. He sees me now." The three men with Kunz bent their heads toward him.

Meanwhile, Synge pushed past a fat waiter and led us up the long aisle to the gang at the last table. Synge was quite a sport to hang with, a modern-day Eliot Ness.

He pulled out his wallet and flashed his badge. "Mr. Kunz, Francis Synge, FBI."

"How do you do?"

Each of the three men sitting with Kunz looked as if he was going to shit in a different way. I took a good look at them. All white men, two middle-aged, blue-collar guys who could be brothers and a guy in his twenties with greased-back hair and a big crucifix dangling in front of his shirt.

"This is Detective Sabbatini, Saint Paul Police," Synge said. "Isn't he a hell of a dresser for a cop?" Everybody turned to look at Bobby in his linen coat and slacks. "And I think you know Augie Boyer."

Kunz looked as if he wanted to spit. "Mr. Boyer, good to see you."

"Nice to see you, Kunz. Hey, I'm still waiting for my Christo Snoopy."

Kunz forced a laugh. "A little joke between us."

"I didn't think it was a joke," I said.

"Sorry to disturb your lunch, gentlemen," Synge said with a wrinkle of contrition. "How's the pastrami, by the way? I love the pastrami here. I could fantasize about it, like another guy fantasizes about some babe to cheat on his wife with. I don't do that shit. I keep it clean. But a nice Russian Reuben, a bowl of matzo ball soup, a bottle of Vernors ginger ale. Hey, that's what you're having, Mr. Kunz. What do you know?" Synge shot Kunz his Curious George smile. "Look, we need to talk with you guys. We can either have a little chat here or we can go over to Minneapolis."

"I'm not talking to anybody," Kunz said, "without my attorney. And neither are they."

"That's a mistake, Mr. Kunz. We could have a very comfortable conversation here."

Kunz looked up at Synge. "You're fishing, sir, but there are no fish in this lake."

"Aw, there's plenty of fish, Kunz," Synge grinned. "We've got a couple of dozen e-mails you sent, all very fishy, if you ask me. We've got you soliciting the 'elimination'—that's your word—of three abortion doctors in the Twin Cities. We've got you offering shooters fifty grand a pop. Is that you guys?" Synge asked, giving the three men a big smile.

"You're fishing," Kunz said.

"The fuck I'm fishing."

Kunz, smirk-faced, said, "You've got a national political convention coming into Saint Paul, a huge gang of anarchists and other disreputables ready to disrupt it, and you guys are out fishing."

Sabbatini jumped forward and was about to grab Kunz by the collar until Synge stood between them. I noticed people from other tables turning their heads to get a look at us.

I took a step toward the table. "Tell me where Elizabeth is, Kunz."

"How should I know? I sent her home with my driver last night after dinner."

"You know where she is."

"You have a rich fantasy life, Boyer."

Once Synge had gotten Sabbatini calmed down, he pulled a digital camera out of his pocket and moved around to the side of the table. "Let me get a shot of you guys. My daughter just gave me this camera for my birthday. I can't believe the technology. To think I used to get excited about a Polaroid. Okay, let's get a nice table shot first." Synge backed a little away from the table and looked in the window at his composition. "A photographer I used to know told me that the history of photography is the history of figuring out where to stand." Synge backed up a little, leaned to the left, then to the right. He finally snapped a picture of the four men, sitting expressionless. He took a moment to look at what he got. "Not bad. Let's get another shot, but this time with you smiling. Say cheese, you guys." Synge demonstrated with a wide, cheesy grin. "Come on, say cheese. Say cheese, you fuckheads!" A quiet chorus of "Cheese" followed. "Good," Synge said, looking at the picture he'd just taken. "That's a nice one." He leaned his head close to them now. "Listen, gentlemen, we are going to be on your asses so tight that you'll be able to feel our fingers wiggling around up there."

Back in the car, Synge said, "Made one fatal error in there— left without any pastrami."

We went by McCracken's clinic, which was dark and looked as if nobody had been in it for years. On the drive across Selby, I mentioned what I'd heard from Nina about McCracken.

"Yeah, I remember that case," Synge said. "It was quite a while ago. I worked on the investigation. On the front end. I never got as far as McCracken. They called that shit 'false memory syndrome.' Something like that. You had therapists practicing 'recovered memory therapy,' convincing their patients that they were repressing a trauma, usually incest. Some lost their licenses. McCracken came along later, when the parents got outraged. He did a little reverse brainwashing. I don't know what they called that; 'reversed recovered memory therapy'? Trouble is, McCracken was indiscriminate and convinced some real victims that they hadn't been touched. He was sued later and settled out of court. I remember the press exposé. One of McCracken's former patients called him 'the king of mind control,'" Synge said with a giggle.

"Yeah," I said, "well, I think he's trading in his kingdom for a bit of Nazi gelt."

Sabbatini perked up. "And the guy's mode is outdated. He should be using poetry to manipulate her behavior. Just a little assonance could go a long way."

Synge grinned in the mirror. "You're right, Bobby. Think what a guy could do with a handful of spondees."

"I figure Kunz is having McCracken erase the violinist's incest memory," I said. "But there's something else."

"Maybe he's still banging her," Sabbatini said.

I shook my head.

"She knows what Kunz is planning," Synge said, taking out a handkerchief and blowing his nose. "She's been trying to spill the beans. A loose cannon like that, I wouldn't be surprised if he has her eliminated."

RELATIVE ANGST

"How about a quick one?" Sabbatini asked, after Frankie Synge dropped us where we had left our cars, on Selby and Western.

"Sure."

"There's something I've got to tell you," he said, not looking happy about it.

"Yeah, you haven't been quite your mellow self this afternoon, Bobby. Frost's or Moscow on the Hill?"

Sabbatini flashed five cents of bravado. "Hey, if I wanted vodka, if I wanted blinis and caviar, Augie, I'd say Moscow. But what I want is a good, stiff Maker's Mark."

The bar at Frost's was practically empty in the midafternoon, and we took a window table near the front. Sabbatini excused himself to the bathroom and I thought about Rose and Jesse Ventura, as I do every time I go into Frost's, even if I'm on the bar side. Then I thought about Erica and how I saw trouble coming there.

I ordered a Surly Furious, a tart-forward ale from the sorry suburb of Brooklyn Center. It would have been better if I could have lit up a doobie to go along with it. But I'd been smoking so much lately I could pretty much call up the condition. I stared absently out the window at the Blair House, a beautifully restored brick and brownstone monolith. It was pure Edward Hopper in the winter.

Garrison had his good bookstore in the basement of the building. I liked the place, with its checkerboard floors and cave-like feel. A decade or so to smudge the patina, and it would really have some character. Garrison had a desk down there with a sign pinned to it that named the books he'd written on it and the various typewriters he used. It was almost as good as being at the John Steinbeck museum in Salinas.

I sipped my ale, wondering if Garrison carried any Hannah Arendt. He had a honorable poetry section, a heroic collection of Fitzgerald, and his people knew how to put the right new books down on the tables so you were tantalized by most everything. I could have spent a fortune in there. But who has time to read? Garrison also had a big self-help section, but I doubted he went deep into Hannah Arendt. If it were Woody Allen's bookstore, there'd be a whole wing of Arendt.

It seemed to me that Lutheran angst didn't hold a candle to the Jewish version. The Lutherans went in for self-help, the Jews for self-flagellation. Of course, the Catholics seemed the sorriest when it came to guilt. It dripped off them. As for the born-agains, they were as angst-free as a can of Fresca. They carried a guarantee, right beside their Wal-Mart charge card, that they'd be saved.

Anyway, I figured that Nina had probably polished off *The Human Condition*. It would be fun to find some more light reading for her. Pick up a copy of Hannah Arendt's *Men in Dark Times* and have it gift wrapped. The idea made me chuckle and I was laughing out loud by the time Sabbatini came back with a glass of bourbon and sat across from me.

DON'T BLAME IT ON THE POETRY

Sabbatini shook his head. "You're scaring me, Augie. I leave for a minute and by the time I get back you've gone daft."

"I just had a funny thought."

"Yeah?"

"My wife in bed with Garrison Keillor."

"She slept with Garrison, too?"

"Not that I know of."

"You need a vacation, Augie."

"Probably do. I'd sure feel better if we came up with a search warrant and I could find that damn violinist."

Sabbatini lifted his glass of bourbon and sipped it slowly. "Don't worry, Augie, all this stuff is going to sort itself out."

"I wish I believed you."

"So what did you think of Frankie Synge?"

"Hell of a guy, but he kind of put the fear of God in me when he started talking about the poetry epidemic at Guantánamo Bay. I don't see poetry as the big problem with Gitmo."

"He was joshing, Augie."

"I'm not sure he was joshing. He's quite the bureau spook."

Sabbatini nodded. "He takes his job seriously."

"Agreed." I faced Sabbatini directly. "Hey, Bobby, you wanted to talk to me about something."

"About the violinist . . ."

"Yeah?"

Sabbatini took a swill of Maker's Mark. "Blossom and I weren't exactly forthcoming with you."

"What are you talking about?"

"I happened to be over at Blossom's when Elizabeth disappeared. She was tucked away on the futon the last I saw her. Blossom and I were in her bedroom. I performed a few Kenneth Patchen love poems for Blossom, and one thing led to another. Afterward, when I went to the kitchen for a glass of water, I saw that the violinist was gone."

"What time was that?" I asked.

"About three in the morning."

"So you went out looking for her."

Sabbatini shook his head.

"You left her to wander around Lowertown at three in the morning?"

"She could have left much earlier. We were in the bedroom for a couple hours."

"What did you do, go back to bed? You didn't even call me."

"It was three in the morning, Augie."

I stood up and glared at Sabbatini. "You're a fucking police detective, supposed to be one of the best, but you just blow this off."

"I think it's the poetry, man. It's having a strange effect on me."

"Don't blame it on the poetry, Sabbatini; you fucked up."

THE GHOST IN THE MANOLOS

Back in my car, I realized that I'd left my phone off for hours. Among my messages were two from the violinist. The first one, left nearly three hours earlier, was spoken in an amused if weary voice: "I'm sorry that I left Blossom's like that. I was a little jumpy and couldn't sleep. I wandered around Lowertown for a while. I must have been quite the sight—a hobo with a violin and a rolling leather suitcase. Eventually, I took a cab home. I'm sitting outside at Joe's Garage now. Should I not be sitting outside, Augie? I just can't stand to be cooped up, worrying. Please call me on my cell."

A second message was brief and desperate. "Augie, now I'm really scared. There's somebody across the street watching me and I just got a call from my uncle, who wants to know your whereabouts."

After I called both of the violinist's numbers and got no answer, I bombed back over to my office and walked next door to Joe's Garage. The violinist was no longer sitting outside. I peeked in, hoping against hope that she might be tucked away at a corner table, but there was no sign of her. I approached a shaved-headed meatball, who doubled as busboy and host. I'd seen him before at Joe's.

"Have you been here all afternoon?" I asked, holding out a ten-dollar bill. "I'm looking for somebody who was here earlier."

The guy, who couldn't have been thirty, nodded his bald crown and looked at the ten spot as if it should be more. He took the bill and led me to a quiet corner near the take-out counter.

"I've been here since we opened," the guy said, "and I'm not gone until we're closed."

"So, you're getting rich today."

"Yeah, really rich. What can I do you for?"

"You remember seeing a tall blond woman this afternoon? Rather attractive. Often wears these long pointed shoes. I don't know what they are—Ferragamos?"

The guy shrugged. "The lady I'm thinking of wears Manolos."

"Those are Manolos?"

"I don't know if they're Manolos, but I think of her as 'the lady in the Manolos.'"

The ghost in the Manolos, I thought.

"She lives around here, doesn't she?" the meathead asked.

"Did you see her today?" I asked.

"Yeah, she was here. Landed at an outside table for a while."

"What time did she leave?"

The dude gave me a weary look. "Hey, I didn't pay attention to when she came or when she left. She's a nice-looking lady, but we were busy, man." The guy closed his eyes as if he were trying to remember something more. When he opened them, he smiled at me. A smile that turned quickly to a smirk. "She ordered a chicken caesar that she didn't eat. That's all I can tell you. Except that you're not the only person looking for her."

"Who else?"

The guy shrugged.

I pulled out my wallet. The smallest bill I had left was a twenty. I handed it over.

"Tall guy in a suit. Was here looking for her before she came."

"What'd he look like?"

"Like I said, tall guy. Kind of old-school."

"Did he stand really straight as if he'd gone to college to study posture?"

"Yeah, I guess."

"Did you tell her somebody was looking for her?"

"Hey, man, I'm not working for anybody here. Customers deserve their privacy."

"Did you see her leave?" I asked, anxious, wanting to grab the punk by the collar. "Did she leave by herself?"

The guy shrugged. "Hey, I must have been inside when she left. I took a peek out and she was gone. Tell you the truth, I was disappointed. Woman's kind of a babe." He took a close look at me. "You work around here? I've seen you around here."

I nodded.

"Hey," he said, "when you see the lady with the Manolos, send her my regards."

With that, the guy dismissed me and walked quickly to the back of the restaurant.

I dashed up the three flights to my office. There was no indication that anybody had been there. Both deadbolts were still locked. No notes on the door or underneath. No messages that mattered. I called both of the violinist's numbers again. No dice. By leaving my cell phone off I'd screwed up just as badly as Sabbatini.

NEITHER SIDESHOW NOR CATHARSIS

What followed was a crooked trail. After picking up a couple of bottles of zinfandel at Surdyk's for the evening ahead with Erica,

I checked my left pocket for the tin of joints I'd rolled in the morning and shook it back and forth. Comforted, I drove across the river and parked near Mill Ruins Park and the Guthrie Theater and plugged a meter full of quarters. I found a bench beside the Stone Arch Bridge and fired up a joint. What did it mean, I wondered, that I'd have preferred a solitary evening with a fatty and my iPod to a night with Erica?

I took several deep tokes of the Pootie—what I liked to think of as defining tokes—then walked up the hill to the new Guthrie and wondered how long I'd think of it as new. Although I appreciated the giant faces—Shaw, Strindberg, O'Neill, Williams, and Tyrone Guthrie himself—looming on the ground floor of the exterior, I didn't care for the massive edifice. I found the deep blue monolith forbidding. The building projected a cool arrogance and lacked the grace and wit of the Frank Gehry museum across the river. After a number of visits, however, I began to dig the interior. The ghoulishness of it. The fractured views of the river. The chimera of past performances growing out of the walls from new-age daguerreotypes.

It was Saturday night and there were Arthur Miller productions in each of the three theaters. Patrons could decide whether they wanted to spend the evening with Miller in Vichy, in Salem, or on the Brooklyn docks. More than an hour before curtain, the space was bustling with the dinner crowd. I climbed a hundred feet on the magnificent escalator and strolled past the proscenium theater and the raw bar, thinking it would be nice to dawdle over a dozen oysters and a pint of Anchor Steam. But I was living on borrowed time.

The air was lovely on the "endless bridge," the open-air, cantilevered jobby that shot out spectacularly from the rear of the complex toward the river. After the 35W bridge went down, I walked to the end of the "endless" a number of times. From that vantage, you could see a bit of the wreckage, but I was more interested in watching the other people, who seemed greedy for a view of the tragedy. Were they interested in a catharsis that they couldn't find at a Guthrie performance? No, their interest was more sideshow than catharsis.

Now, I took a peek at the new bridge, just beginning to assert itself, and found a fine, tucked-away perch so that I could see everybody in front of me while gazing at the river and at the city's east bank. I sat there for a while, forgetting my responsibilities and enjoying the pure buzz of the Pootie. I was like a dude in a cool blue cape. Superman's deadbeat cousin, devoid of ambition, interested in neither sideshow nor catharsis.

Of course, perfect moments don't last for long—my phone rang, and it was Erica. I thought not to answer, but hit the green button just to shut up the ringing.

"Where are you, Augie?"

"Caught in traffic. There's been a crash on 94."

"I hear people around you."

"Traffic's come to a standstill; folks have their windows open."

"Damn you, Augie. Where are you?"

"I'm on my way," I said, gazing down at the river. "On my way."

CHINESE TORTURE

For the first hour I was at Erica's duplex on Blaisdell, she gave me the freeze treatment. I rather liked it. Erica answered direct questions with little more than a grunt or a monosyllable, so

I stopped asking. The situation hadn't prevented me from ingesting more than my share of sushi and swilling two lush glasses of ancient vine zinfandel. I preferred Erica like this—simmering, but quiet. I found her sexy. The young attorney didn't know how lovely she was when she stopped talking. But after catching up with me in the wine department, she showed signs of returning to her voluble self. Pity.

"I don't know if I'm going to forgive you, Augie."

I really didn't think she should.

"I made such an effort to get Ritchie out of here early, so we'd even have a little of the afternoon. I went out and got all the food together. I mean, I'm not complaining about that. I'm happy to do that. But when you don't come and you don't come, I begin to feel like you don't want to come. I'm not exactly unattractive am I, Augie? I'm not a fright, am I?"

I held my silence. It seemed as if there might be hope for the evening if at least one of us refrained from speaking. Erica might not mind the arrangement, now that she'd found her voice. I uncorked the second bottle of zinfandel and poured us each another glass.

"I've been getting to the gym five days a week. I want to look good for you, honey."

If I'd been speaking, I'd tell her that she'd be better off with someone who truly appreciated her efforts, someone who kept himself in shape for her.

"You know what you mean to me."

It was like a form of Chinese torture, in which the torturer and the tortured continually changed places. Every other straight man in America would go mad for a woman like Erica, and she deserved one of them. How had she ever managed to find me?

"You make me feel good about myself."

I only wished that were true.

"The thing I need to get from you, Augie, is a real commitment."

The thing I knew she'd never get from me was a real commitment. I had always known that it was coming to this. I'd tried to tell her. She just didn't want to hear it.

"Everybody says I've been very patient with you."

And everybody was right.

"Believe me, I've had friends and colleagues who've advised me that you'd end up being nothing but trouble. I was outraged that anybody could say that without even meeting you. I wouldn't listen to them. The age difference, they said, was one thing, but worse than that was the fact that you're still married. They said you were just using me to bide time. Certain women, they said, fall for married men because the situation's doomed, and I told them, 'Well, I'm not one of those women.'"

But you are, poor thing; at least in this case.

"Augie," she said plaintively, wanting something from me, anything.

But I was thinking about all the years with Nina, how I'd shut her out for no real reason. I didn't want to be bothered. My behavior wasn't the result of any repressed trauma, as the therapists and the twelve-step gurus might have it. I wasn't an incest survivor; nobody had abused me. I just wanted to smoke my weed and disappear. All the noise, all the chatter—there comes a time when the whole world seems like a leaky faucet and I just wanted to turn it off.

Erica's head was tilted, her mouth open, expectant. "Say something, goddamn it, say something!"

I took a long sip of zinfandel but had nothing to say.

Erica looked up at me with a fierceness I'd only seen when we'd made love, but this time she turned it on me. "Get out of here, you bastard," she shouted. "Get out."

THE END OF SOMMERFEST

Once I got to the car, I drove a few blocks without any idea of where I was going. I pulled over and talked myself out of firing up a roach—such discipline—and hit both of Elizabeth Odegard's numbers, to no avail. I called Blossom, whom I'd been avoiding since Sabbatini fessed up at Frost's, but there was no answer. She'd probably gone out with Bobby.

I started the car up and was going to drive home when I remembered that there was a symphony concert that night—I'd seen an ad in the *Star Tribune*. It was the last Sommerfest concert of the year. I'd practically forgotten that the violinist was a member of the symphony.

At the point I slipped into my seat in the balcony, the orchestra had just launched into the second movement, the Moderato, of Shostakovich's Cello Concerto no. 1. The movement began with such glorious restraint—a sweet horn solo, a pliant oboe weaving around the cello—that I almost forgot that doom was close by. I scanned the first violin section for a sight of Elizabeth Odegard but, given my distance from the stage, I couldn't make her out. I saw a couple of violinists who might have been her, but neither seemed quite right.

After making myself bleary-eyed trying to spot the violinist from the balcony, I noticed that the third box, stage right, was empty. Once I'd hoofed down the stairway and was comfortably ensconced in the box, I pulled my chair up to the rail and studied both of the violin sections. Elizabeth Odegard wasn't there. I tried to sit back a moment and gather myself, but the agitation of the Allegro con Moto was making me frantic. I did a quick breathing exercise and, in my fresh clarity, it occurred to me that Elizabeth Odegard might not be playing the Sommerfest season. I flipped through the program until I came to the page that listed orchestra members. Her name was not on it.

At intermission, I went backstage. I'd spent a lot of time there while investigating the disappearance of Pieter Haus's violin. Now I nodded to several musicians I recognized and, finally, Pieter Haus appeared, cradling his precious Goffriller.

"Augie," Pieter said, hurrying over to give me a one-armed hug. "You never come around anymore."

"You guys are too careful with your instruments, so there's no business for me."

"I thought you got rich enough off me to retire," said Pieter, a dashing young man with a family fortune. I used to wonder what it'd be like to be Pieter. Young, rich, talented, good-looking. But it was hard not to like the man, with his curly blond hair and dimpled grin. He winked at me. "So, what's new?"

"Well, actually, I was looking for Elizabeth Odegard, thinking she played Sommerfest."

"Who's Elizabeth Odegard?"

Pieter was a sweet guy, but I was in no mood for joking. "Come on, the violinist."

Pieter pushed out his lips and shrugged.

I felt a panicked energy rise. "Maybe she goes by her maiden name in the orchestra—Elizabeth Kunz."

"Betsy Kunz?! God, I haven't heard that name in a long time."

"What are you talking about, Pieter?"

"You used to hear a lot of speculation about her. She's in Minnesota?"

"Are we talking about the same woman, Pieter? A tall blonde. Rather attractive."

"I never really knew her, Augie. You heard about her. She was a few years younger than me. I set eyes on her a time or two before she left Oberlin, maybe fifteen years ago."

"Yes," I said, "she went to Oberlin! What did you hear about her?"

Pieter, a little surprised by my intensity, took a step back in a comic gesture. "Geez, Augie, what do you have going on with this woman?"

"Tell me what you've heard," I said, grabbing Pieter's right arm, the one holding his bow.

"Yeah, sure, Augie." Pieter scanned his colleagues for someone to rescue him.

I let go of the violinist's arm, but looked at him hopefully.

"She was quite the prodigy. She'd soloed with several major orchestras by the time she was sixteen. I believe her uncle was her manager. She went to Oberlin for a bit of finishing, but didn't last a semester. Lots of stories about what might have happened. She got pregnant; she had a baby. You heard about her audition-ing for orchestras around the country, playing in the pit at Broadway shows, busking with an open fiddle case on Michigan Avenue. But you never knew if any of it was true. The gossip among musicians can be pretty brutal. Why are you asking about her?"

"She's married to a violin dealer named Odegard. Perry Odegard."

Pieter exploded with a surprised laugh. "That's the best one I've heard yet, Augie. Outstanding. Betsy Kunz married to that gypsy."

"You know him?"

"I avoid him. We all avoid him. Well, most of us."

I pulled out a photo of the violinist I'd snatched the first time I went by her apartment. "Is this the woman?" I heard the desperation in my own voice.

Pieter took hold of the photo and peered at it. "My, she's grown up, Augie."

"And you're telling me that she doesn't play in the orchestra."

"Never has, Augie. At least not in my time here."

"I've been hoodwinked," I said, bowing my head toward Pieter.

"Happens to the best of us, Augie."

YOUR DAUGHTER'S A STAR

I woke up late on Sunday morning and was disappointed to discover that Rose was already out of the house. I brewed a small pot of French press coffee and hoped to sit quietly for a few moments without thinking about anything. But I couldn't keep Elizabeth Odegard, the violinist without an orchestra, out of my head or my nervous system. There had been no sign of her since her phone messages the day before. I worried about her as if she were a child. And I was pissed at myself. A fucking moron. I should have checked her orchestra connection as soon as I took her business. God knows why she hired me. I still had no idea if she was working with her uncle or trying to get away from him.

From the start, I sensed that something about her didn't add up. I'd figured she was a heavily medicated maze of personalities. Maybe one of those poor depressives surviving on a not-quite-adequate cocktail of medications. Add the creep husband and the Nazi uncle who abused her and you had one big mess of a woman. But where the hell had she gone? I tried her numbers again, but nothing.

At eleven, Bobby Sabbatini called. "You still talking to me, Augie?"

"Sure, Bobby, I got no choice."

"You're still angry at me."

"I don't hold grudges, Bobby."

"Good man. Listen, Synge got the search warrant this morning. He wants us to meet out in Woodbury at noon."

"Great. Hope it's not too late."

"Hey, Augie, look on the bright side. . . ."

"The bright side. I've got a missing client, Bobby."

"She'll turn up. Hey, Augie, hell of a piece on Rose."

"What are you talking about?"

"Don't you read the paper, man? Big spread across the front page of the Arts and Entertainment section today. Your daughter's a star."

"Did they say where she was going to be performing?"

"Not that I saw."

"Good." I took a final sip of coffee that was full of tarry grounds.

I went out to pick up the paper from the front porch, but it wasn't there. Rose must have taken it with her. I checked in with her blog.

MINNESOTA ROSE

SCHEDULE　　PRESS　　GALLERY　　LYRICS　　BLOG　　ACTION

Sunday, August 31, 2008

Hello Friends,

I want to let you know about the shit that's going down around the national antiabortion rally tomorrow, Labor Day, on the capitol grounds in Saint Paul. This is the megaevent I came to Minnesota to protest, though I'll stay on for the Republican convention to see what other damage I can do. But the antiabortion rally is my main concern. Watch the site, as I plan on making several updates a day.

I went out very early this morning to get a feel for the scene. A large crowd of evangelicals is already gathered on the capitol grounds. It's a kind of tent city turned into a banner-making factory. Kids and even old people are down on their knees with markers and signboards.

The main stage is set up right beneath the capitol. It has an enormous banner that reads: "God Is Pro-Life." On the east side there are medical stations and tents for women in labor who plan to give birth here. Born Free, the event's sponsor, is trying to reclaim the term "Labor Day" for the antiabortion movement. I thought that was a hoax at first. I couldn't believe women would allow themselves to be induced for a cause. But pregnant women are arriving from all over the country and the ones at full term will induce. Apparently, it's being sold as a great honor, a way to become a true patriot. To my mind, the patriots are abortion doctors, who take great risks to uphold our freedom.

Flash Action: Tomorrow, September 1, at noon, meet up at the site of the counterrally, just south of the capitol grounds in Saint Paul. To demonstrate our solidarity with abortion doctors, always under threat, I'd like everybody to show up in doctor's whites, a medical face mask, and a stethoscope, if you can round one up. That's how I'll be dressed, and the more of us like that, the more powerful the statement we make. The idea comes from the Danes. They wore yellow stars during WWII to be in solidarity with the Jews, who were required *by the Nazis to wear yellow stars. Sorry for the short notice on all this. Hope to see a great crowd full of doctors tomorrow.*

—Rose

ODE TO GEFILTE FISH

The first person I saw when I got out to Kunz's house was Lionel Ross. He'd just stepped out of his Buick Century and was walking toward the twin Snoopys.

"Hey, Lion," I called, "what the hell are you doing here?"

The violin dealer kept walking and said over his shoulder, "Detective Sabbatini asked me to come out."

I remembered that Sabbatini had bought a couple of violas from the man. "Something the matter, Lion? You're walking away from me."

"Damn right, something's the matter," Lionel said, turning to face me. The violin dealer had a little round bandage covering the cancer on his right nostril. Damn thing must have gone nasty on him again.

"First you drop a stolen instrument on me, unannounced," Lion shouted, "and then you don't return my calls."

"I'm sorry, Lion. I've been running around like a madman."

"I've begun to think you are a madman, Augie."

Agent Synge, in a khaki sport coat, pressed Levis, and his plantation-style Panama hat, stood in the front hall, grinning at Kunz, when Lion and I walked in.

At the sight of us, Kunz threw his hands into the air. "What is this, an open house? We going to let anybody in here?"

I nodded to Synge and then faced Kunz, who was dressed in a blue blazer with gold buttons, a yellow bow tie, and a pair of pleated gray slacks.

"I'm not anybody, Kunz," I said, "I'm the thorn in your side. And this gentleman is Lionel Ross. He knows violins like you could only dream to."

"Lion's Stringed Instruments on LaSalle. I know you," Kunz said, giving Lion a friendly smile.

"Well, I don't want to know you," the violin dealer said.

Synge laughed and shook Lionel's hand. "Francis Synge," he said, "FBI. Thanks very much for coming out, Mr. Ross."

Synge turned to Kunz and flashed his monkey smile. "So, you never told me how your pastrami was yesterday, Mr. Kunz. And those boys you were with, I've been wondering about them. They didn't exactly look like your people. That's always been one of the most interesting things to me about crime—the way the classes interact. It's a sociological wonder, don't you think? United in crime. I mean, none of those guys looked like the kind of people you'd have over for an evening of quartets in the mansion. Am I right?"

Kunz looked directly at Synge but did not answer.

"Who exactly were they, those gentlemen, Mr. Kunz? We've got their pictures, so we'll figure it out. But it'd sure be nice to talk with you a little. We could send out for some sandwiches. I tell you, I could go for a Russian Reuben right now. How about you guys?"

"Sure," Lion said, nodding.

"I don't know," I said, "I think I'm more in the mood for a bagel dog."

"All right," Synge said. "And you, Mr. Kunz?"

Kunz remained mute.

Synge took out a notepad and started scribbling. "Okay, so far we got two Russian Reubens, a bagel dog, and the beginning of a hunger strike. I'm feeling pretty confident I can put Sabbatini down for a third Reuben. I'm thinking coleslaw all around, a little bucket of pickles . . . last chance, Mr. Kunz; care for a bowl of matzo ball soup?"

"Hey, Augie," Sabbatini said, walking toward us from the direction of the library. Bobby was dressed in a maize-colored suit and his crocodile shoes. A large blond man with a baby face, a plainclothes cop, walked beside him. "This is Dave St. Clair, Woodbury chief of police.

I shook hands with St. Clair and introduced Lionel around.

"Mr. Ross," Sabbatini said, shaking Lion's hand with vigor, "I'm so glad to see you again. We've got some instruments out here that I'm sure you'll find interesting."

"I can't believe you let them all in here, Davy," Kunz said. "Where the hell's my lawyer? Don't I have the right to have my lawyer here?"

"First things first," Synge said. "Bobby, we're sending out for a little repast. I've got you down for a Russian Reuben."

"Sounds great."

"Dave, you care for one?"

"Sure."

"All right, that gives us four Russian Reubens and a bagel dog."

Kunz looked at the Woodbury chief. "This is ridiculous," he said.

Synge, who had his phone out, said, "It's not too late, Mr. Kunz; we can still put you down for some gefilte fish. Gefilte fish is one of the wonders of the world, if you ask me. Bobby, you ever seen a poem about gefilte fish?"

Sabbatini shook his head.

Synge threw his hands in the air. "If Neruda can write odes to conger chowder, to the onion and the artichoke, I don't see why somebody can't write one to gefilte fish."

Sabbatini nodded. "I think the territory is open for you, Frankie."

"Yeah, I'll try it after I finish my sestina to celery root."

Kunz turned toward the Woodbury chief. "Why do I have to put up with this inanity?"

Synge flashed the rest of us his Cheney-twist-mouth smile, and said, "He thinks we're inane."

Everybody, except for Kunz, roared with laughter. Even Lion hooted, and the Woodbury chief giggled enough to get his milk mustache rippling.

"And I'm sure that's a phony search warrant," Kunz said.

"There's nothing phony about it, Fred," the big blond man said.

"Wait," Frankie Synge said, "I think I've got the first line. 'How much easier to salute the stately salmon than the gelatinous gefilte.'"

"Oh, yes," Sabbatini said, "you can go anywhere from there, Frankie."

I'M NOBODY, WHO THE FUCK ARE YOU?

As Synge stood back to make a phone call, I stepped toward Kunz. "Where have you stashed your niece?"

"I don't know what you're talking about."

"You have her somewhere?"

Kunz squinted at me. "You're nobody, Boyer."

"I'm nobody and, to give Emily a tweak, who the fuck are you?"

"That was good, Augie," Sabbatini said.

"How about your wife?" I asked Kunz.

"She's out of town for the weekend."

"That's convenient."

"And Galina?"

"She's got the day off."

"She gets a lot of days off. Maybe that's because you have her working nights."

Kunz turned to the side and straightened his bow tie.

Synge flipped his phone shut, and said, "All of us are here; we might as well get started. My daughter's bringing out the chow from Cecil's. I figure we're going to be here awhile. I've got a couple of more agents coming, each with a van, but we don't have to wait for them."

Sabbatini looked at the Woodbury chief. "Dave, how about sticking with Mr. Kunz?"

"You don't have my permission to search this house," Kunz shouted, and then made the mistake of reaching into his pocket.

"Hold it!" Sabbatini said, drawing his sidearm.

"I was just getting my phone."

"Careful," I called, "this asshole pulled a gun on me the other day."

"Take your hand out of your pocket. Put your hands in the air," Synge said, his gun drawn and aimed at Kunz as well.

Sabbatini had Kunz's hands cuffed behind him in a flash. After a quick frisk, Sabbatini reached into Kunz's front pocket, pulled out his cell phone, and flipped it over to Frankie Synge.

"I was just going to call my lawyer. See where the hell he is."

"We have phones down at the station. Should we run him in, Frank?" Sabbatini wondered.

"Let's do the search, first. Mr. Kunz can stay here with the chief and enjoy the spectacle."

I was beginning to enjoy the spectacle. Nice to have the guns aimed at someone else. Even Lionel, who was bouncing a bit on the balls of his feet, seemed to be getting a kick out of the action.

"You can't leave me in handcuffs," Kunz shouted.

"They're not very comfortable, are they?" Synge said with a nod of sympathy. "If you want to talk with us, tell us who you've contacted about the doctors, we'd be happy to take those cuffs off."

Kunz held his head high. "I'm not talking to you, not without a lawyer. I know my rights. And you can't tie me to your fantasy plot with a bunch of phony e-mails that anybody could have written."

"You're already tied, Mr. Kunz, and now you're cuffed. And if anything should happen to one of these doctors this weekend, you're going to go away for a long time, maybe the rest of your life."

"You guys," Kunz said, turning from Synge to Sabbatini, "are so ineffectual at your jobs that you make up fantasy crimes. You're like a bunch of old high school athletes, like Dave here," he said, nodding to the baby-faced Woodbury chief, "who, instead of sitting around playing fantasy baseball, play fantasy crime. Why not buy yourself a good video game instead of harassing law-abiding citizens?"

Synge massaged the two-day growth on his chin for a moment. "I don't know if it's in your best interest to offend us, Mr. Kunz. Listen, I happen to be a Catholic and I'm opposed to abortion. But the law of the land gives a woman the right to have an abortion, and I'm sworn to do everything in my power to protect that law." Synge took off his sport coat and tossed it over a small table. His revolver was now visible, tucked in its shoulder holster. "I'm warning you right now that if you've set anything in motion that interferes with the law, you're going to be severely punished, Kunz." Synge reached into his pocket and pulled out Kunz's cell phone and put it into the man's cuffed hands. "So, call it off right now. Because we're not going to stand for some Nazi-loving pansy in a blazer taking the law into his own hands."

"Hear, hear," Sabbatini said.

"There's a higher law," Kunz shouted, "you self-righteous prick. You think you're going to your Catholic heaven for protecting murderers? You're going to get yours."

"Are you making a threat, Mr. Kunz?" Synge asked.

"I'm not making any threats; I don't need to. But here's a fact," Kunz said, nodding his head toward Synge, "not a threat, but a fact. I'm going to sue your ass for everything you're worth."

"It's not much, I'm afraid, Mr. Kunz." Synge chuckled. "I'm putting my daughter through college and I have a wife who doesn't work. It's old school, I know, but I like it that way. I've refinanced my house so many times that there's hardly any equity in it. But my wife does have a very nice collection of clocks. She's got grandfathers, Big Bens, cuckoos. An art deco clock that's a real beauty. She's big into nostalgia clocks. I bet she's the only person on our block to have both an Annette Funicello clock and a Fatty Arbuckle. I got to tell you, the Fatty Arbuckle clocks are rare. So, worse comes to worst, we sell the clocks."

Sabbatini and I began laughing hard and were joined pretty soon by the Woodbury chief. Lion, with a smile on his face, bounced up and down on the balls of his feet.

"Let's go," Synge said, "and see what we can find in this dump." Synge and Sabbatini started up the hall.

Kunz shouted after them, "The hell you're going to search my house."

"Not just this house, Mr. Kunz," Synge said, turning back.

"We've also got a warrant for White Bear Lake. I hear that's where you keep most of your Nazi crap."

"You can't go out there." Kunz looked from face to face to see if this was some sort of joke.

"Sure we can," Synge said. He faced the Woodbury chief. "He thinks that because he bankrolled the Police Athletic League, and has a recreation center named after him, that he can keep Woodbury law enforcement eating out of his hand."

"To hell with that," the big blond man said. He waved a folder at Kunz. "We've got the warrants right here, Fred."

Kunz rolled his eyes. "I'm sure they're phony. How do you get a search warrant on a Sunday morning?"

Synge flashed his monkey grin. "Believe it or not, we have the governor in our corner, Herr Kunz."

ONE-UPPING HITLER

I led Lion down to the sunken, marble-floored gallery where the instruments were encased.

"My God," Lion said as he walked from one glass display to another. He took a small pad from his shirt pocket and began making notes. "I've never seen anything like this. The man has collected some legendary instruments. I've heard about this Carlo Bergonzi, and the del Gesù. Christ, half the world's been looking for that instrument. It was owned by a violinist in Vienna named Mosky. Supposedly, Heifetz and Mischa Elman played it when they traveled through Vienna. I'd just like to hold it for a minute. It's been years since I've had a del Gesù in my hands."

I was surprised to see tears welling in Lionel's eyes. "We'll see if we can get the case open, Lion, so you can hold it."

"Do you realize the arrogance of this man?" Lion said as he continued walking past violins. "He makes a point of showing off when and where each instrument was captured. Do you know how many broken dreams are in this room? This man one-upped Hitler. He got to do something the Führer wasn't able to do—gloat over the Nazis' plunder."

"He said he was having friends in town this weekend who could really appreciate the collection."

"Who the hell would that be?" Lion asked. "The Sheikh of Araby?"

"He said he was still missing an instrument or two."

"Like that Guad."

"Wonder why Odegard didn't sell it to him, Lion."

"Probably waiting for his price."

"What do you s'pose it's worth?"

"Well over a million."

I shook my head. "Nobody's getting it now." I gazed around the huge room. "It'd be nice to return these instruments to their rightful owners. To their heirs."

"That would be a lifetime's work, Augie, but worthwhile, certainly worthwhile."

THE BIG STINK

An hour and a half later, after helping Sabbatini, Synge, and a couple of more agents haul three computers and a half-dozen file cabinets to the van, Synge's pretty, dark-haired daughter, Maria, arrived with two large sacks from Cecil's.

"Sorry," she said sheepishly. "I got lost on the way."

"Happens to me all the time," I said, and introduced myself.

"Are you Rose's father?" she asked.

"That's my claim to fame."

"I admire her," Maria said simply, nodding her head a few times for emphasis.

Synge gave his daughter a hug and handed her two fifty-dollar bills from his wallet. When the rest of us started pulling out money, Synge waved us off. "It's on me, fellas. You can all buy me a sandwich after Mr. Kunz sues me for all I'm worth."

Synge had ordered a couple of extra Reubens for the late-arriving agents, and even offered half of his own sandwich to Kunz, who only glared back at him. I looked around at the others, who, like me, leaned against a wall in the entry hall, quietly devouring their sandwiches. Like horses, I thought, eating at the trough.

When Sabbatini and the Woodbury chief led Kunz out the front door, he went crazy. Standing between the Snoopy sculptures, he hollered, "I'm just trying to save lives. The lives of innocents."

"Shut up, Mr. Kunz," Synge shouted. "I've really had enough of you."

"It's not a few lives, but a million and a half a year."

"Shut up!"

"The Jews talk about their phantom six million, but they've killed forty million since 1973!"

Francis Synge walked over to where Kunz stood between Sabbatini and the Woodbury chief and put a hand on Kunz's shoulder. "Listen, Mr. Kunz, I can't put my finger on it, but I find something false about what you're saying, something disingenuous. You talk like you're some kind of lifesaving patriot at the same time you're aching to become a murderer."

"It's simple math," Kunz shouted.

"I don't think it has anything to do with math, Mr. Kunz; I think it's all about timing. I think you want to make your killings at the time when you can create the biggest stink. You have all the evangelicals in town, all the Republicans, an entire circus of elephants stinking up Saint Paul." Synge sniffed the air. "You can get a whiff of it all the way out here. But you, you, Mr. Kunz, want to make the biggest stink of all."

Bobby Sabbatini piped up: "The Big Stink. The Big Stink in Saint Paul. The Big Stink. Make a great title for a poem. Theodore Roethke would have nailed it."

I smiled at Agent Synge. "The trouble with Bobby is that everything sounds like a poem to him."

As they forced Kunz into the Woodbury squad car, the two FBI agents came over to Synge and asked if he still wanted to take the two Snoopys.

"Absolutely," the FBI agent said. "Let's see what light the Snoopys can shed on this fiasco."

Everybody, even Kunz, from the backseat of the Saint Paul Police squad car, watched as each Snoopy was lifted from its perch and wrestled into the back of the second van. I've got to admit it was quite a sight to watch the two FBI agents, in nylon jackets that said FBI FORENSICS, working with ropes to dismantle the Snoopys from their mounts. Frankie Synge beamed and lurched around snapping pictures. At a certain point, Synge, in the midst of his photographic frolicking, hollered, "I've switched it to video now. Maybe it's not as iconic as the toppling of Saddam's statue," he gloated, "but, I guarantee you, this is going to be a YouTube favorite."

I grinned at Kunz in the squad car. He stretched his neck out the open window toward me and said, "Don't worry, Boyer, you're going to get yours."

GO SMOKE A FATTY

"I trust I'll see you tomorrow at the capitol, and after that nonsense blows over," Frankie Synge said to me, "we'll deal with your violinist and all those stolen violins."

The rest of the afternoon was a bust. Synge decided that Kunz and his threat to the abortion docs had become an exclusive FBI matter. He wanted to examine the takings at the headquarters in downtown Minneapolis. "I've got a team waiting for me, even though it's Sunday. Even though all this other shit is going down." He shook hands around. "I'll call you as soon as we find anything relevant. If we don't find what we need here, we'll consider going out to White Bear Lake."

I felt deflated on the drive back to Saint Paul. I dialed the violinist's numbers to no effect and then called Blossom, filling her in on the events of the afternoon. I decided to go light on the violinist's disappearance during Blossom's little love fest with Sabbatini.

"Sounds like Agent Synge is on top of it," Blossom said.

"Maybe, but I don't feel good about this thing. I'm sure Kunz still has something up his sleeve."

"Look, Augie, the doctors are safe; they've got protection."

"And the violinist?"

"Still no word? I'm so sorry about that. I feel terrible. But I really think it's a separate matter."

"Not me, I don't think anything's separate anymore."

"Hey, been meaning to ask," Blossom said, the pitch of her voice rising with excitement, "what did you think about the piece on Rose?"

"I haven't seen it yet."

"Oh, man, I hope there's a paper left out there. I bought ten copies. Guess what, your famous daughter's going singing with me tonight."

"Karaoke?"

"Yeah. You should come, Augie. Ten o'clock at Grumpy's. Relax a little bit. You're all wound up. You're seeing ghosts. Go smoke a fatty, man, a real torpedo."

THE END OF THE WORLD

I took Blossom's advice and fired up a big J, walking down Grand Avenue with it cupped in my hand. One of these days, I figured, I'd get my ass busted for smoking pot in public, but until then I'd go on pretending that so innocuous an act carried its own immunity.

I traipsed through a lot of pretty streets in Crocus Hill, and then up Grand Hill, taking the turn to Summit Avenue. Obama signs had been planted in front lawns everywhere. It's as if they'd sprung up overnight. A traditionally Democratic city in a deeply Democratic time was welcoming the Republicans. There were also Hillary, Edwards, and Richardson signs left over from the primary. The Al Franken for Senate signs were ubiquitous. A few vintage and handmade signs for past Minnesota luminaries added character. Hubert Humphrey and Eugene McCarthy, Walter Mondale and Paul Wellstone. I saw a single Republican sign during my outing, on a lawn near the James J. Hill mansion. It called for a Harold Stassen victory in 1948.

At the corner, beside the cathedral, I looked down to the capitol. Nearly a mile away, too far to pick up any of the activity Rose described in her blog. I hoped she'd gotten the hell out of there a long time ago. I stopped at the corner and called Rose's cell. "Rose, this is your dad," I said in a message. "Nothing is resolved to my satisfaction for tomorrow. I don't want you to play at the rally. I know it's why you came to town, but I don't believe it's safe. Please do not play at the rally."

It must be some sort of multiple sin for a stoned nonbeliever to walk into a cathedral, but that's what I did next. I'm not sure I wanted to pray, or if I even knew how, but I did feel some need for the place. I'd been inside the cathedral a few times before to hear the chamber orchestra or a stray *Messiah,* and always found my perch strangely misaligned, sitting in a set of pews that had me facing sideways toward the orchestra or toward one of the multiple altars. It had never occurred to me that my misalignment might have a spiritual consequence.

But on that Sunday afternoon, between masses, with only a couple of dozen stragglers making their way through the enormity of it, I felt perfectly centered and, though I did not say a prayer or light a candle, I did make a wish: that everybody be safe, tomorrow and beyond.

I walked outside into the heat of the summer afternoon feeling momentarily blessed. But it was a short moment. After I headed a block or two up Selby Avenue, the cathedral glow dissipated. I started to wonder if I was depressed. I certainly felt ineffectual. Maybe the Pontchartrain Pootie was bringing me down. That's what I deserved for smoking grass grown from a ruin.

Next I ducked into Nina's, a high-ceilinged café across from Frost's and on top of Garrison's bookstore. I dug the fact that Nina's was named after a Victorian madam, who did business just a few blocks from the cathedral.

"Your Saint Paul namesake is a whore," I'd told my wife, after first hearing about the original Nina.

"Not a whore," Nina corrected, "a madam."

Since the advent of Wi-Fi Nina's is always packed. There's somebody with a computer at nearly every table. I liked the place better in the old days when quite a few of the customers wandered over from the halfway houses in the neighborhood.

I ordered a double espresso from a cute young woman in a Batman T-shirt. A stack of discarded newspapers were piled beside one of the tall windows. I rummaged through them until I found the Arts section of the *Star Tribune*. There was Rose, splashed in color across most of the front page. It was an old photo of her with flaming red dreadlocks and a gamine smile showing off the gap between her front teeth.

There had been a number of other features on Rose in the local papers—and, of course, the cover stories in *Rolling Stone* and *Spin*—but this one was surprising because Rose wasn't even here on a concert tour. Thankfully, the piece didn't mention why she was in town. It talked about the clubs she'd played in town when she was starting out, about her rare talent and the amazing trajectory her young career had taken. There were ample quotes from *Rolling Stone* and *Pitchfork*. The *Star Tribune* writer was rhapsodic in his praise of Rose. "The quirky songwriting and rock-and-roll flash that brought Rose her initial prominence has given way to a warmer and wiser style of both song and performance. Even when her songs are fueled by a topical political rage, they end up grabbing you by the heart." Somehow, it never seemed to go to Rose's head.

I turned to Dexter Dunn's column. He did a decent job of setting the stage for the next day.

> So when you come back from the lake tomorrow evening, you may cross paths with a procession of pilgrims on their way out of town. Hardy evangelists, hemorrhaging salvation, and leaving afterbirth on the state capitol grounds.
>
> But fret not, the Republicans have just towed their sorry coronation ceremony into town. If only it were winter and they were reindeer coming instead of all the beautiful losers—Rudolph and Huckabee, Brownback and Tancredo, Romney and Ron Paul. And Governor Holsom, fresh from the adoration of the born-agains, will lay as low as Lazarus until he's offered the vice presidential nomination.

It sounded to me as if the end of the world was coming. I figured a night of karaoke at Grumpy's was in order.

KARAOKE QUEEN

After zipping through an order of ribs at Lee's and Dee's, I called Sabbatini. "Listen, Bobby, unless you've got some earthshaking news, I don't want to hear it."

Sabbatini laughed. "Good, 'cause I ain't got nothin'."

"So how about heading over to Grumpy's to listen to a little karaoke. Rose and Blossom are supposed to sing."

"I was just on my way," Sabbatini said. "I'm thinking of reciting a couple of Seamus Heaney poems on top of some Van Morrison."

"That sounds daring."

"My middle name. I'll pick you up in fifteen."

✳ ✳ ✳

I saw Rose, once we turned into the karaoke side of Grumpy's. She was low-riding in a booth, in a pair of shades and my Twins cap. I figured that despite the camouflage, she'd been recognized and people were sending over complimentary treats—I counted three tumblers of whiskey and a couple of plates of Tater Tots in front of her.

Sabbatini and I slid into Rose's booth and she gave off a hoot of pleasure at the sight of us, then reached her hand across the table and shook Sabbatini's. "Detective, it's good to see you."

Blossom returned to the booth with a fat karaoke book filled with song titles and artists. She smiled at Sabbatini, who'd dressed down for the occasion in a pair of pressed khakis and a knit shirt in a beautiful shade of teal. "Look what the wind blew in," she said.

I nodded to Sabbatini. "Somebody's glad to see you, Bobby."

Sabbatini shrugged. "I don't know about that."

"The woman thinks she's inscrutable," I said, "but I know how to read her."

Blossom glared at me.

"Well, I'm glad to see her," Sabbatini said, "and glad to see Rose. Either of you done a song yet?"

Blossom shook her head. "No, but I've put one in. Rose hasn't yet."

I noticed people sneaking looks at our booth. A tall Asian

woman walked by and snapped a photo of Rose with her phone. "People sure as hell know you're here, honey."

"Yeah, I know. Either of you care for some Bell's Irish?" Rose slid a tumbler to each of us.

"How about the Taters?" I asked. "I haven't eaten for almost an hour."

"They're all yours." Rose pushed the plates our way. "I wonder what people make of you guys."

Sabbatini lifted his glass. "They think we're your protection."

"And they're right," I said.

Blossom flipped the karaoke book open to a certain page and slid it over to Rose. "See, they've got two of your songs."

I noticed "Mothers, Daughters" and "The Yours Truly of the Tale" listed across from Rose's name.

More people kept gawking at our booth.

"I'm kind of used to this," Rose said, "but if it wasn't for that damn article in the paper, it might not be so bad. So, I do a phoner with some guy from the *Strib* while I'm in LA. He wants to talk about my career, but all I talk about is women's rights and the antiabortion nuts gathering in Saint Paul. None of which makes it in the article; it's just about my career."

"He did you a favor," I said.

Blossom stabbed a couple of Tater Tots from Sabbatini's plate and then took a long sip from her pint of beer. "Take a look at this crowd, Rose; nobody here reads the newspaper."

I followed Rose's gaze around the room. Save for a booth full of college kids, everybody looked older than her, a too-cool crowd in their late twenties and early thirties. A few of the women in their thirties were wearing vintage summer dresses. Most of the others, both boys and girls, were in tight T-shirts. People had their heads cocked to the side as if they were operating in bullshit-detector mode. Folks continually flowed in and out the door to the smokers' patio. The currency in the room, it seemed to me, was irony, which made me wonder why people were so interested in Rose. She didn't trade in irony. She was doomed, like her old man, to be earnest. But celebrity, I realized, even trumped attitude.

Up on the small stage, a guy in a black T-shirt that said PUMP IT was making people laugh as he did a send-up of Billy Ocean's "Get Outta My Dreams, Get into My Car."

A kinky-haired waitress brought over another round of Tater Tots and whiskey, and then pointed to a man in a Minnesota Wild T-shirt, who winked at Rose. Sabbatini and I placed a beer order. The waitress, wary of us, bent toward Rose and whispered, "Are you going to sing?"

"Maybe in a little while."

Sabbatini appraised the crowded table with its plates of potato snacks and tumblers of whiskey. "We've got the history of Ireland right here."

A woman in a cute pair of yellow pedal pushers came up behind the waitress and snapped a phone picture of Rose. Next, a tall man, about my age, came by and took a snap. "For my daughter," he said.

Blossom sipped her beer. "They're not going to stop gawking until you sing, Rose. I'm up pretty soon. Look," she said, and pointed to the stage.

A couple of tall, lean women had gone up together.

"Check them out, those are the Roller Derby girls. They're either with the Atomic Bombshells or the Dagger Dolls. You can tell they're used to kicking ass. They're not the best singers, but they own their bodies, and when they're up there they own the room."

The two women, both in short skirts and tights—one in fishnet, the other in faux leopard skin—strutted, beautifully in sync as they fell in with the song's intro.

The opening lyrics of Paula Abdul's "Opposites Attract" flashed onto the screen. It was just as Blossom said: the women had no voices to speak of, but the way their muscular bodies rippled and swayed was enough to make you believe in Roller Derby.

When Blossom got up to sing, there was a sense of expectancy in the air—here was the woman palled up with Rose. The opening lyric of "What a Little Moonlight Can Do" ran across the screen and Blossom's flat, nasal voice was so unlike Billie Holiday's lilting, languorous sound, I wondered how she felt any affinity with the song. And yet she looked beautiful and brave standing up there in her black lace gloves, leather skirt, and green jersey knit top, which showed off her little boobs nicely. Aside from pushing out her large, beautiful lips in that way she has, Blossom kept herself very still. A torch singer holding her torch close. Rose and I both checked out Sabbatini as he watched Blossom. He was a man in love.

After a smattering of applause for Blossom, a chant started up: "Rose, Rose, Rose!"

We congratulated Blossom when she got back to the booth, even as the chant grew thunderous: "Rose, Rose, Rose!"

"You don't have to if you don't want to," I said.

"I don't mind." Rose stood and took off her cap and shades and had a gulp of whiskey.

A huge cheer went up as Rose held up an arm to greet the crowd. Camera phones flashed through the room like a hundred fireflies. I found the intensity a little scary as Rose walked up front and picked up a mic. "Thank you. I didn't really mean to disrupt karaoke night. You've got such a nice scene going here. But I'd be happy to sing one of my songs that's actually in the book—'The Yours Truly of the Tale.'"

There was some wild cheering amid the flashes. Rose closed her eyes as the DJ punched in her song. The intro was a synthesized version of what the band had recorded. Dozens of people stood up and moved closer to the front. I was scared for Rose. Anybody who wanted to could hurt her. As the intro drew to a close, Rose opened her eyes. I tried to calm myself by reading the first lines of the song, stretched wide across the screen. Rose's voice knifed its way into the room.

> *"You're spinning your wheels to find a solution*
> *Getting tired of all this mental pollution."*

A cheer went up and Rose raised an arm to acknowledge the crowd.

> *"You're not gonna fix it by changing the clocks*
> *Or knitting your baby a pair of new socks."*

The Roller Derby girls, back by the door to the smokers' patio, flung each other around in a wild form of swing dancing.

> *"The whole blooming world's in a frightful dilemma*
> *So you do up your hair with a fistful of henna."*

Others started dancing.

> *"Your lover, he's cheating, yet you're afraid to bail*
> *Honey, it's time to honor the yours truly of the tale."*

Blossom stood up and started dancing in the center of the floor.

"They tell you to take it one day at a time
Tell you to sit tight and suck on a lime."

A small crowd formed a circle around Blossom as she gyrated, tossing off one black lace glove and then the other. Rose belted out the song as if she were Janis Joplin.

"The whole blooming world's having a fit
Be safer for everyone if you'd take a great shit."

A big whoop went up in the room.

"What if you'd rather not take it at all?
Eve's in the garden, but she ain't gonna fall."

Sabbatini shot me a wary smile as Blossom shimmied in the middle of the circle.

"If you take no risk you're as good as in jail—
It's time to become the yours truly of the tale."

The small crowd roared and Rose lifted her arm and then bowed. I could see that she was craning her neck to get a look at me. I was standing beside Sabbatini, but from her vantage, the room must have appeared very different. People were screaming for more. "Rosie, Rosie!"

When I finally caught Rose's eye, she called into the mic, "Dad, Dad, come on up here."

I shook my head.

"Come on, sing a song with me."

Sabbatini had me by the arm and was urging me forward.

The crowd hollered, "Come on, Dad, come on."

I figured I didn't have a choice. When I got up to the little stage, Rosie hugged me and said, "'Like a Rolling Stone'?"

"All right," I said.

"Then let's duet to it."

The crowd had grown quiet but the flashes kept going off. I didn't care for the feel of that. I didn't want to be in anybody's picture.

As soon as the familiar intro began, everybody started whooping again. Rose and I'd had a good time singing the song on the trip to Memphis.

"This is my father," Rose said into the mic. "He's got the real voice in the family."

We launched into the first chorus, singing a jagged unison into the shared mic. By the next chorus it seemed as if everybody in the room was dancing, and when the "How does it feel?" bridge came around, the decibel level in the room rose tenfold. We might as well have been a ship in the ocean, swaying from side to side.

When we finished the song, Rose gave me a hug and, for once, nobody called for more. Could it have been that satisfying? Then a man's voice shouted, "Hey, Rose!" I didn't like the sound of the voice. There was some sort of barb in it.

"Hey, Rose," he shouted again. "You singing at the Born Free rally tomorrow?"

I could feel myself grow tense.

"At the counterrally," Rose said, not facing the man.

"That mean you're for killing babies, Rose?"

With that, I rushed toward the man, pushing people out of my way. I could see Sabbatini starting toward him from across the room. When I caught up to the wiry punk, who must have been twenty years my junior, he was standing in the doorway.

"Who the fuck are you?" I hollered.

"This is who I am." He threw a single punch that hit me square in the jaw. I flopped backward and was caught by a couple of people before I hit the ground. The crowd was stunned. A couple of people sneered at the punk, but everybody stood watching as he dashed through the door and up the street. Sabbatini went after him on foot, but the guy was gone like a rat.

HOME

I woke very early the next morning with a dull throb in my jaw that I could live with. It was the fateful day. Labor Day. I, for one, wasn't expecting a miracle. I went through my morning rituals just as if it was an ordinary day. At the mirror, finally, I recited a section of McGrath's poem about the poet returning to his childhood home in a dream.

"Away to the north,
Stark in the pouring light, on a page of snow,
The black alphabet of a farm lies jumbled together
Under its blue spike of smoke.

The coulee is full of moonlight: it pours that water
South toward the river dark.

> *I have come home*
> *From the river. Come up the coulee, come past*
> *The buckbrush breaks where the rabbits lurch and leap,*
> *Where the hunting hawks of the summer make their kill,*
> *Past the Indian graves and home."*

How different one man's sense of home is from another's, I thought. If I were to choose, it would be this house in Saint Paul, where I'd lived for years, rather than any home from my childhood. And yet, even with Rose staying in her old room for a few nights, the house was empty without my wife.

CHILL

"What happened?" Rose said, frightened.

"Nothing. Yet."

"Then why did you wake me at six in the morning?"

After taking a couple of Advil, I'd roused Rose. She sat up in her bed and rubbed sleep from her eyes. I remembered her as a girl, sleeping in the same bed, her big-girl bed, and thought of all the times I'd sat on a corner of the bed and read her stories. The time on her clock, the Sony Dream Machine of her childhood, flashed 6:06.

"Rose, I want you to promise not to sing today."

"No, I've made a commitment."

"It's not safe, Rose."

"I'm sorry, Dad. I'm going to sing."

"Please."

Rose rubbed some more at her eyes, and then dug to China

for a yawn that might have lasted a minute. "I appreciate your concern," she said finally.

"It's more than concern, honey."

She nodded. "Blossom told me you've been going a little bit off the deep end."

I protested. "I'm not going off the deep end."

"She thinks you should take some time off."

"The hell with what she thinks."

"Maybe stop smoking so much weed for a while."

"I can't believe she talked to you about that."

"She thinks the cannabis is making you paranoid."

"The fuck I'm paranoid."

"She's concerned about you, Dad, and so am I."

I stood up, wondering how the conversation had shifted to concern for me. "Do me this one favor, Rose."

"Sorry, Dad." I watched her slide down on her pillow, flop over to her belly, and pull the single sheet that was covering her up over her shoulders.

I waited a half hour and called Blossom. The phone rang five times before she picked up. I could hear Sabbatini grumbling beside her. I told Blossom that I wanted the three of us to meet for breakfast at seven thirty. We needed to plan a strategy for the day. She passed the phone to Sabbatini.

"What the hell's the emergency?" he wanted to know.

"Oh, no emergency. It's just an ordinary day, Bobby. They're forecasting ten thousand at the state capitol, with live births and a counterrally."

"They're all still sleeping, Augie."

"Plus forty-five thousand folks fresh in town for the Republican convention."

Sabbatini perked up. "Does that last number include the press and the prostitutes that have come in to service the delegates, Augie?"

"I'm gonna check on that, Bobby."

"And have you factored in the number of overlaps you're going to have? Plenty of born-again delegates and politicians will be hanging out in Miracle Land."

"Yes, but I haven't counted all the protesters outside the convention center, Bobby, not to speak of the anarchists crawling out of manholes and trying to block bridges and freeway on-ramps all over town, or the Obamathon participants, who the Swift boaters on the Mississippi plan to shoot with poisoned arrows. And let's not forget the Hilary Hijackers, and the Hilary Hotties, and the Reverend Wright lookalikes, just out of their training camp."

"Enough, Augie. You woke us too early. Those people in the tents at the capitol haven't even rolled over yet."

"I've got a bad feeling about today, Bobby."

"Smoke another reefer, Augie."

"I'm serious, man."

"So am I."

"I tried to get Rose to promise me she wouldn't sing, but she said no. She's defying me."

"She's nearly twenty-five, Augie. You've got no authority over her. Anyway, she's going to be perfectly safe."

"Wish I believed you. Listen, I need you and Blossom to meet me over at Highland Grill in an hour to figure out what we're doing."

"Whatever you say, Chief. Meanwhile, you need to chill. I'm going to give you something that will help, a poem by Buson.

"The coolness:
The sound of the bell
When it leaves the bell!

"If you say it over to yourself five times, I guarantee it will bring down your temperature."

THE SCARY SILENCES

I have to admit that Sabbatini's prescription—the three lines of Buson repeated five times—was effective. By the time I left the house I was mellow. I told myself that it might be wise to add a sampling of haiku poets to my morning ritual along with the McGrath. I drove down Grand wondering how the poets would interact. The styles were so different. McGrath's clotted syntax spilled out of him with a proletarian sense of doom, while the haikuists distilled a solitary image of acceptance. I doubted that the interaction of styles would be fatal. But when my phone rang, flashing an area code I didn't recognize, I half expected it to be a poetry authority begging to differ.

"Mr. Boyer?"

"Yeah, who's this?"

"McCracken."

"Where are you?"

"That doesn't matter."

"Where's the violinist?"

"I don't know."

"She's not with you?"

"No."

"Did you see her yesterday?"

McCracken didn't answer.

"Did you?"

"Yes, but I couldn't do it anymore."

"Do what?"

McCracken remained silent.

"What were you doing to her?"

"I . . . I shouldn't have . . . ," McCracken said, and began sobbing.

"You shouldn't have what?"

There was a long pause and I remembered Nina's talking about some of the calls she used to field as a volunteer for the Suicide Prevention Center. The scary silences. The only thing that mattered was to keep people on the line.

"I shouldn't have taken the job," the shrink said finally.

"You felt bad about working with her?"

"I thought I could help her, even though I was working for him."

"Kunz?"

"Yes."

"Help her how?"

"To a clear identity."

I pulled my car over when I crossed Fairview.

"It wasn't brainwashing. People always think of it as brainwashing. But for a woman with multiple personalities . . ." He began sobbing again. "You don't understand, to have a clear sense of who she is . . . would be a very positive result."

"And who was Kunz having you shape her into?"

McCracken sniffled on the other end of the line.

"Come on, Julie."

"He wanted absolute loyalty on her part. A loyalty that was stronger than a sense of right or wrong. Just like with the cults. But I was trying to set her free."

"Even though he was paying you well?"

"It's not what you think," McCracken said, spitting out the words.

"So even though you were taking Kunz's money, you were working against his wishes."

"Exactly."

I thought of Goya's trick of painting the Spanish royal family as grotesques, but somehow having them feel flattered by the portrait.

"There are certain things we can do with hypnosis."

"I'm sure."

"We can take a dark moment in the past and aim it toward a positive action."

"What sort of positive action?"

"An acceptance of self," McCracken said solemnly. "But she told me things yesterday."

"What things?"

McCracken was silent.

I said the Buson poem over to myself three times, listening to make sure McCracken was still on the line.

"You can hardly believe a word she says," he said, sobbing.

"What did she tell you?"

"How can you believe a woman like that?"

"What did she say?"

"She told me his plans for this pro-life rally."

"What are they?"

"There's only so much madness that I can listen to."

"What did she tell you, Julie?!"

"The woman is profoundly delusional."

"You have to tell me, Julie."

"I only called," he said, sniffling, "to say that I've had no part in it."

"No part in what?"

"I knew nothing about his plans until yesterday."

"What the fuck are his plans, Julie?"

With that, McCracken hung up.

LIMITATIONS

Blossom and Sabbatini sat across from me in a booth at Highland Grill. Blossom, clearly irritated about being awakened so early, wore dark glasses and a black cotton sweater with the sleeves stretched over her tattooed hands. It was as if she'd decided to expose as little of herself to me as possible. Sabbatini, on the other hand, was his usual congenial self, decked out in a gorgeous silk coat, a navy-and-red windowpane pattern that whispered Brooks Brothers. He began reciting a long poem by a beat poet named Jack Spicer while we waited for our eggs. Blossom interrupted him. Holding up a sleeve-covered hand toward Sabbatini, she said, "It's too early in the morning for Spicer."

I told them about the call from McCracken but tried to stay cool until everybody had eaten their breakfast. Sabbatini could sense my agitation.

"So you get a hysterical call from this crazed shrink," he said, breaking a link sausage in half with his fork, "but what does it tell us?"

"That the guy was freaked," Blossom said, shrugging.

Sabbatini put a bite of sausage in his mouth. "Sure the guy was freaked. Let's take him at his word. Maybe it's the first time he's heard Kunz's fantasies. You know, to off the abortion docs.

We've already heard all this shit. We've already acted on it. Taken suitable precautions. Kunz is in custody. The docs have protection. We've put out the word to the bad guys. They know we're on to them. Synge took their pictures, for Christ's sake."

"I think there's something more," I said. "I think we're missing something big that's going to happen today."

"So you've got a hunch, Augie." Sabbatini shrugged, then used his fork to jab a link sausage into each of the yolks of his sunny-side-up eggs.

"What are you thinking, Augie?" Blossom asked, raising her shades to the top of her head and staring at me.

I didn't answer right away.

Blossom shrugged, and then squirted a pool of syrup onto her hotcakes.

"I don't know what to think," I said. "I just hope we have a huge police presence at the capitol."

"It's not going to be huge, Augie. You know what else is going on."

"So, you didn't find out anything about the violinist's whereabouts?" Blossom asked.

"Nada."

Sabbatini kept pushing the mess around his plate, and it began to look like a gaudy finger painting. Never had such a well-dressed man made such a mess on his plate. "I bet she ran off with the husband, Augie," he said.

"She hates that man."

"They're probably on an Alaskan cruise by now. Flew up to Vancouver. On their way through the inside passage."

"McCracken said he saw her yesterday."

"All right, they're on a casino boat on the Mississippi." Sabbatini dipped a handkerchief into his water glass and sponged a coffee drip on the sleeve of his coat. He looked up at me. "Some things remain a mystery, Augie, and it doesn't help to crowd them."

"You're a detective, Bobby."

"Which means that sometimes circumstances require me to wait, to honor the mystery until it decides to reveal itself, if it does. I've got an apt poem for you, Augie."

"Surprise, surprise," said Blossom.

You know Wisława Szymborska's 'ABC'?" Sabbatini said, pronouncing the poet's name with great relish. "Do you know it?"

"Not intimately," I said.

"But you know Szymborska?"

I nodded. "She's quite different from Milosz," I ventured.

"Of course," Sabbatini agreed. "You know," he said, gesturing for emphasis with a forked hunk of sausage in his right hand, "nothing makes me happier than the fact that both Czeslaw Milosz and Wisława Szymborska won the Nobel Prize."

Blossom shook her sleeved hand in the air, with a forked hunk of syrupy pancake. "And I'm pleased as punch that the Serbian Charles Simic is now our poet laureate," she said, in a fair impression of Sabbatini.

"The kid's really funny," Sabbatini said, sticking his chin out toward Blossom, "but guess who's been memorizing Simic."

"Have not," Blossom said.

"Come on," Sabbatini said, "give us one, love."

Blossom turned her face to the side and then said, " 'War,' by Charles Simic."

"The trembling finger of a woman
Goes down the list of casualties

On the evening of the first snow.
The house is cold and the list is long.
All our names are included."

Sabbatini shook his head with wonder. "The greatest war poem of our generation."

Blossom looked up at me sheepishly. Sabbatini had made a convert of her.

"Now, try this one out, Augie," he said. "Here's Wisława Szymborska's poem 'ABC.' Every detective on the street should be required to memorize it.

"I'll never find out now
what A. thought of me.
If B. ever forgave me in the end.
Why C. pretended everything was fine.
What part D. played in E.'s silence.
What F. had been expecting, if anything.
Why G. forgot when she knew perfectly well.
What H. had to hide.
What I. wanted to add.
If my being nearby
meant anything
for J. and K. and the rest of the alphabet."

"Isn't that wonderful, Augie?" Sabbatini said before shoving a forkful of yolky sausage into his mouth. "Some things we can't know, and if we want to go about our work strategically, we need to accept our limitations."

I wasn't buying it. My limitations were so prodigious that if I accepted them I'd never get out of bed. I looked down at my plate. Two poached eggs, untouched, four half slices of toast, neatly stacked. I stood up and put some money down on the table.

"You haven't touched your breakfast," Blossom said with a surprisingly maternal concern.

"I'm just trying to accept my limitations."

ATTITUDE ADJUSTMENT

The size of the crowd was daunting. It was hard to know how many people were there—maybe fifteen, twenty thousand. Pro-lifers staying at the Kelly Inn, just west of the capitol grounds, had turned sheets into banners and draped them over some of the windows. I THINK . . . THEREFORE I'M PRO-LIFE, one said. Another, rendered in huge red block letters, said, ABORTION: A DOCTOR'S RIGHT TO MAKE A KILLING.

I'd parked on Summit Avenue near the cathedral and sat in the Mazda discreetly smoking half a joint. You could hear music and amplified voices and the swell of the crowd rising up the hill from the capitol grounds.

I'd wanted to take my time getting there. I needed to figure out what the fuck I was doing. I'd been getting myself beat up since I met the violinist. My instincts were for shit. They never were great shakes but at times I could be clever. At least I usually kept myself from getting slugged in the jaw and having jokers pull guns on me.

Of course, both the aging and the reefer had set me back, but they weren't entirely responsible for my disarray. If I were another kind of guy, I'd say my chakras were clotted, my energy was doing the boomerang. I'd roll out a couple of baseball injunctions—you need to let the ball come to you, to hit it where it's pitched. Perhaps that is what Sabbatini was telling me. You can't control what you can't control, I told myself. But I didn't like it. By the time I repeated Buson's haiku five times, I was ready to join the general parade to the capitol.

I remembered walking with Nina and Rose to Taste of Minnesota when it was still held at the capitol. None of us was interested in the little city of food booths that gave the annual event its name. The music was what mattered. Nina and I pretended to care about the aging bands that excited Rose, just to be with her in her rapture. I'll never forget the look on Rose's face when she believed that Ringo Starr, appearing with a British band of all-stars, waved directly to her, and the way she blushed when Eric Burdon, of the barely revived Animals, signed an autograph and, in his deep British voice, said of Rose's cornrows, "I really like your hair." Later, I made the mistake of telling her, in Nina's presence, that Burdon's nickname with his friends was Eggman, because he used to like breaking eggs over naked girls. This was one of the images that haunted Nina when she thought about Rose going on the road with her band.

At John Ireland Boulevard traffic had come to a standstill. Cars filled with Republicans were heading downtown to the Xcel Energy Center. It was fun to think of the VIP Republicans mounting the same stage where Marilyn Manson had just performed. I fantasized for a moment about a line of Minnesota Wild, who also played at the Xcel, shooting slap shots at the Republicans, but then I came to my senses—surely, most of the American hockey players, like most sporting millionaires, were Republicans.

People were walking in twos and threes, carrying banners. I

met the eyes of a pixie-faced woman pushing a baby stroller. Somehow she managed to carry a banner in each hand while pushing the stroller. One sign read I CAME, SO THEY MIGHT LIVE. The other said DARWIN IS DEAD! AND HE AIN'T COMING BACK.

But from the looks of the crowd heading toward the capitol, it was clear that there were plenty of pro-choice folks on their way to the antirally—stylish young attorneys and university instructors, exuberant college kids, and white-haired matrons who'd been sexually active before abortion was legalized. A blue-haired dame, pushing eighty, held up a sign that read KEEP YOUR LAWS OFF MY BODY. Another sign that amused me said MAY THE FETUS YOU SAVE BE GAY.

A group of high-spirited pro-choice men and women had commandeered the freeway overpass on John Ireland Boulevard. They held up HONK FOR CHOICE signs. I enjoyed the interplay between the honking drivers and the choicers doing a loony bit of dance.

As I got closer, I saw that the police had used Martin Luther King Boulevard to separate the pro- and anti-choice demonstrators, which meant that the anti-choice folks got the prime capitol grounds and the pro-choicers were wedged together in a far smaller piece of property, with a dozen squad cars parked between them and the big rally.

A fleet of antiabortion trucks, with their images of bloodied fetuses, had been allowed to park in a long line along John Ireland Boulevard, just west of the capitol steps. I counted thirteen of them. The trucks struck me as some sort of twisted religious imagery. Maybe anti-choice fanatics would start wearing cameos of bloodied fetuses around their necks along with their crucifixes. As a born-again agnostic, I'd always thought of bloodied Christs as a curiously grotesque symbol, better suited for appealing to hate and vengeance than to love and faith.

One thing I hadn't accounted for was all the national press. They'd come for the Republican convention, but there was a hell of a lot more human interest here than at the first morning of the convention, which would be all about credentials and putting the right spin on their bullshit platform. There were several communication towers on the grounds, beaming signals off the satellite. Parked around the bend from the abortion trucks were radar-equipped vehicles from Fox News, CNN, ABC, and CBS. I hadn't seen so much press since the bridge collapsed. I imagined Katie Couric stationed by the tents with the labor-induced mamas.

It was nearly ten and Rose wasn't supposed to play until noon, so I decided to wade into the enemy crowd first. Would they be able to tell that I was an infiltrator? I carried nothing with me, no banner, no baby, not even much of an attitude.

THE NEW MATH

Once I'd walked into the crowd it felt as if I'd entered a small city in the midst of a carnival. Banners and helium-filled balloons were ubiquitous, attached to trees and light poles and benches. The mood of the crowd was more buoyant and festive than I'd have expected. I heard snatches of what the minister onstage was saying. "We are the prophets . . . let nobody tell you . . . and when they talk about being modern, beware." I stopped near a speaker to listen more closely. "When they talk about how man walked on the moon, remember where Jesus walked. When they talk about the so-called new age, remember that the new age is nothing but recycled paganism. And when they talk about being good feminists, remember that real feminists don't kill their babies."

I was surprised by the number of men in the crowd. For some reason, I'd pictured a rally made up almost entirely of women. I knew how pigheaded and beastly certain women could be, but the men, here as everywhere, were the scariest. The righteous ministers. The conservative politicians. The pedantic professors who walked around in the haze of their own superiority. The tight-assed civil servants and post office clerks. The blue-collar punks who craved a fistfight, an enemy. The ones who drank, and then beat their wives and abused their children.

I took a deep breath to regain my calm. Was anybody watching me? Could anyone in the partisan crowd tune in to my thoughts? What was the point of spooking myself? Maybe Blossom was right and all the weed was staring to turn me paranoid. I walked to the east side of the grounds and saw the long row of tents. Was it really true? Had a number of women actually chosen to bring their babies into the world as part of a bizarre spectacle?

I remembered the afternoon that Rose was born. Nina had been in labor most of the night before. I stayed with her the whole time. I'd brought a tape player with cassettes of very calming cello music. The nurses, who shuttled between birthing rooms, loved the peacefulness of our room. One of them said, "Most of the others are watching game shows. Can you imagine giving birth with the *ding, ding, ding* of a game show in the background?"

I thought of our room with the late afternoon light. Pablo Casals playing Bach's Unaccompanied. Nina's legs were spread open. Fluid was everywhere. She was screaming. *Fucking cocksucker!* I held her hand and told her to breathe. To push. Breathe.

Push. *Enough with the asinine commands,* she shouted. And then the head. Push. A fresh excitement in the room. Push. Push. And then it was done. And she was crying. Crying still when I put the baby in her arms and said, *She's a girl, and she's beautiful.*

I wove my way toward the tents, past knots of people and banners and balloons and news teams. How close would they allow me to get to the tents? Did I hope to hear the screams of labor, or witness a live birth? Why was I doing this? There was a phalanx of cops standing guard in front of the tents. They weren't regular cops, but some sort of private security force. Probably survivalist freaks down from the wilds of Montana. Did the organizers actually think the pro-choice folks might break into their camp and try to prevent a live birth? I saw a small crowd keeping vigil. Several people were sitting on lawn chairs with Bibles on their laps while others sat cross-legged on the grass. I decided I'd better get my ass out of there before one of the survivalists keyed on me.

As I wended my way back toward the big stage, I passed a senator I recognized. It might have been Lindsey Graham, the almost sensible dude from South Carolina, but I couldn't tell for sure. I paused for a moment to read a sign held aloft by a serious-looking man in overalls. The sign read BORN ONCE, DIE TWICE. BORN TWICE, DIE ONCE. It sounded like the new math to me.

DEUTERONOMY 30:19

There was a sudden bustle around me. I spotted a couple of Secret Service agents hustling toward the stage, followed by none other than Geraldo Rivera and his camera crew. A local news anchor from KARE 11 applied lipstick as she cantered toward the stage. What fun. A brass band struck up "The Star-Spangled Banner." The reverence with which the crowd turned to face the huge American flag hoisted atop the stairs of the capitol put a fright into me.

I got close enough so that I could see the stage. A lineup of politicians in summer-weight suits was assembled up there, everyone turned to face the flag. I've never considered myself unpatriotic, but I have no use for the national anthem except before baseball games. I turned to look at the crowd behind me. Caps held over hearts, a motley chorus singing the words of the anthem. I joined the ranks, taking off my Amsterdam Ajax cap and placing it over my heart. I felt as if I had gotten myself trapped in the enemy's church. If only I'd had the courage to holler "Play ball" when the anthem concluded.

Next, a number of political officials spoke and, finally, Governor Holsom was introduced: "And now the man who brought Minnesotans and all of America together after our tragic bridge collapse last year, Governor Jim Holsom." A huge cheer went up and people hoisted HOLSOM FOR VP signs into the air. Some of the signs had JIM HOLSOM spelled out in red, white, and blue. Others featured a thoughtful photograph of Holsom, with his inevitable dimples, looking toward the sky. The skyward glance was meant to suggest Holsom communing with his God. He looked more like a turkey in a hailstorm to me.

For some reason I stood there through the five-minute, fully orchestrated demonstration for Holsom. A bunch of 4H kids, liberated from the State Fair, burst into the crowd wearing T-shirts and handing out signs that read JIM, IT'S HIM. This seemed like a fair preview of what would take place on the convention floor. I watched the news cameramen hustling around for the best position. This was a story. Governor Jim Holsom was preempting the great Republican convention.

Finally, Governor Holsom came to the rostrum as the crowd chanted, "Jim, It's Him, Jim, It's Him, Jim, It's Him." Jim Holsom bowed deeply to the crowd. As had been widely observed during his term and a half in office, the governor had two trademark gestures: the Japanese-style bow, dubbed the Jim-bow, and the hand over the heart, meant to indicate how moved he was by the public's acceptance. The man was the king of false humility. The gestures really resonated with his crowd, who must have seen them as an extension of "Minnesota nice." False humility was something to aspire to. Sort of like compassionate conservatism. And, indeed, I noticed numerous people in the crowd at the capitol bowing back to Governor Holsom.

People were impressed with the way Holsom utilized the Jim-bow during the bridge collapse and the tragic flooding a couple of weeks later. He'd perfected a slow, keening bow that projected just the right measure of solemnity. And somehow, given the darkness of the times, he managed to dial down his dimples. Holsom had played it right. Now that Minnesota's mood had recovered, and the Republicans had got to town, now that miracle births were set to commence at the state capitol, a fresh buoyancy followed the Jim-bow, and the broad dimples returned.

I figured that if the guv, by some series of nightmares, ever ascended to the presidency, the Jim-bow might become the crowd participatory event of the day, sending the Wave and the Macarena into oblivion. Given the proliferation of fast-food fatties in America, a crowd of Holsom supporters might be mistaken for a convention of sumo wrestlers.

At the rostrum, Holsom placed his hand over his heart and

held it there for a long moment. He blessed the crowd with a wide smile, the deep dimples seeming to flutter with an other-worldly joy. Then he spoke in his high tenor, his man-child voice.

"On behalf of the great state of Minnesota, I would like to welcome you all to this amazing gathering. It does feel like a miracle to me. All of us are gathered here with a simple message: Choose life. Choose life so that you and your descendants may live. Deuteronomy 30:19. Choose life so that you and your descendants may live—it's as simple as that. This is not rocket science. This isn't even creation versus evolution. It's a matter of owning up to our responsibility as human beings. It is an awesome responsibility, but, ultimately, we are the deciders. Are we going to be remembered as a species who killed their own? Or as a people who chose life?"

The crowd began to chant: "Choose life! Choose life! Choose life!"

Governor Holsom bowed to the crowd. Many returned the bow, while others pumped Holsom signs up and down in the air. Along with the planted Holsom signs, a flurry of ideological slogans were hoisted into the air. Among my favorites were a peace sign with the words FOOTPRINT OF THE AMERICAN CHICKEN, and a hand-colored steak with the words LIBERALS, THE OTHER RED MEAT.

HALLELUJAH TIME

As soon as Governor Holsom laid his hand over his heart again, I figured it was time for me to ditch the scene. Time to check in with Blossom and Sabbatini. But once I got to Martin Luther King Boulevard, the demarcation between the two rallies, I ran into, of all people, my pregnant wife. Once again, Nina spotted me first.

"Augie, Augie," she called, and ran up to me. "You'll never guess who I saw."

I shook my head.

"Mel Gibson. He was signing autographs for the evangelicals."

"Did you get one?" I asked.

"No," she said curtly.

I could see that she wanted me to give her a hug. So I did. I'm not sure why I did it. For old times' sake?

I took a good look at her. She was lovely in her straw hat and sleeveless blouse. "I'm a little surprised to see you here," I said.

"I thought it would be a good way for me to have my reckoning."

"Your reckoning?"

"As I told you, I'm planning to have an abortion, Augie. I wanted a feel for how the other half live."

"Aren't you making it a little hard for yourself?"

"Should everything be easy, Augie?"

I figured that she was making some comment about my life and didn't answer her.

"I sat over by the tents for a while," she said.

"I was over there, but I didn't see you. I'm surprised they let you near. You don't especially look like an evangelical, Nina."

She reached into the pocket of her skirt and pulled out a huge round button that said ABORTION. IT'S NOT A CHOICE, IT'S AN INDUSTRY.

"You put that on, Nina?"

"Well, it was easier for me than wearing a cross. I was sitting there for over an hour. No births yet. You'll never guess the anchor I saw doing a story by the tents."

"Katie Couric?"

"No, Anderson Cooper."

"I should have guessed. Well, I saw Geraldo," I said, enjoying the absurdity.

"Wow."

"So, you going over to hear Rose?" I asked.

"Yes." Nina looked at her watch. "Less than an hour now."

Just then a huge roar of HALLELUJAH came through the speakers near the capitol stage.

Nina and I moved toward a speaker. "HALLELUJAH! HAL-LELUJAH! We have a new baby born among us. Just as Jesus was born in a manger, we have a fine baby boy born in a hallowed tent, among all of us, among people dedicated to LIFE." A roar went up in the crowd.

Beside us, a group of women with their heads covered in white doilies sang a lullaby that turned into an anthem for the cause. "We came so they might live," they sang in a rather pretty harmony. People were pushing forward. Everybody wanted to bathe in the aura. I noticed Nina laying a hand over her belly. A woman at the periphery rode past on a bicycle with a bouquet of blue balloons. She wore a T-shirt that said THANK GOD MARY AND JOSEPH WERE PRO-LIFE. For some reason, the quote made me laugh. Suddenly, a man, dressed in the brown robe of a monk, came running through the crowd. He shouted, "It's illegal. The mother's an illegal. The baby's a wetback." A hush broke over the crowd.

"I guess they can't count it," I said to Nina. "Maybe it will be like Barry Bonds—go into the book as a miracle with an asterisk. Look, I think I'm going to split rather than wait for an Aryan birth." I gave Nina another hug and told her I'd see her a little later over at the other rally.

As soon as I worked my way back to no-man's-land, I got Sabbatini on the phone. He and Blossom had been over at the counterrally the whole time. "Everything's copacetic over here," Sabbatini said. "I hope you've chilled a little bit, Augie."

"Yeah, I'm mellow. We just had the first live birth, but they're not going to count it. Hey, I'll trade places with you guys. Maybe you'll catch the first official birth."

I strolled past a dozen uniformed cops standing around on the strip between the two rallies. They might as well have been at a picnic. But by then I'd pretty much lost sight of any danger in the air. I was actually having a good time. I walked off into the bushes and lit a joint. So much for vigilance. When I returned to civilization, if you could call it that, I passed through a gaggle of boisterous chanters—"Pro-child, pro-choice, pro-child, pro-choice." There was a good mood and a little more humor on the pro-choice side.

I noticed a few plainclothes cops sprinkled through the crowd. One of them wore a large Obama button on his shirt and waved a banner that said MINNESOTA ROSE. That gave me a chill.

The speaker onstage was yapping about the perpetual threats to clinics that perform abortions. I wished she'd be quiet. It was as if I feared her words would summon another attack.

Rose was due to appear soon. The cop's banner reminded me to be worried for her. But I was excited to hear her sing. It had been awhile since I'd heard her do anything aside from karaoke.

There were quite a few men in the crowd, but when I looked

around, all I really noticed was women. God, how I loved women, but the women in my life seemed to be disappearing. I thought of Nina, pregnant by another man. Rose out in front of her band, on tour forever. The missing violinist with too many personalities. Blossom, finally letting herself fall for Bobby. I thought of the look of anger on Erica's face when she kicked me out of her house. And again about Nina. Had she come over to this side with the pro-choicers? Or was she staying with the evangelicals? If I were a praying man, I'd have said one for Nina.

MINNESOTA ROSE

A spirited whoop went up from the crowd as Rose walked onstage dressed like a doctor, with a stethoscope dangling around her neck. At first, I didn't understand what I was seeing. Then I remembered Rose's blog entry. With her head down, Rose didn't even acknowledge the cheering crowd, but glanced at her watch. Pretty soon everybody was checking the time. It was a couple of minutes before noon. As Rose finished tuning her guitar, a great cheer went up and a gang of maybe fifty young women, and two or three men, outfitted in doctor's scrubs and stethoscopes rushed toward the stage. The kids close to the stage stepped aside, leaving the fake doctors room to fill in up front. Rose applauded the doctors, and a mighty cheer went up from the crowd.

I have to say, Rose mesmerized me from the start. She stepped up to the microphone and commanded the world in front of her. "We thank you for coming, doctors. It seems appropriate to honor the doctors who are willing to perform abortions, especially now when they are under such great threat. To have a safe, legal abortion is one of our rights. And it is these doctors who are preserving our rights.

"You've all heard the story of Christian the Tenth, the king of Denmark, who wore a yellow star and encouraged his country-men to do the same, to show sympathy with the Jews when the Danes were under German occupation. I'm told that the story of Christian the Tenth and the yellow star is really an urban legend, but maybe that means it's more than true.

"So, we borrow that legend to start our own. Instead of cowering in the face of the fear and intolerance being expressed across the way, we have taken back the day; instead of yielding our rights, we stand up to protect them. So these doctors gather for the first time in public to say that we get to make a choice, and if we choose abortion, it doesn't again have to be a back alley activity.

"It's great to be back in Minnesota. I'm always so proud of the progressive tradition of this place and to carry its name with me everywhere I go." A booming cheer went up, followed by a chant, not just from the faux doctors but from all of the crowd: "Rose, Rose, Rose!" Several Minnesota Rose banners waved in the crowd.

Rose raised her arm in greeting and then stepped back to the mic. "So how about I sing a couple of songs?"

WHERE YOU GOING, GIRL?

Rose had gotten her "doctors" and the rest of her fans so roused by her first two songs that they were still dancing while she stopped to say a few words. Even I had started to move a little bit toward the end of the second song, "Girlie Man Meets Girlie Woman." Somebody had passed out Minnesota Rose banners and suddenly there were dozens waving. Then I saw a man holding a sign that troubled me. It read: MINNESOTA ROSE = TOKYO ROSE. I weaved through the crowd toward the man, but he disappeared with his sign almost as soon as I spotted him.

"Thank you. Thank you," Rose was saying. "I think we have a little more life happening on this side than they have over there." A big cheer. "Some of you are familiar with my song 'Coat Hanger, Meat Hook.'" Another cheer. "Well, I'm not going to sing that now. I've written a new song, a little less graphic, not really graphic at all, but I hope it will have some relevance. It's called 'Where You Going, Girl?'"

As Rose played the soft, open chords of her introduction, I spotted Frankie Synge. He was standing quite a distance away, nodding his head, in his Panama hat, to Rose's light beat. When he finally saw me, he lifted his hat purposely and raised his thumb in the air. I thought of working my way over to him to tell him about the infiltrator I spotted, but I decided to stay put and listen to Rose.

> "I've been drinking cup after cup of emerald green tea,
> Wondering what the hell's gonna happen to me.
>
> They been telling me since I was really small,
> That the world's no place for a sinner at all.
>
> Where you going, girl, where you been?
> Killing your baby is the evilest sin.
>
> Don't give 'em a mallet, don't give 'em a gong,
> If you listen, they'll make you feel wrong.

They will shame you into a corner
Want you to live your life as a mourner.

This is your daughter, singing a song
Isn't this the place where I belong?"

AUTOMATIC PILOT

The buzz in my pocket didn't register at first. Rose had just begun another verse. As I pulled out the phone, I could see it was Sabbatini on the other end, but I could hardly hear him. "Let me get out of here," I shouted into the phone. In a moment, I was standing beside the line of patrol cars between the two rallies.

"Can you hear me, Augie?"

"Yeah."

"Well, get over here to the big rally quick. You gotta see who's up on the stage."

I hurried into the crowd and did a high-speed shimmy, weaving my way through knots of evangelicals.

At first I couldn't see the stage but the amplified voice was sure familiar. "I'm not saying that I was coerced or that it happened against my will," said the voice in a surprisingly even cadence. "It was my *choice*."

A huge, woeful "Boo!" thundered through the crowd, and I realized that in this crowd the word *choice* had become a blasphemy.

"But it's a *choice* that I've regretted every day since I made it. Women should not be faced with this *choice*!"

A great, quaking roar went up from the crowd as I slid forward and was finally close enough to see the speaker.

Elizabeth Odegard stood absolutely poised at the podium, neither acknowledging the response of the crowd nor shying from it. She was wearing the same tan fitted-waist dress she'd worn on her first visit to my office. The damn woman was on automatic pilot! This is what she'd been hypnotized for.

"Our Savior did not die," the disembodied voice said, "so that we could become murderers. He did not die for that. He did not!"

A chant started up in the crowd: "He did not die for that. He did not! He did not die for that. He did not!"

"I will take my sin with me to the grave," the voice said.

The poor woman was pitiful. I wanted to cover my ears.

By the time she'd finished her speech, I'd worked my way to the steps at the edge of the stage. A couple of men in dark suits—paid security—escorted her away from the podium. They were coming my way. I could tell from a distance of twenty yards that the violinist was a phantom inside her skin. I'd never seen her like this. It was more than stage zombie stuff. I wondered what they'd drugged her with.

When the violinist, with her two handlers, had gotten close to the stairway, I could see that her eyes were focused inward rather than looking out. McCracken had planted a trigger in her brain and a device for pulling it.

"Elizabeth," I called, but there was no reaction from her.

Her guards each flinched and crowded closer to her as they tried to pick out the enemy. The taller one, a big blond boy with a juicy wen in the middle of his forehead, had his hand on his gun. I called her name again. "Elizabeth." Although the violinist's eyes were still not focusing, I saw her mouth my name.

"She doesn't know you, mister," said the shorter guard, whose hair was slicked back with plenty of product.

"Of course she knows me, Slick. She's my client. She just said my name."

"She doesn't know you," the guard repeated. He, too, had a hand on his gun.

As the two guards conferred, the violinist opened her mouth: "I'm sorry, Augie."

"What are you sorry about?"

The guards turned the violinist, intending to take her off the other side of the stage.

"I'm sorry about your daughter," she said, just loud enough for me to hear.

OUTSIDE LINEBACKER

I may have knocked over a couple of people as I dashed toward the pro-choice rally. I was hoping against hope that Rose had left the stage by then. But once I broke free onto the other side, I could see that the stage was filled with faux doctors, standing around as if they were expecting a hospital photo shoot. I barreled through the crowd like a man being chased, though I was the one doing the chasing, hoping to change a fate I couldn't accept. "Get down, Rose," I screamed. "Rose, get down."

It's amazing the fright a single man running through a crowd can create. People scattered. Banners and signboards flew up into the air and were trampled as soon as they hit the ground. Voices rang out. I heard hysterical gibberish. Moans. Snatches of prayer.

High-pitched screams. Stern warnings to loved ones. People were cowering everywhere. Single-handedly, I'd created a fetal village.

Although I've never been known for my vertical leap, somehow I bounded onto the stage. Panic hit before I arrived. It did not bring clarity. Many of the faux doctors ran around in circles. It was a curious dance, choreographed by the devil.

I couldn't tell which of the doctors was Rose. All I saw were women in scrubs. "Get down," I screamed, "all of you, get down." A few were already down, their arms over their heads as if they'd been trained. Others kept scattering. Had they lost any sense of survival? I ran toward one woman who seemed Rose's size, then another. Sirens began to blare. Everybody onstage, whether upright or curled in fetal position, was screaming. Frantic, I nearly tripped over a tangle of abandoned stethoscopes.

Then I spotted the hair, Rose's red hair. She stood there, numb, the mic still in her hands. I tackled her and draped myself over her body as if I were a bearskin rug. I have to say, I felt a split second of exhilaration. For just that long I was an outside linebacker, nailing a running back in the open field. Then I heard a shot. It skipped off the stage beside us. The next one hit me. The chorus of sirens no longer sounded urgent. They seemed like an afterthought, commentary on a civilization whose time had passed.

Rose managed to turn her head to claim a bit of breathing room. I don't think she realized that I'd been hit. She whispered, "How did you know, Dad?" I can't remember if I answered her.

LOCAL HERO

The next days went by in a haze of morphine and happy visitors. I was in a private room at Regions Hospital. At first I couldn't understand why everybody was so happy. Were people simply pleased that Rose and I had survived, or were they still cracking up about where I'd been shot? It turned out that I'd been hit twice in the ass by 5.56 mm bullets from an M-14. "One for each cheek, Augie," as Sabbatini so delicately put it. Except that both bullets penetrated my right buttock. One of the bullets ripped through muscle and fractured my hip rather dramatically.

Along with a hip replacement, I got my fifteen minutes of fame, due almost entirely to being the father of Minnesota Rose. There were plenty of news items, and I was the subject of a Dexter Dunn column. I actually trumped the Republican convention for a day.

The column, titled "The Adventures of Augie Boyer," was a profile of yours truly filled with lies, perpetrated by Blossom and Sabbatini. Here's a lone sample: "When Augie isn't busy saving lives and tracking deadbeats into the suburbs, he enters chicken-wing eating contests. It's said that he once polished off three dozen plump ones from Shorty & Wags in a single sitting."

It seemed as if everybody I ever knew came by to see me. Rose, Blossom, and Sabbatini were there from the start. They cleared out for other visitors but always seemed to return. Rose brought me an iPhone, loaded with music and pictures.

"I'm writing a couple of songs for you, Dad."

Great, I thought, now I'll become an international laughing-stock.

Blossom brought a pumpkin-zucchini spice cake and told me to go light on it because she'd packed it with a lot of bud. I nibbled on it from time to time and began to feel like myself again. Sabbatini brought a hardcover copy of Ezra Pound's Cantos. "I want you to memorize these, Augie," he said. I still didn't reveal that I had nearly ten thousand lines of McGrath's poem to memorize first.

One afternoon I woke from a fevered sleep to see Rose and Nina sitting on either side of me. As I smiled at each of them, they both began to cry. Quite an effect I had. Nina muttered something about being so happy we were both safe, then began crying again.

"Mom told me her news," Rose said, and the two of them smiled at each other as if they had a secret.

A while after Nina and Rose exited, Erica came in with nine-year-old Ritchie and planted a big kiss on my nose.

"I'm not supposed be here," Ritchie whispered.

"Then why are you here?" I asked, dumbly.

Ritchie rattled the rails of my bed. "I had to see you, man."

Erica was planting kisses all over my face by then.

Ritchie boosted himself up on the bed rails and teetered on his belly right above me. "Can I see where the bullets went in?"

I shook my head but pointed to the affected area.

"In the butt? You're kidding me!"

A little later, as the light through my hospital window was turning toward dusk, Trevor the geek popped in to say, "Dude!" He was wearing a Dizzy Gillespie T-shirt, the bent bell of Diz's trumpet aiming north. Trevor had something else he wanted to deliver to me. "So, here's the thing," he said, "I ran into Blossom and Detective Sabbatini the other night at Roller Derby. The man is very persuasive, Dude, so I, like, have a poem for you, by Michael Dennis Browne: 'Driving South, Sunset, February.'

> *"House on fire, but only the glass*
> *Fence on fire, but only the wires*
>
> *Horse on fire, but only the eyes."*

I nodded in appreciation, and Trevor said, "Don't you think that's the best sunset poem you've ever heard, Dude? That's what Sabbatini said. And I timed my visit right for sunset, man."

Next, Lionel arrived, the whole of his nose bandaged this time. He talked a blue streak about Nazi violins and a Jewish agency he'd been in touch with. "They work to find the rightful heirs of lost instruments. They want to talk with you, Augie."

Everybody wanted to talk with me. Even my endocrinologist, Dr. Jacks, came by, his Adam's apple jumping around in his throat. Apparently, I'd had a standing order to have my testosterone levels checked and when they ran all the tests on me, those numbers went to the lab with the others. I confessed to Dr. Jacks that I'd stopped rubbing on the AndroGel some time ago, after weeks of itching. "Doesn't matter, Mr. Boyer," he said, "your numbers have shot through the roof. You have the readings of a man of thirty." Dr. Jacks threw a nice left-right-left combination in the air. "Who can explain it? I think what we're witnessing is the Labor Day Miracle."

DRIPPING WITH CODE

Agent Frankie Synge came by on the second or third day and brought me a box of Irish linen handkerchiefs. He leapt around the room for a while in his Panama, snapping pictures of Blossom, Sabbatini, and me.

After Synge exhausted himself, he had a seat near the bed. "I've got a new Bill Holm poem for you, Augie. I've finished memorizing *Boxelder Bug Variations,* and now I'm on to his recent book, *Playing the Black Piano.* Some very interesting symbolism in there."

"Symbolism or code?" Sabbatini asked.

"Yeah," I said, perking up. "How's the office of metaphorics coming?"

Frankie Synge flashed us his Curious George smile. "Have a listen," he said. "Here's 'Practicing the Blumenfeld Etude for the Left Hand Alone.'

> *"Forget, after a while, the right hand exists at all.*
> *Whatever it's up to is no concern of yours,*
> *whether pulling a trigger, counting change,*
> *unfastening a dress. Maybe it's even*
> *practicing yet another etude*
> *for some silent interior piano. Meanwhile*
> *your single sinister hand plays over and over*
> *a stretch of notes, till even the fourth finger obeys,*
> *wrist rotating on the pivot of the magisterial thumb,*

an airplane doing show tricks in midair
banking this way and that to dazzle the crowd.
Such music your five fingers make!
The right hand is jealous now, an ignored
lover waiting for the phone to ring."

Sabbatini nodded his head. "It's a lovely poem."

Synge, looking a bit solemn, said, "It's dripping with code."

"How do you figure, Frankie?" Sabbatini wondered.

"Come on. We've got the right hand not knowing what the left's doing. We've got the trigger, the airplane in midair, the counting of change, the banking, and the impending phone call. Not to speak of the sinister repetition, the rotations, and the deadly pivot. I can tell you right now, I don't like the fourth finger obeying, one bit. And you can imagine what I think of the magisterial thumb."

"It sounds like you're taking it a little too far, Frankie," I said. Even in my woozy state, I realized that Agent Synge had gone mad.

"It's a crazy reading, Frankie," Sabbatini said.

Francis Synge got to his feet, jerked a quick Cheney twist-mouth at me, said, "Good luck, Augie," and was gone.

THE MAN IN THE BLIZZARD

"See what all this poetry nonsense can lead to," Blossom said as soon as Synge left the room.

"No," Sabbatini said. "There are always abusers ready to take advantage of good things. But I really liked that Bill Holm poem. The way the right hand's divorced from the left. It reminds me of another poem."

"Surprise, surprise," said Blossom.

"From Mike Tuggle, the poet laureate of Sonoma County. It's called 'Divorce.' I give it to you, Augie, as you lie in bed contemplating your own.

> *"The ring finger, aching for its ring*
> *months after it has been removed,*
> *feels naked and scared.*
> *The thick gold band, which had become*
> *almost like another knuckle over the years,*
> *lies now in a box somewhere,*
> *circling nothing but air,*
> *dreaming of its finger."*

I closed my eyes for a moment to contemplate nothing.

"Now, Augie," Sabbatini said, "Blossom and I have some big news for you. I've asked her for her hand in marriage and she's said yes."

"Congratulations, you two," I said, rousing myself from my morphine stupor.

Sabbatini stood beside my bed now and beckoned Blossom. She got up and stood next to him. He took her sad, scarred hands and held them open for a minute. "I have a little benediction from Robert Bly," he said, "'Taking the Hands.'

> *"Taking the hands of someone you love,*
> *You see they are delicate cages . . .*
> *Tiny birds are singing*

In the secluded prairies
And in the deep valleys of the hand."

"That's very moving," I said.

Blossom rolled her eyes. "Yeah, Bobby's such a romantic it makes me ill," she said. "All right, Bobby, I have a poem for you."

"You do?"

"Yeah, by Joyce Sutphen."

"Oh, Joyce, the jewel of Gustavus."

"Be quiet, Bobby," Blossom said, and announced the poem the way a kid in the third grade would. " 'How We Ended Up Together,' by Joyce Sutphen.

"He was good in an emergency, calm
in the middle of a storm. Accidents
didn't surprise him; he was always

ready for whatever came along. You
could count on him; you could make
a deal and he would keep it, even if you

couldn't. His deals were impossible;
his deals were meant to make you fail,
and failing you found yourself in some

sort of emergency, someplace you didn't
want to be, and he was good at getting
you back to the ground, back to your feet.

I chose him for what he could not give me,
and he chose me because I would not ask
until I was desperate and only he could help."

Sabbatini looked stunned. "I don't know what to say."

Blossom smiled at him. "Then don't say anything, Bobby."

I wished that I could disappear from the room, or slip back into my morphine sleep.

"I've got a ghazal by Bly," Sabbatini said.

"Enough Bly," Blossom said. "You've just tattooed my hands with Bly."

"Oh, Blossom, but I'm just sick about not getting you over to see Bly's 'Peer Gynt' at the Guthrie."

"It wasn't meant to be, Bobby. But I've got a ghazal for you, by Mary Logue."

"Oh, I know that one."

"Shut up, Bobby. 'A Ghazal,' by Mary Logue.

"There's an inside of me and an outside of me.
The clouds block the sky and the grass has dried golden.

Only a fool would try to love when the heart's in the wrong place.
The tree is trying to tell me something but I'm deaf with longing.

Take away my pen, my paper, the table, and I am only
a woman crouched over the air, thinking.

My bed sags in the middle and my dreams get caught in my
 throat.
The wind comes in my window but the stars are stuck on the
 screen.

It doesn't take very long to realize you're dead, but alive,
you can go minutes without knowing it. Take a deep breath."

"What a wonder," Sabbatini said.

I feared that the battle of poems would go on until I was

released from the hospital, and knew that only I could stop the hemorrhaging. It was time for Thomas McGrath. I wasn't yet ready to deliver any of his "Letter," but I'd tucked away a little nugget of McGrath's in the corner of my brain.

"All right, all right," I said, "I have a poem for you both, which pretty much describes my life as a pothead and a detective. After I recite it, I'm going to need to be alone to contemplate it. 'The Man in the Blizzard,' by Thomas McGrath.

"Even his tracks are gone!
And, of course, his shadow . . .
But he keeps walking around,
Searching
Certain that someone
(Himself perhaps)
Was here before—
Or will be."

"That's you all right, Augie," Sabbatini said, standing. "The man in the blizzard."

"Stay cool, Augie," Blossom said.

I nodded from my chilled vantage and watched Blossom and Sabbatini walk arm in arm out of my room.

ROUNDUP

Nearly a year's gone by since the shooting and everything's pretty much back to normal. We have a new president as well as a new senator from Minnesota. After Election Day, I finally cleaned the spitballs off the TV.

In local news, Jim Holsom is back in the governor's mansion after a spirited dash as John McCain's running mate. Dexter Dunn dubbed the pair "the living and the dead." Not surprisingly, the guv converted a frightening number of Americans to the Jim-bow. The I-35 bridge has been completed, but Minneapolis and Saint Paul are down to a single newspaper and nobody knows who the publisher is.

I'm back at the office, with a sensible load of workers' comp cases and an occasional wave of infidelity. I've cut way back on the reefer madness, reserving a fatty now and then for special occasions. My new addiction turns out to be cooking. I've been taking a couple of courses every season at Cooks of Crocus Hill. My recent favorite was Calamari Kalamata: The Squid and Olive Cookery. And, not to brag, but I now have three thousand lines of McGrath's "Letter" under my belt.

In a couple of weeks, Frederick Kunz's trial for conspiracy and attempted murder begins in Duluth. I can't say I'm looking forward to it. The shooter, one of the brothers who had his pastrami sandwich interrupted at Cecil's, plea-bargained a few years off his sentence for giving up Kunz.

Sadly, Jules McCracken took his own life shortly after the shooting. The poor man followed his suicidal son to the grave. Perhaps there is only so much that we can change others, only so much that we can change ourselves.

The violinist and her husband are long gone. Pieter Haus calls me periodically with fresh rumors about her. She's been installed as the concertmaster of the Guadalajara Philharmonic, she's teaching master classes in Beijing, she's playing in the pit for Cirque du Soleil at the MGM Grand. I had a bit of my own information about the violinist. Shortly before Christmas, I received an envelope from a motel in Cheyenne, Wyoming, with a check for ten thousand dollars. It was drawn from a bank in Salt Lake City and signed by Elizabeth Odegard. I stood for a moment and said a silent prayer that she wasn't some Mormon's fifth wife, and then I went and cashed the check.

I half expect the prodigy to come walking into my office one of these days in her turquoise ferrets.

Rose, who cut a record with Prince in the spring, has been rumored to be dating Conor Oberst. "It's not true, Dad," she told me in a teary conversation. "We're just good friends." She's back in LA, about to make a solo, acoustic album, dedicated to me. I've been tempted to try and talk her out of the project, or at least the title, *Hero for a Day*, which reminds me of the pathetic *Queen for a Day* of my childhood.

Against my better judgment, I've started seeing Erica again. She's quit her job and is doing a fair amount of pro bono work when she's not buying foreclosed properties and flipping them. I turned her on to William Carlos Williams's beautiful love poem "Asphodel, That Greeny Flower," and she promptly had a field of yellow bog asphodels tattooed across her back, just below her shoulders. Her son, Ritchie, who texts me all day long from his iPhone, has taken to calling me Pops.

Lionel is doing a little work on the side for the Jewish agency he'd mentioned, whose mission is to reunite musical instruments and art confiscated by the Nazis with their rightful heirs. It sounds like a quixotic project to me, but I've hooked up Trevor the geek with Lion, and together they always seem on the brink of a breakthrough.

Francis Synge took early retirement. He and his wife moved out to the town of Minneota, where they bought a four-bedroom fixer-upper for twelve thousand dollars. I received a letter from Synge a few months back.

"I had an epiphany over the winter, Augie. I realized that instead of trying to crack other people's code, it was time for me to crack my own. Picked up an old Underwood with a case of ribbons in an antique shop in Montevideo. I've got enough ink to peck away for the rest of my life. We moved in across the street from Bill Holm. Every Monday I send new poems to his PO box in town and a week later I get them back in my PO box with his comments. Bill can be a bit ruthless, but he's not unkind. I realize that it's not fair for a novice to expect the achievement of a man who's worked a lifetime in the art. Every once in a while Bill and I will go up to the café for a carafe of weak coffee. My goal is humble, to write a half-dozen good lines, someday, that a guy like you might want to memorize."

Blossom and Sabbatini bought a pretty little house in Cherokee Heights. Sabbatini's taking viola lessons again and has leased an old workingman's bar in Northeast Minneapolis that he hopes to turn into a poetry-karaoke establishment. Blossom has a nice vegetable garden going. Not long ago she gifted me with a few pounds of the ugliest heirloom tomatoes I've ever seen. Recently, she started doing yoga, and she has been memorizing Adrienne Rich poems. On the day that she delivered the tomatoes, she recited "Diving into the Wreck" for me. Although she'll still work with me on an occasional case, Blossom has become quite the homebody. She's expecting in early spring.

GIFTS

Yesterday I went over to visit with Nina. It was my first time to see the new baby. Before walking out the door, I caught a glimpse of myself in the full-length mirror. Twins cap, pressed Levi's, wrinkled oxford cloth shirt, and my new pair of red Converse high-tops. I reminded myself of the jaunty young man I was when I first met Nina. The cap was necessary for maintaining the illusion.

I'd decided that I shouldn't arrive at Nina's empty-handed, so in my usual manner I brought too much, subscribing to the flawed theory that three imperfect gifts were better than one. But what exactly is the right gift for a man to give to his estranged wife after she's given birth to somebody else's baby?

I stood in Nina's doorway with a large basket of fruit from the co-op, a bouquet of long-stemmed Brazilian roses, and a bag of board books from Wild Rumpus for baby Claire.

Nina welcomed me inside. "What's the idea with all the gifts, Augie?"

"I wanted to give you something proper for the baby."

"Isn't this a little overkill?"

I told myself not to react and glanced around the living room for Claire.

"We had a nice run this morning and she just went down for a nap."

"I see." I noticed the baby monitor on the coffee table and listened, with a smile, to Claire's even, staticky breath. I looked around the small living room, which had a trio of reproductions from Matisse's *Jazz* series on the wall.

"I just got those framed. Like them?" Nina asked.

"Absolutely."

"I don't have your eye, Augie."

"Nobody does."

"You look good, Augie."

"Good? I don't know about that."

Nina took the roses from me. "Come with me while I get these into water."

A jogging stroller sat in the corner of the kitchen. "So, Claire likes to run with you?"

"Yeah, she seems to love it."

I watched Nina's hands as they held down the stems, careful of the thick thorns, and cut a good inch from each stem. She smiled at me the way she used to when she wanted to know how much she meant to me. "I'll get a vase for these," she said.

"Can I help?"

"No, I think I can manage." She caught my eye for a second, and then reached for a vase from an upper shelf.

Nina was wearing a sleeveless top, a blue heather running tank, over what must have been a sports bra. It was hard for me to take my eyes off her. The sports bra had a way of spreading her breasts at the same time that it accentuated their roundedness. As Nina reached for the vase, I could see the outlines of her nipples stand at attention. This was my wife, I reminded myself. We were still married.

Nina had both hands around the tall vase. She stood there holding it for a moment. She knew I was watching her. She'd done a remarkable job of getting herself back into shape so quickly, especially at her age.

"Do you have it?" I asked.

"Yes, I have it."

"You know, Nina, you still have a radiance about you. I thought it only lasted while you were pregnant."

I'd managed to make Nina blush. "Well, I'm still nursing." She ran water into the tall clear vase. "Can you imagine, a forty-six-year-old woman nursing?"

"I'd love to see it."

"Augie."

"I'm sorry. I'm just being honest. That's all I know how to be anymore," I said with a wink.

"Honest Augie."

As Nina arranged the roses in the vase, there was something watchful about her, as if she were hoping for more. Nina carried the roses out to the living room.

I followed close behind her. "So, what gives with Manny?"

"He came by once to see the baby," she said, keeping her back to me.

"Just once?"

"Yes. And after that he sent me a check for a thousand dollars. I sent it right back to him."

"That must have made him angry."

"Not angry exactly. There's something blithe about Manny."

"Blithe, huh?"

"Yes." She turned and looked at me. "Do you want to see the baby?"

"Of course."

She took my hand and led me into the bedroom.

"She'll sleep for another hour."

I stood at the crib, almost afraid to look. Nina pulled back the baby's quilt. Claire, asleep in her waffled red pajamas, was splayed beautifully across the mattress, her arms and legs stretched out in a lovely, balletic pose.

"Pick her up, Augie."

"What are you talking about? She's sleeping. You don't wake a sleeping baby."

"That's sleeping dogs that you let lie. Pick her up; she'll go right back to sleep."

"Really?"

Nina nodded.

I reached down and plucked the small bundle out of the crib. It was all I could do not to rub my nose against her rosy cheek. I loved the warm, powdery smell of her. Slowly, she opened her eyes. Did she see me? "Hello, Claire. Hello, sweet Claire." I turned to Nina. "She's beautiful." The baby's expression was as poised as her body had been, stretched across the small mattress. I wondered who she looked like. Not me, of course. But in the eyes, Rose, maybe; surely Rose.

After a few moments I handed baby Claire back to her mother, who kissed her and settled her back in the crib.

I smiled at Nina. It was quiet in the room. Just the baby's sleeping breath.

ACKNOWLEDGMENTS

Many thanks to Philip Patrick, my good friend and publisher, for encouraging me to think "romp" with this novel. Thanks to Mary Logue, a fine writer and my excellent editor here, who suggested I meditate on the idea of suspense, even if I had no affinity for it. To George Rabasa, trusted buddy, whose novels inspire me, and who responded to more than one draft of this one. Bouquets to Lisa Leonard for all her loving-kindness, and for the numerous suggestions and corrections that made their way into this book. To Jim Moore, for his poems and for his loyal friendship through the years. A final thanks to my children, Simone and Anton, a pair of wonderful adults now, for their love and wisdom.

also by

BART SCHNEIDER

Race

An Anthology in the First Person

978-0-517-88728-8

$14.00 paper ($19.50 CAN)

In a range of twenty first-person idioms, some of the finest American contemporary writers and social leaders explore the issue of race.

Beautiful Inez

A Novel

978-1-4000-5443-5

$14.00 paper ($21.00 CAN)

Set against the vivid backdrop of San Francisco in the early 1960s, *Beautiful Inez* is an unexpected journey into the lives of two masterfully drawn, unforgettable women.

Available from Three Rivers Press wherever books are sold